CLASSYWELL'S SECRET

Also by John Robins:

Follow the Leat
Rambling On

CLASSYWELL'S SECRET

A Nineteenth Century Dartmoor Story

John Robins

UNITED WRITERS
Cornwall

UNITED WRITERS PUBLICATIONS LTD
Ailsa, Castle Gate, Penzance, Cornwall.

British Library Cataloguing in Publication Data
Robins, John
Classywell's secret : a nineteenth century
Dartmoor story.
I. Title
823.914 [F]

ISBN 1 85200 037 6

Printed in Great Britain by
United Writers Publications Ltd
Cornwall

For Patricia.

I am indebted to my daughter Patricia, and to my great friend John Pegg, for their constructive criticism and helpful suggestions during the writing of this story; and to John in particular for checking as I wrote, and for his diplomacy in blaming my typewriter for the many mistakes he found.

PREFACE

All the place names in this book are factual, though the spelling of some of them may differ from that found on maps. For example, Nillacombe is the vernacular pronunciation of Newlycombe. Classywell, Classiwell, Classenwell, Clakeywell, Clazywell, Crazywell, are variations of the word used by some authors, or on some maps or in census returns. Eylesbarrow, as shown on the Ordnance Survey maps, is variously spelt Ailsbarrow, Ailsborough, Hillsborough, and again in the vernacular, Yelsborough. The mine map dated 1823 is entitled Ellisborough Mine. The description given of the mine is based on this map, the reading of articles concerning it, and personal exploration of the remains. The story of its development is purely conjectural.

Whilst the principal characters in the book are fictitious, some are real, such as Deacon, Leger, Rowe and Uren. The names of other minor characters are taken from the 1851 census return for Walkhampton Parish, such as Zachariah, Sharack, etc. The overcrowding in the houses at Foggin Tor Quarry is also taken from this census.

The author has walked (or in some cases was only able to view) most of the length of the Plymouth and Dartmoor Tramway track, from Princetown to Sutton Harbour in Plymouth, and as a schoolboy actually walked part way into Leigham tunnel and saw the circle of daylight at the far end.

All the farms or cottages mentioned in the book, with the exception of Wapsworthy, Willsworthy and Cox Tor, are now in ruins, or in some cases do not even survive as ruins, such as the Mount Pleasant Cottages, later to be named West View Cottages, and by William Crossing as the Red Cottages, the stonework from them being taken to help build the television station at North Hessary Tor.

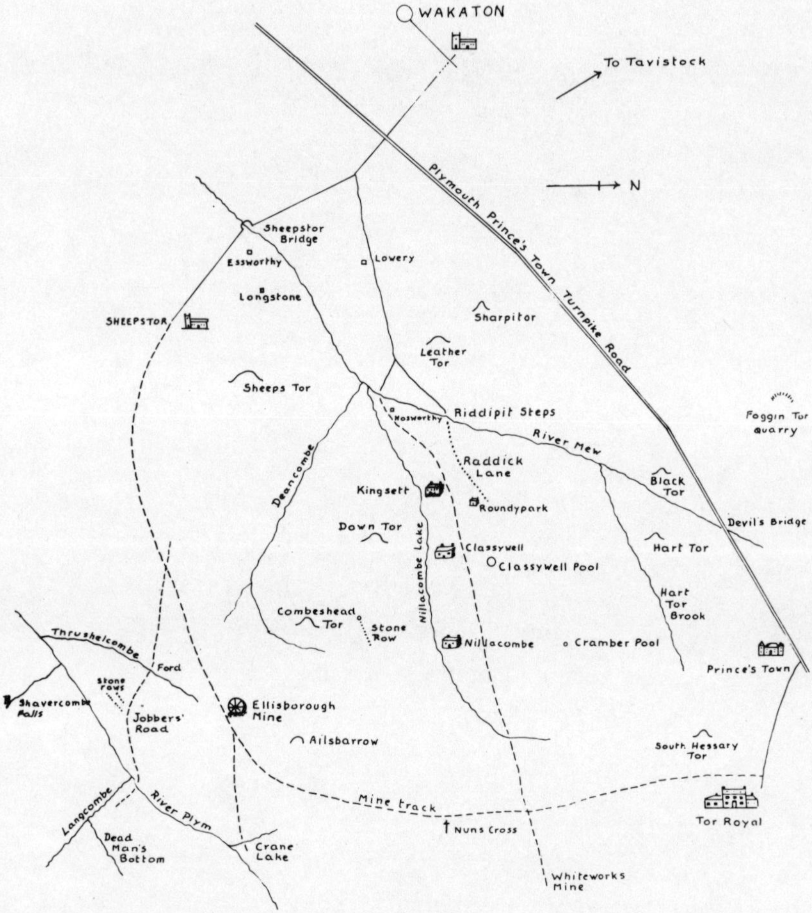

Reference map covering the story to Chapter 14.

Chapter One

A steep lane leads from the village to the church on the hill. So prominent is this church, with its imposing tower on its lofty eminence, that it can be seen for miles around, a focal point for a very large parish. The Domesday Book records this parish as Wachetone, the village bearing the same name. The word is pronounced Wakaton, and that is what we will call this village, for indeed its inhabitants pronounce it thus, though its spelling has undergone many changes over the ensuing centuries.

Roads, lanes and footpaths lead to this church from all directions. Mostly they are steep, some rugged, some stony, others muddy. For the population of this parish is widely scattered, consisting mostly of outlying farms, Gnatham to the west; Burham, Welltown, Peakhill and Horseyeat to the east; Waytown, Eggworthy, Daveytown, Parktown, Routrundle, Babyland, Crabbyland and others to the north; Lowery, Leathertor, Roundypark, Kingsett, Nosworthy, Classywell, Nillacombe and many more to the south.

In all probability there would have been a church here even before this noble structure had been built, in 1500 or thereabouts. In such an exposed position the fabric of the old church had suffered from the buffeting of the elements on many occasions. By 1813 a document reporting on its condition stated '. . . The church and the tower belonging thereto are become so ruinous that the parishioners cannot assemble for divine worship without great danger to their lives, and the said church cannot any longer be supported, but that the great part thereof as well as the tower must be taken down and rebuilt . . .'

By the year 1820 those repairs and rebuilding had been completed. The tower rose again to its full height, all eighty-five feet of it, and that is how it was seen, in the spring of that year, by a solitary figure climbing that steep lane from village to church. Elbow Lane it was called, for it was necessary to make a sharp turn left from the lane to reach the church. But though it was a Sunday it was not to the church that the young man was bound, it was much too early for morning service anyway. Instead he turned right at this point, down one of those many approaches to the church, this one a narrow, stony track between high hedges. At the bottom of it a sparkling brook fussed over impeding stones and hurried headlong down the valley to the village, and from there past Knowle Farm to join the River Walkham below Huckworthy Bridge. Knowlebrook it was called in those days.

A lane passed over the stream, leading to Welltown Farm. But again, that was not where the youth wished to go. Instead he crossed the brook and climbed the opposite side of the valley, up that lane that seemed much longer than it actually was, so steep was it. At one point he turned to view the land from whence he had come. There was the church, boldly lit by the early sun, its tower sharply outlined against a sombre hill beyond. Beside the church were the white walls of the church house.

Further up the lane the new highway from Plymouth to Prince's Town cut across it. But still the lane continued to climb. Eventually the crest of the hill was reached, and there the young man paused and gazed about him in wonder at what he saw. Low walls had taken the place of the hedges that had lined the lane. Flanking them on their left was a lofty, smoothly rounded hill; on their right a more gentle slope led to open moorland, both hiding what lay beyond, both treeless and pristine as nature had made them, untouched by man. But ahead a great expanse of Dartmoor was to be seen, dominated in the foreground by a massive bulk of hill shaped like a crouching lion. In front of it was a broad green valley. Behind it range upon range of hills faded away into the distance. Facing about him, the church had paled into insignificance in comparison with the great panorama of rugged-topped hills now to be seen to the north.

For this country was all new to the young man. He had only recently arrived at Wakaton with his mother, from the far west of Cornwall. He was a miner's son. At the age of fourteen he had gone down the mine with his father, who had taught him all he knew about mining. For that was traditional in Cornwall. Sons followed in their fathers' footsteps, there being little other employment available for them. It was dangerous unhealthy work which usually shortened their lives and sometimes prematurely ended them. That had been the sad fate of his father. In search of new ground some ancient workings had been broken into. Water had poured into the level in sudden and increasing volume, carrying all before it. His father's body had been found near the mouth of the adit. Overcome with grief, his mother could no longer bear to live there, and had come to Wakaton to live with her sister.

There was little room on the farm for such an addition to the family. Tom, for that was the young man's name, felt unwanted. He did not get on too well with his uncle who rather resented having someone on his farm who was so obviously unsuited for the work he was asked to do. Thus it was that he had set out on this journey in search of other employment.

Mr Bicknell, an old retired miner in the village, had told him something of the mines that had been worked on Dartmoor, and had advised him to go and see a Mr William Dawe, who would be able to tell him more about the mines that were still working. He had had considerable experience of those mines, but now he was a man of independent means. It was common knowledge that he had married into a landed family, much to the disappointment of the parents who considered that their daughter was marrying beneath her social status. But the father had a soft spot for his daughter and had bestowed on her a comfortable dowry. At the time of their wedding Classywell Farm had become vacant. They bought it and made a comfortable home of it. Mr Bicknell had given Tom instructions as to how to get to Classywell.

Resuming his journey, Tom turned left at a fork in the road. The right fork, he understood, would have taken him to

Sheepstor Bridge. The lane he was on now was narrow and winding, with high hedges which obscured his view. His pace quickened at the easy descent. His long legs were clad in knickerbockers and cloth gaiters; a loose-fitting waistcoat only partially covered a long-sleeved open-necked shirt. A tousled mop of brown hair crowned a pallid, rather sickly looking boyish face, signs of the long hours spent in the humid bad air and dark depths of those Cornish mines. Yet his brown eyes were bright and intelligent, the set of his jaw determined. Quite recently he had celebrated his twentieth birthday.

At the bottom of the hill Tom saw Lowery Farm, confirmation that he was on the right road. Once past that, slightly rising ground took him to where a waterway crossed the lane. Mr Bicknell had not told him anything about that, yet it ran beside the road for a considerable distance. It was little more than a wide ditch, but obviously man made. What could it have been made for? Where did it go? From where had it taken its water? He now had a clear view across the valley, to that huge hill and the beautiful green valley below it. A new cone-shaped hill appeared ahead. Once more the lane crossed the waterway and now departed from it, descending past Leathertor Farm to Riddipit Steps. These names he had written down to ensure that he remembered them, and would know what to look for on this journey into the unknown.

Tom was not sure what to expect at Riddipit Steps. Why 'steps'? When he got there and saw the line of boulders spaced evenly across the river, he realised they were so placed to enable one to step across the water dry shod. He did so with ease. Then paused to admire the sylvan beauty of the scene. Trees, resplendent in new leaf, lined the river banks. Rays of sunlight penetrated their branches and dappled the waters with dancing reflections. Such crystal clear water it was, splashing over or swirling round the grey granite rocks that littered the river bed. The very sound of the rushing waters adding enchantment to the place. He stooped beside the stream, cupped his hands and drank; a sort of baptism to the land he was destined to know so well.

For a long time he sat and quietly enjoyed this unique experience, near mesmerised by the sight and sound of the river, the purpose of his mission momentarily forgotten. This was the very antithesis of the squalor, noise and harshness of a Cornish copper mine.

That thought roused him, and made him realise he must continue his journey. With reluctance he rose and turned away, with a mental expression of thanks for this delightful interlude.

Not far away he found the start of Raddick Lane, the next point on his list of instructions. It proved a steep, storm-rutted track between grey stone walls, of seemingly interminable length, hard on the feet and wearying on the mind. With relief, at the top, he found himself on open moorland, where he turned downhill, past Roundypark, to a rough cart road. Threading its way eastwards it was flanked on one side by the rising ground of Cramber Down and on the other by dry stone walling. Beyond the wall a maze of fields descended to the depths of a long almost treeless valley. A high, uncultivated heather-clad hill rose on the far side.

Tom followed the track as he had been instructed, glancing every now and again over the wall for any sign of the farm he was seeking. He came eventually to a gateway, and there below it were the unmistakable white walls and undulating thatched roof of Classywell, its two square dome-topped chimneys rising from each end. Resting his arms on the gate Tom stood there for a while, absorbing the rural scene. Sheep grazed peacefully in the fields, lambs pranced about, bleating, or jabbing eagerly at their mother's udder. Cawing crows wheeled around hunting for any scraps of food they could find. Overhead a kestrel hovered motionless, skylarks twittered incessantly. Somewhere in the distance a cuckoo called.

How is it possible, thought Tom, as he unlatched the gate and forced it open, to associate this scene with that of tin mining? Yet Mr Bicknell had said that this valley had been worked for tin.

When, after descending through a large field, he reached the gate to the courtyard of the farm, a dog sprang out from a kennel which seemed to Tom to be but a part of the wall. The sound of the barking brought a man to the door of the cottage.

"What do you want, young man?" he called. The tone of

his voice was not so much a reproach as one of surprise that anyone unknown to him should be calling.

"I have a request to make, sir; may I have a word with you?"

The man approached the gate and quietened the dog.

"Well, what is it?"

"I was told to come and see you by a Mr Bicknell of Wakaton, sir, do you know him?"

"Yes indeed I do, though it is a long time since I've seen him."

"He thought you might be able to help me."

"Oh well, come in, come in." He opened the gate for Tom and led him towards a seat beside the door of the cottage.

They sat facing the opposite side of the valley. Tom's eyes became riveted upon the scene, particularly the noble rock-topped hill which he had seen from the distance, cone-shaped then but different from this angle. It dominated all else.

"Well boy, are you tongue-tied?"

"No. I'm sorry sir, I have never before seen land like this. What is that great hill?"

The young man's interest in such things mollified the man, for he also had never ceased to enjoy that view.

"That's Down Tor boy, that's what they call these hills with rocks on them, tors. Are you a stranger here then?"

"Yes sir, I have recently come from Cornwall, my father was a miner there. He . . . he lost his life there recently."

"I'm sorry to hear that, boy. I understand. 'Tis a dangerous life. What can I do for you then?" The man's voice was now kindly, for such news was nothing strange to him; he himself had been in some such tragic situations.

"You are Mr Dawe?"

"Yes."

"Mr Bicknell thought you might be able to tell me about the mines here and help me to get a job."

"You still want to go mining after what happened to your father?"

"I don't know how to do anything else. I have tried farming but . . ."

"Yes, yes, I know boy. I can understand that. Anyway, what's your name?"

"Thomas Tremain. Everyone calls me Tom though."

"Well Tom, there's been lots of mining in this valley, but nobody ever made much money out of 'em, though tin was always found. Only about ten years ago there was that Wheal Hughes further up the valley. Nice little mine it was. They used part of an old leat to bring water to the wheel, but it wasn't enough to do the job and they got more water from Willabeam, on the other side of the valley, and brought it across the river on a launder. Built a nice little shelter for the men they did. But it didn't last long. The wheel is still up there in the pit."

This wasn't what Tom really wanted to hear, but Mr Dawe was now lost in his reminiscences and continued.

"Then further up the valley, at the fork in the stream, there was another little working which some people call Wheal Chance. Whether it was a good chance or a bad one I don't know, but there's a shaft and an adit, wheel-pit and so on still to be seen there, so I suppose they got something from it. The best of them was Nuns Cross Mine. My father was the Captain there, one of the shafts is named after him. I worked there too, in the levels and cross courses that this new leat flows through, comes out of the old adit mouth it does."

But Tom did not ask what leat it was or where it went, though he did wonder if it had any connection with the one he had seen on the way to Classywell. He broke into the diatribe by asking if there were not some working mines in the area.

"Well yes, a bit further away. About thirty years ago they built that cart road from Nosworthy to Whiteworks, a mine beyond Nuns Cross. Supposed to be good prospects there amongst the old surface workings. Lots of lodes there, mostly got at by adits, but there's a few shafts too, of no great depth. Then the mine was up for sale about ten years ago and while the mine was idle two bullocks were lost down one of the shafts. Always a bit of trouble there was there. Now I believe they have cut a new leat and got a new wheel, only for the whole lot to be put up for sale again, water-wheel, bobs, connecting rods, whim, all the blooming lot; tragic it is, because there's good tin to be had there. Regular shambles the way they run that mine."

"So it's not much good my applying there for a job?"

"No Tom. I reckon your best bet is to go a bit further afield still. About five years ago they started working new ground at Aylesborough which showed some promise. It is now run by a Mr Deacon. What he doesn't know about tin mining is not worth knowing. I reckon if he's got a say in it there will be every chance of success. They call it Ellisborough for some reason. From what I hear they are laying things out in a proper tidy manner. And the wages are good too, about £7 a month, more for the skilled men. I believe there's talk of having their own smelting house. If they do, that'll save them a whole heap of money, for everyone else has to send their stuff to Cornwall for smelting. And of course other mines will send their black tin to Ellisborough for smelting and that will be more profit for them. They have already built barracks for the men and a new house is being built for the captain. You go along there Tom, for a start anyway."

"And how do I get there?"

"Did you come here along that new cart track?"

"Yes."

"Go back to it and follow it until you come to the new leat; then walk along the footpath beside the leat until you come to where it gushes out of the adit. Carry on in the same direction until you see Nuns Cross, a fine old granite cross about seven feet high. When you reach it you'll see the new track to the mine, going south. " 'Tis a good two miles or more, but nothing to a young man like you."

Tom rose to take his leave.

"I wish you luck Tom, come back and tell me how you got on."

Tom thanked him and promised to return. At the gate the dog came out of his kennel and gave him a quizzical look, but decided since he had been there so long he must be a friend of the family and forbore to bark. As Tom closed the gate he heard a sweet voice call, "Father, your dinner's ready."

Tom had brought no food with him. To go to Ellisborough now would add another four or five miles to his journey, and he may have to be there some time to find anyone to talk to. Anyway, being a Sunday, it was probably not the best day for such a mission. He would go there tomorrow.

With his mind full of his plans, of what Mr Dawe had told him, and how he was to explain to his mother what he was determined to do, Tom was not concentrating on his route and was suddenly brought to reality by the barking of another dog. He found himself in the courtyard of Roundypark Farm. Old Mr Bicknell had given him careful instructions as to how to get *to* Classywell, but things looked different in the opposite direction, and now Tom was confused as to where the top of Raddick Lane was. He went to the arched doorway of the house and was intrigued to see the date 1668 on its lintel. At the same time the door opened and the aged farmer appeared, wiping bits of his dinner from his lips with the back of his hand. Tom apologised for disturbing him and asked to be directed to that lane that led down to the river.

"Au yes, you mean Raddick Lane, goes down to Riddipit it do. Go up beside this yer wall, hundred yards or so, you'll soon see en. Where you from then?"

Tom explained that he was a stranger here but had been to see Mr Dawe at Classywell.

"Au yes, Mr Dawe. 'E don't know nothing about farming but 'e's a good neighbour. He or 'is wife or that there darter of 'is comes to see if us need any 'elp; getting on in years the missus and me be, and us welcome a bit of help at times us do. Where do 'e live to then?"

"At Wakaton, but I am hoping to get a job at Ellisborough Mine."

"Ellisborough, Ellisborough, never 'eard of 'e."

Tom explained where he was told it was.

"Au, you means Yelsboro, Yelsboro, that's what us calls en. Proper old mess them miners are making of the land, diggin' great 'oles in it, cutting great long leats, making roads to 'em. Where be us farmers goin' to graze our cattle then, eh? Didun ought to be allowed. 'Tis ruination of Dartymoor it be. You mark my words, before long they'll all know that none of 'em is goin' to make any money out of 'em, then they'll all pack up and go and leave the land one unholy mess full of pits for our cattle to fall in. 'Tis wicked."

Expressing his thanks Tom took his leave before the old man could go further into his complaints. But his outburst gave him further food for thought as he trudged up the hill to the lane. Was mining going to turn this lovely land into another devastated area such as he had seen so often in Cornwall?

The next day, with his uncle's simulated permission, for really he was hoping that his useless nephew would get a job, he returned by the same route, but continued along the mine road for a mile or so to where it crossed the new leat on a bridge of granite slabs. As Mr Dawe had instructed he now walked beside the leat, in a long curve around the hill, the ground falling away on his right to reveal glimpses of the stream that flowed down the valley, soon to broaden out and join the main valley of Nillacombe, whose name he was now familiar with. Down this valley he could see the stationary water-wheel of Wheal Hughes and the line of the leat that brought water to it, though it was obvious that it extended for a considerable distance beyond. As Mr Dawe had said, it was an old leat, only the first part of it reused for this mine. The curving course of the leat he was following took him now in the opposite direction to that scene, until he eventually came to the astonishing sight of its water gushing out of an adit mouth. He had seen many an adit mouth in Cornwall with water draining from the mine, but never in such quantities as this.

The hillocks and pits of Nuns Cross Mine were now all about him. He threaded his way through them until he saw, ahead, the venerable old cross of that name. He went up to examine it. What a curious shape it was, getting wider as it got higher, the top above the arms widest of all and stumpy, the short arms projecting too near the top, in his opinion. There was a cross engraved upon it between the arms, and some letters below it, not very clear and rather roughly chiselled. There was another word on the other side, across the arms, rather like a child's writing, letters of uneven size and not in a straight line. He could not spare the time to decipher the words; another time perhaps, but he did wonder when, by whom and for what purpose it had been erected in this remote position. This was the first of the puzzling monuments he was to find abounded on Dartmoor.

The new mine track passing it was quite obvious, and as he strode along it a different scene unfolded before his eyes as he looked towards his left. A vast desolate flat-bottomed bowl surrounded by hills, with further hills extending eastwards into the distance. Further to the left he saw another stationary water-wheel and realised it must be the Whiteworks Mine mentioned by Mr Dawe. A leat could be seen carrying water to it. Another larger leat above it, he realised, must be part of the one he had been walking along and that it was carried through the high ground on which Nuns Cross stood via the adits of Nuns Cross Mine. He now began to understand the importance of water as a source of power for these Dartmoor mines. In Cornwall only a very few water engines were in operation, there were too many mines there, especially in west Cornwall where there were no major rivers. The steam engine had solved their problem for all purposes and was now almost universally used.

For another mile Tom walked along the mine track until the disturbed ground on either side of it gave tell-tale signs of ancient workings, and a little later he saw a familiar sight, the vertically mounted drum of a horse whim, slowly revolving as the horse plodded round its circular platform, hauling the ore from a shaft, whose headgear shortly came into view. Further on a line of flat-rods was moving backwards and forwards, operating a balance-bob at the head of another shaft, transferring the motion from horizontal to vertical rods down the shaft to the pumps.

All these sights and methods were familiar to Tom, but he was astonished at the primitiveness of the apparatus, accustomed as he was to the massive structures of the Cornish mines. The flat-rods were sliding on their pulleys in conventional manner, but incredibly the pulleys were supported by pillars of rough moorstone, grooved at the top to take their axles. He had never seen anything like it, yet it worked.

The path he had been following now developed into a wide cart track, descending now beside these flat-rods. He came to a reservoir on his left, the waters passing beneath the track to flow into a short length of leat and a wooden launder to the head of a fair-sized water-wheel, the source of power for the flat-rods. A crank on the other side of the wheel was operating another set of rods. In spite of its simplicity it seemed to Tom that it was all well thought out and certainly economical.

At last Tom found someone to enquire where he might find the mine captain.

"Down there lad, by that bit of walling, on t'other side of the track."

As Tom approached that bit of walling he found, as that rhythmic clatter of sound had led him to suspect, that here was a small stamping mill, a small wheel operating only four head of stamps; a toy compared with the banks of perhaps twenty head of stamps operated by a massive beam engine that he had been accustomed to.

The figure now leaving the mill Tom recognised as the mine captain, for not only was he better dressed than anyone else, his fine head sported a luxurious growth of beard. All the mine captains that he had known had impressive beards, it seemed to be the hallmark of their profession.

Tom waited for him to approach so that he would be able to make himself heard away from the clatter of the stamps.

"What do you want my boy?"

Damn it, thought Tom, why does everyone call me lad or boy. But he stifled his resentment and said, "I'm looking for work sir, can you offer me anything?"

"What sort of work can you do? Have you any experience of mining?"

"Yes, I have worked on mines in Cornwall for the last six years."

"Then what are you doing up here?"

There was a slight hesitation before Tom replied.

"My father lost his life in a mine accident. My mother would not stay there. We live at Wakaton now."

Once again Tom found that such a tale of mine tragedy softened the tone of his interrogator's voice.

"And you still want to go down a mine?"

"My mother is all against it, but it is the only work I know."

"We have a full complement of men here at present. But this mine has every prospect of being successful, we may expand later. I haven't anything to offer you now, but come back and see me every week. If there's a job going you shall have it. On trial." He added as an afterthought.

"Thank you sir."

During this conversation they had been walking back along the track and had reached the Account House to which Mr Deacon was turning as they parted company. Tom had only gone a few yards when he heard him call, "Come back. What's your name?"

"Thomas Tremain, sir."

"Ay, a good old Cornish name. You look half starved boy. Here, get yourself a good meal," as he thrust a coin into Tom's hand.

Tom was so surprised and overwhelmed by the gesture, Mr Deacon had gone before he could utter a word of thanks. Perhaps he did look undernourished, and that was why he was referred to as 'boy'.

He had much to think about as he wended his way back along the path to Nuns Cross. That mine. What an extraordinary place it was. Primitive, yet efficient. The debris and squalor of mine trappings softened by the magnificent scenery all round it.

The noise and bustle of mining activity gave way, after the meanderings of the track through those ancient workings, to the silence of the open moor, broken only by the occasional bird song. If mining was in the young man's blood, this new scenery was captivating his mind. What a contrast between the fetid atmosphere and dim candlelight of the depths of a mine and this sparkling clear air he was breathing. Did he really want to go down a mine again? Perhaps there was no choice. He had to live. He had to break from the ties of that temporary existence on his uncle's farm.

As he strode along the Whiteworks track he remembered his promise to return to Mr Dawe and let him know the result of this visit. At the gate of the farm he was once more confronted with some furious barking. But the dog remembered him and soon quietened down, allowing Tom to open the gate and pass into the courtyard. Mr Dawe came to the door and welcomed him.

"Well Tom, have you been to the mine then?"

"Yes, Mr Dawe. There is nothing for me there at present, but Mr Deacon thinks the mine has good prospects and may expand. He will give me a job if one becomes available. He was very kind."

"Ah, that's good. What are you going to do in the meantime then?"

"I'll just have to carry on at my uncle's farm and come out here once a week to see what's doing."

Just then Mrs Dawe came to the door.

"Is this the young man you were telling me about, Will?"

"Yes. Meet me wife, Tom."

"We are just sitting down to our dinner. Will you join us?"

"If it is not putting you to too much trouble, Mrs Dawe."

"No, no, come along in."

And thus did Tom meet Mary Ann.

Chapter Two

When, a week later, Tom was returning from a fruitless visit to Ellisborough Mine, and as he approached the vicinity of Classywell, he wondered if he should again call on Mr Dawe. He wanted to, but wondered whether it might not look as if he was hoping for another invitation to dinner, it being about that time of day. As a matter of fact he had found that last invitation a bit of a strain. Amongst strangers he became rather reticent. At table he had sat opposite Mary Ann who was equally as shy. When their eyes met she had lowered hers quickly. Mr Dawe saved the situation when he asked Tom to tell them something about the mines in Cornwall. This was a subject he could talk about. He told them of the wonderful new steam engines that were now being used for pumping the mines. Since the patent held by Boulton and Watt had expired in 1800, he said, the Cornish foundries now had a free hand in the design of their engines and many improvements had been made. Not only were they increasing in size and power but they were using much less coal, and as coal had to be imported from South Wales this had been a great saving in the cost of running the mines. Tom was warming to his subject now and went on to explain the improvement in the pit work, the substitution of the old bucket pumps by a new type of plunger pump. If it hadn't been for these improvements the mines would not have been able to go any deeper because of the impossibility of keeping the water level down. Good ground was being found in depth and some of the mines were now reaping rich rewards.

Suddenly, and covered with embarrassment, he had realised that only Mr Dawe was listening to him. He apologised to Mrs Dawe for being so rude.

"Not at all," Mrs Dawe had said, "very interesting I'm sure."

He had finished his meal in relative silence again. But he *had* enjoyed that apple dumpling and cream.

He had passed Classywell by now and was about to leave the track for the ascent to Raddick Lane when he saw a figure leaving Roundypark. It was Mr Dawe's daughter. She had seen him too and waved. He waited for her to approach and for the first time was able to get a more comprehensive impression of her. She was a slim girl, her long grey skirt swaying gracefully as she walked down the grassy path. Her tightly fitting bodice ended in a frilled collar that becomingly encircled her neck. She wore no hat and her fair hair was tied at the back with a large blue bow. She walked with the assurance of one accustomed to the rugged terrain. She seemed to have lost her shyness when at last they met and she greeted him with, "Hullo Tom."

He was pleased to be called by his Christian name.

"Hullo, and may I call you Mary?"

"No you may not. But you may call me Mary Ann." A half smile and a dimple showed on her face.

"Mary Ann. Yes, I like that. But why two names?"

"There were so many Marys at our school that we had to have a second name to distinguish us. Mother liked it and so I have been called Mary Ann ever since."

"And what school did you go to?"

"Lady Modyford's at Wakaton, I expect you know of it. Father has been telling me that you are living at Wakaton but looking for work in the mines here. He told me to look out for you and to tell you he would like a word with you."

They had been walking back towards Classywell whilst this conversation was taking place and were now at the gate to the farm field.

"Will you come down now and talk to him?"

Tom did not need any pressing. This was a new experience for him to be walking and talking with a girl. He wanted to get to know her better.

Once again Tom was asked to stay to dinner. This time it was a happy occasion, all restraint gone.

As they entered the living-room Tom noticed how comfortably furnished it was. On the previous occasion he had been too ill at ease to notice his surroundings. Opposite him a door led into a kitchen from which emitted an appetising smell of cooking. On the wall beside the door hung a portrait of a bewhiskered gentleman of noble appearance, perhaps one of Mrs Dawe's ancestors, or would it be her father? The room was a fair size but did not admit of much more than the essentials of table and a variety of chairs. At the end wall was an enormous fireplace with a massive stone lintel. A fire was laid but not lit on such a warm spring day. A doorway at the opposite end of the room presumably led away to the bedrooms.

Mr Dawe explained that it had once been an old longhouse, that is a simple home of past centuries when one room was occupied by the family and the other, separated by a passageway and the entrance porch, by the livestock. The latter part had now been reconstructed and extended to form the bedrooms.

The long refectory table was highly polished and set tastefully for the meal. As they sat themselves down Mrs Dawe entered from the kitchen carrying a dish of rabbit pie, setting it down before Mr Dawe. She returned with a tureen of potatoes baked in their jackets and another of vegetables.

Mrs Dawe was a woman of middle age and knew well how to dress herself and make the most of her still comely good looks. This day she was vivacious and kept them all amused by the stories of escapades she and her brothers used to get up to in their youth. The obvious reference to a previous life of wealth in no way suggested that she regretted its passing or reflected on the simple life they were now living. The meal finished in a mood of bonhomie and homeliness.

Mr Dawe and Tom remained at the table whilst the ladies removed the dishes and retired to the kitchen.

"I understand you wish to speak to me about something, Mr Dawe."

"Yes, Tom. It is a long walk for you from Wakaton to Ailsborough every week. It takes up all the day when you could be earning a bit of money. I have been speaking to old Samuel Hocaday up to Nillacombe. He and his missus could do with a bit of help. He can't pay you much but you will get free meals and he's got a small room there you can have. What do you say?"

"That would suit me fine. What sort of work would I have to do?"

"They keep a few sheep, a couple of goats and some chickens. But the old place is in need of repairs, falling down about their heads it is. They thought you might be able to help there."

Tom was relieved to hear it wasn't all farming that he would be expected to do. On the mines he had proved himself very capable at effecting repairs to a variety of apparatus. He loved working with his hands.

"What say we take a stroll up there and see the old chap?"

"I'd love to," said Tom. Apart from the prospect of a job he was only too pleased for the chance to see a bit more of this lovely valley. In due course they walked up the narrow lane that connected the two farms.

Old Samuel Hocaday lived up to his Biblical Christian name. He looked a real old patriarch with his long flowing white beard and wise old head. His missus, as he always referred to her, was a typical old grandmother with her long black gown, white apron and white poke-bonnet framing her wrinkled kindly face. Yet they had had no children and had lived in this old farm for most of their lives, eking out a precarious existence, and in their old age unable to keep the old place in repair as well as to look after their livestock. In spite of its sad worn-out appearance Tom fell in love with the place. Its remoteness (it was the last of the farms in this valley), its isolation, its aspects and its prospects, and not least, its occupants. Already he was planning how he could repair that shippen, with only half a roof left. But he was seeing it in high summer conditions, though it was still only May. He gave no thought to what it might be like in winter.

"I see you'm takin' a good look round young man, d'ye reckon you can help us out yer?"

"I'm sure I can, Mr Hocaday."

"Au, call me Samuel, nobody calls me Hocaday, let alone mister in front. And me missus 'ere, she'm just Nancy. What us would do 'ere without the help of Will 'ere and 'is good lady, I dunno. Proper kind they've been, and now they brings you along. Will 'e stay my boy?"

"Yes Samuel. And please call me Tom."

But of course Tom had to return to Wakaton to explain to a tearful mother what had been arranged for him, collect what meagre belongings he possessed, and with these on his back and in a shabby old canvas bag, returned the next day to his new abode.

When Will Dawe returned to his home and told his family of the result of their visit to old Samuel, there was mutual satisfaction. Though neither he nor his wife mentioned it, and perhaps it was but a subconscious emotion shared by both, Tom seemed to take the place of their own son who had died of the dreaded whooping cough. Mary Ann had also had it but not so badly and had soon recovered. Their son, aged eleven, now lay in Wakaton churchyard. He also had been Tom. There was room enough at Classywell to have had the new Tom here, but they decided it would not be seemly, and to have fixed him up at Nillacombe was the next best thing.

On the next occasion when Tom went to Ellisborough Mine, he was offered a temporary job. One of the miners had sustained an injury and was likely to be off work for some weeks.

"Are you prepared to go underground?" asked Mr Deacon.

"Yes, of course," said Tom.

Mr Deacon called over one of the miners named Harry and drawing him aside whispered, "Keep an eye on him and let me know how he gets on."

He was taken to a shed and fitted out with the conventional attire for a miner working underground; trousers and coat of tough wearing material known as ducks, and a wide-brimmed hard hat. Then Harry handed him two items as a test to see if he knew what to do with them. "Here are your yorks and skiddy-bags." Tom looked at him quizzically, unsure whether to believe him; he had not heard these names applied to the items before but he was quite familiar with their use. He donned the leather gaiters and tied the yorks (laces) below his knees so as to raise the trousers and enable him more easily to bend the knees. Thus attired, with a bunch of candles tied to his waist and one stuck in his hat, they walked over to the ladder shaft, a circular stone-lined hole no more than six feet wide.

"Down yer go, Tom."

Harry waited for Tom's reaction. Without hesitation Tom got on to the top few rungs, then pausing, looked up at Harry and asked:

"How deep is it?"

" 'Bout twenty fathoms."

Tom nodded. He had been in mines hundreds of fathoms deep, taking half an hour or more to climb to grass, and that after a core of eight hours.

At the bottom and as they walked along the level Tom paused to examine the walls.

"Easy stuff to work, isn't it; what is it?"

"Mostly tourmaline and quartz in a clay base."

"What's the width of the lodes?"

"Two to three feet mostly."

Eventually they reached the end where stoping was taking place and relieved the two men working there. Harry explained to Tom how to distinguish the cassiterite. Tom had only worked in copper mines but he was eager to identify this new mineral. He was quick to learn and proved an able assistant. Harry had nothing but praise for him when he reported back to Mr Deacon.

For the next three weeks Tom's days were full. With eight hours core at the mine, the walk there and back, repairs to old Samuel's shippen, and other odd jobs on the farm, he slept the sleep of exhaustion on his hard bed in his tiny sparsely furnished room. There was no time during the week to see the Dawes, but they asked him to share their dinner on a Sunday. After the meal on those blessed days he asked Mary Ann to show him more of the Nillacombe valley. Initially they were short walks. The first was down through the fields to the river and up the opposite bank to Wheal Hughes. Crossing the river again here they walked up that impressive gert which went by the name of Willabeam. Beam, Tom was to learn, signified old surface workings when these deep excavations were dug in the search for tin.

Water naturally drained into them to form rivulets. Usually there was quite a copious flow of water in this gert and that is what the miners of Wheal Hughes had laundered across the river to augment their supply. Now, however, in this dry weather, only a trickle was flowing down.

The second walk had been to Classywell Pool, quite a lake in another deep excavation, silent, rippleless and rather mysterious. From there they had ascended to the leat and walked beside its banks for a short way before turning down past Roundypark. In answer to Tom's question about this leat, sections of which he kept coming across, Mary Ann had explained that it had been cut about twenty-five years ago for the Naval Dockyard at Plymouth, and was generally known as Dock Leat, to distinguish it from the Plymouth Leat, which had been cut two centuries earlier. Sir Francis Drake had something to do with that leat, it was often called Drake's Leat.

On the third occasion they had walked beside the river, which he was surprised to hear was called Nillacombe *Lake*, past Kingsett, the largest of the farms in this valley, to where the River Mew joined it from the north. Then they walked up the Mew valley and Mary Ann showed Tom a strange ruin of a building with many stones on its floor with hollows in them. She had seen it often but had no idea what it was. Neither had Tom seen such a ruin or those stones before. But he remembered some of the old miners in Cornwall talking about the 'Old Men' who streamed the river valleys in Cornwall for the alluvial tin to be found there, and how they built these small houses and smelted the tin ore in furnaces fuelled with charcoal and fanned by bellows. Blowing houses they had called them. But not many had survived in Cornwall and here he believed he was seeing one for the first time. Tom explained that the hollow stones were the result of stamping the ore to reduce it to a fine powder before putting it into the furnace.

"They probably had a water-wheel here to operate the bellows and the stamps," said Tom, "let's have a look to see if there is a leat to it."

They scrambled up the bank, Tom holding out his hand to help Mary Ann. He released it as soon as she was safely on the path, but wished he could have held on.

"Look, this path is the remains of the leat, see it going up stream; let's follow it."

They walked up it until it could no longer be traced as it neared the river. There was another scramble up a still steeper slope to regain the path that led from Nosworthy Farm to Riddipit. And this time Mary Ann really did need the help of Tom's hand, laughing at the top at the mad escapade. Any restraint that there had been between them was now broken. This little episode of fun and holding hands had brought them together as nothing else could have.

They crossed the river at Riddipit Steps and descended the opposite bank through a meadow dotted with trees. Mary Ann had been shown by Mr Pearse of Leathertor Farm a vooga here, a cave excavated in the growan with a very small entrance. Unless one knew where to look it was very difficult to find. After quite a lengthy search Mary Ann eventually found it. But neither ventured in, the entrance was so small and low down. In any case some form of light was necessary to see inside.

"I have seen something similar in Cornwall," said Tom, "they call them fogous down there."

They recrossed the river at the stepping stones and turned left along the path to an open space on their right where there was another cave. This one had a larger entrance protected by a stone lintel. They were able to go in and when their eyes became accustomed to the gloom they saw that it extended quite a way.

"Mr Pearse told me the farmers used to store potatoes in these caves," said Mary Ann, "many of the farms around here have them."

Then they climbed up a steep and rugged gully, passing a dark hole in the steepest part of it which Tom recognised as the entrance to an adit. Soon after, near the top of the gully, they came to an area of workings which Mary Ann said her father had told her was Keaglesborough Mine. It had worked on and off for many years. Tom of course was interested and spent some time examining the remains. There were two wheel-pits, one above the other. Then he realised that they were part of two separate periods of working, two levelled walled areas with the remains of square buddles, similar to the layout he now had discovered was the plan at Ellisborough, though here the wheel-pits were central in the dressing floors. Beyond the top one was the embankment for the leat, and the leat channel turning away northwards. Wherever he went, thought Tom, he seemed to find the evidence of recent or ancient mining, as well as the present working mines, all on such a small scale in comparison with what he had been used to in Cornwall, for which Tom was grateful, for they were not disfiguring the landscape to the same extent. Nature was quick to cover the scars and blend them in with the scenery, which was taking such a hold on Tom's imagination.

"Come Tom, it is getting late, Mother will begin to wonder what has happened to us."

Indeed Tom had given no thought to the passage of time, so engrossed had he been with all he had seen, and so happy was he to have these intimate wanderings with Mary Ann. They almost ran the rest of the way back to Classywell, to find, as he had feared, a slightly reproachful Mrs Dawe.

When Tom had taken his departure she said to her husband, "Do you think it right for these two to be out so long together?"

"I had been wondering too, Linnie; but I don't think we should worry. If I have read Tom aright Mary Ann will be quite safe with him. Too much depends on his future to risk his chances here. Anyway I'm beginning to have great trust in him, and I like the deference he pays us both, Linnie."

Mrs Dawe nodded with some relief and agreement. Linnie of course was a pet name. Will could never abide her real name, Lavinia, and from his courting days had always called her Linnie. Come to think of it, hadn't they, in those courting days, been out on just such expeditions and escapades?

Back at Nillacombe, much later than usual, old Samuel said, "Where you been to then, Tom, us 'ave been waiting for 'e?"

"Sorry Samuel, I have been exploring this wonderful land of yours and lost all track of time."

"Well the ruddy ceiling has come down in the pantry, can

you do something about it?"

Tom could and did do something about it, and when he had effected some temporary repairs old Nancy brought him his supper.

"There Tom me dear, tuck into that, you must be starvin'." She guessed that it wasn't just scenery that had kept Tom out so late.

After three weeks work at Ellisborough Tom was paid off. The injured miner had returned and resumed work. Tom however was well-known here by now, and liked. Mr Deacon told him not to despair. If what he had in mind did take place, there would be work for him. "Be patient," he said, "and in the meantime have a good look round and familiarise yourself with all that is going on."

Tom walked down beyond the large water-wheel to where he had first met Mr Deacon. He noticed now that there was another small stamping mill on the right of the road, similar to the one he had seen on the left, and with just such a section of wall between wheel and stamps. Its purpose was now apparent. Even with the light summer breeze, water in the form of spray was being blown from the top of the wheel. In a strong wind it would have been almost impossible for the men to work at the stamps without that protection of wall. Also the wall would be returning the sprayed water to the tail-race. Water was too precious to waste.

He took note of the robust steel shaft carrying the cams, its bearing at one end mounted on dressed granite blocks, the other bearing for it built into the wall where the shaft passed through to the wheel. The shaft was obviously strong enough to support such a small lightweight wheel without the necessity of another bearing on the outside.

The arrangement of the stamps was conventional, projections on the cams raising the lifters in sequence, the ore being crushed by the weight of the lifters only.

Tom walked to the second stamping mill, noting its similarity to the first. Two other mills followed downhill, embankments between them raising the leat level to a sufficient height to operate the succeeding water-wheel. There were no walls at these two mills. Presumably the more sheltered lower ground rendered this unnecessary.

Westwards of the fourth mill was a scene of great activity. When Tom arrived there he was informed that the building that was being erected, the walls already of a fair height, was the new smelting house. Massive dressed blocks of granite were being raised by sheer-legs to form the walls of the furnace. Beside it a pit was being dug for the water-wheel that would operate the bellows. A leat from the Thrushelcombe stream was being planned.

Tom spent most of the day finding out all he could about this fascinating mine. He visited the blacksmith's shop; the timber house; the turf house and the powder house. Wherever he went he was treated with kindness and helpfulness. He learnt a lot, but wondered, amongst all these multifarious activities, what sort of job Mr Deacon might have in mind for him.

On the fourth Sunday, when dinner was over, Mrs Dawe said, "and where are you two planning to walk to this afternoon?"

Tom looked at Mary Ann. "Have you anything in mind?"

"What about going to that stone row beyond Down Tor?"

"What is a stone row?" asked Tom.

Mr Dawe explained that there were a number of these long rows of upright stones on the Moor, nobody seemed to know what they were for, but some of them ended in a cairn or a circle of stones. "The Down Tor row is a very good one, but most of the stones have fallen."

"I'd like to see it," said Tom.

And so they set off, walking towards Kingsett and then down the lane to cross the river at Kingsett Ford, where there was also a simple clapper bridge. They followed the river up to where the scarp of the hillside receded from the river to form a large open plain.

"Isn't this where we crossed the river when we went to Wheal Hughes?" asked Tom.

"Yes, but I thought you would like to see more of the valley." She did not admit to herself that to have crossed it there would have shortened the walk!

They turned away from the river now, past the end of a long narrow gert and up to a hollow between the heights of Hingston Hill and Down Tor, providing a much easier gradient than on any other route to the stone row.

The long dry spell of May had extended into June. It was warm, but tempered with a light balmy breeze. Fleecy white clouds streaked the deep blue sky, casting pale shadows on the medley of colours which clothed a rounded hill developing ahead. The grey rocks of another tor appeared and stood out boldly against the sky. "Combeshead Tor," explained Mary Ann in response to Tom's question, "and that hill is Ailsbarrow; your mine lies on the other side of it. I like to pronounce the word 'Ails*barrow*' because there are two cairns on the top of it. You can never see them until you get to the top of the hill."

"And what is that dark streak below it?"

"The source of a little stream, Combeshead Brook. Look, you can see the little white dots of the stone row in front of it."

It did not take them long to reach the row. They stood beside the circle of stones and looked along the length of the row, snaking away into a slight hollow and up the gentle slope beyond. Two large monoliths lay recumbent at the head of the row.

"What an impressive sight it must have been when those two stones were erect," said Tom, "how I wish it could be possible to set them up again. Do you suppose this pit here, in the centre of the circle, means anything?"

"I like to think it was the grave of some important person in the distant past, but I have no idea really. Shall we walk along the length of the row?"

They did so, and noted with sorrow how many of the stones had fallen.

"I'd like to have a look at the source of that stream," said Tom, as they reached the end of the row, "it's not far away from here."

Standing on the edge of an escarpment they gazed down at a broad expanse of very disturbed ground, heaps of barren stones interspersed with heather clad mounds; pools of water reflecting the sunshine dotted the spaces between them. It was a chaotic sight.

"Have you any idea what all that signifies, Mary Ann?"

"There are heaps of stones like that in the Nillacombe

valley; Father says it is the result of ancient workings for tin."

"Yes," said Tom, "the work of the 'Old Men'. That term is used here just as it is in Cornwall, for the old tinners who dug deep into the river beds in search of the tin stone. The men at Ellisborough have been telling me how nearly all the valleys on Dartmoor have been treated in this way. What labour must have been involved, just look at that great width of valley that has been turned over and over. Fancy working here in the freezing conditions of winter."

"I don't think I want to imagine it. Come Tom, tear yourself away before you get another scolding from Mother for keeping me out so long!"

On their return they were passing the foot of Down Tor when Tom said, "Let's climb it."

"Good," said Mary Ann, "I'll race you there." Knowing perfectly well that she hadn't a chance of winning, even without the encumbrance of her long skirts. Tom took the challenge but sportingly let her win by a fraction. Such violent exertion brought colour to Mary Ann's cheeks and enhanced her beauty as they stopped, panting and laughing, at the summit rocks. It made little difference to Tom who was already bronzed with his daily exposure to the almost continuous sunshine. His strenuous life in the open air and the good wholesome food that old Nancy plied him with had filled out his body. There was nothing of the boyish pallidness now in his face, he looked and was a man in the prime of life. They made a handsome pair together as they stopped to admire the marvellous views in all directions from there. To the west, the long broad valley of the Mew dotted with its farmsteads and flanked by Sheeps Tor on one side and Leather Tor and Sharpitor on the other. To the north, behind Nillacombe, was Cramber Down and beyond it a range of tors away into the distance. To the east was Nuns Cross and Ailsbarrow. And to the south, behind Combeshead Tor and Deancombe was the Plym valley and a long mountain ridge beyond, a ridge that gave rise to so many rivers. Those on this side that could be seen were the source of the Plym itself, followed by Calveslake, Langcombe, Shavercombe, Hen Tor Brook and Spanish Lake. When they had completed the circuit of the summit rocks Mary Ann said, "I'm going to the top."

Nimbly she climbed up to the topmost rock, showing a little of her shapely legs as she had to lift her skirts to do so. Tom was about to follow when he was transfixed by the sight of her, sunlit and highlighted against a background of billowing cumulus clouds. She stood up to her full height, her head held high, her fair hair blown back from her forehead. She closed her eyes, clasped her hands behind her head and took a long deep breath of the invigorating air. The wind pressed her clothing against her body revealing the shape of her figure. No sculptor could have bettered that statuesque pose, no artist improve the colourful scene. It was a sight that Tom was never to forget and which was to bring him comfort in the years to come. The vision was all too short. Innocent of the effect she had had on Tom she lowered her arms and asked to be helped down. This time, when they were together again, Tom did not release her hand; nor did she make any attempt to do so. Hand in hand they walked for the rest of the way home.

That evening, at supper, Tom was enthusing about the wonderful views from the top of Down Tor, particularly to the south with that great long ridge and its rivers.

"Ay Tom," said Samuel, "I remember in me young days, when I used to go rabbiting, walking up them valleys. Langcombe was me favourite, though it wadun much gud for rabbits. Nice wide valley it is with a sparkling river and good firm ground. Shavercombe is just the opposite, narrow and rocky, but the water come down in lots o' little waterfalls, very pretty like. 'Bout half way up I remember quite a big waterfall, tumblin' into a dark pool with cliffs all round en. Spooky it was. Yet I always wanted to go back there. Can't say as I knows anything else like it on Dartymoor."

"I reckon you was lucky never to get caught goin' after they rabbits," said Nancy.

"Ay, I 'ad to be careful like, but 'twas gud fun. Anyway you enjoyed them rabbits, didun you?"

The next Sunday Tom surprised the Dawe family by arriving much earlier than usual. Mary Ann came out to greet him with an enquiring look.

"Have you ever been to Shavercombe?" asked Tom.

"No. Why?"

"Old Samuel has been telling me about it. I want to go there."

"It's a long way, isn't it?"

"Does that matter?"

"We won't be back in time for dinner."

"It's a lovely day, Mary Ann, why mess it up just because of dinner? Let's take something to eat with us."

Mr and Mrs Dawe joined them.

"Tom wants to take me to Shavercombe, Mother, an all day outing."

There was a dubious silence.

"Why Shavercombe, Tom?" asked Mr Dawe.

"Samuel says there is a fine waterfall there, he says there is nothing else like it on Dartmoor. I want to see it."

"You could go alone, couldn't you?"

Another awkward silence followed.

"Oh Father, please; I want to see it too."

Their persuasiveness finally won the day and with admonitions to Tom to take care of Mary Ann, they set out.

Once again past Down Tor they went, and to the stone row. They crossed Combeshead Brook below its first little gorge and series of cataracts. Over the plain beyond and around the head of Deancombe to the ford on Thrushelcombe. It was all guesswork on Tom's part, knowing only the direction they had to go. Fortune was with him that day, or call it beginner's luck, but he had chosen the best possible route.

They came across more stone rows on an extensive plain, encircled on three sides by hills and on the fourth by the river which they realised must be the Plym, for they could now see the Shavercombe valley beyond it. There were three stone rows, each of which ended in a low cairn, and at the other end of the rows, a massive long stone lay prone on the ground. Judging by the fact that only one face was visible above the soil, they must have fallen a very long time ago. Near the longest of these stones was a huge cairn, yet isolated from the rows. They scrambled to the top to find that the centre was hollow, possibly, they surmised, as a result of seekers after treasure. They wondered if anything had been found.

They now headed for the Shavercombe and arrived at a track leading to a ford on the river. There were no stepping stones here, nor any suitable boulders to effect a crossing. The water level was low however, and trickled lazily over the pebbles of the ford.

"I'll carry you over," said Tom, and removed his boots, giving them to Mary Ann to hold whilst he took her easily into his arms and paddled across the river. They sat on the opposite bank whilst Tom dried his feet and Mary Ann lived again the pleasurable sensation of being cradled in his strong arms.

The Shavercombe valley is wide at its confluence with the Plym, with gently receding hills, and only gradually narrows as it is ascended. Not far up, at some distance from its banks, they came upon the ruins of an old farmhouse. In their exploration of it they tried, in their imaginations, to rebuild its walls and rooms and wondered what it must have been like to have lived here, so remote and isolated, yet with such a breathtaking prospect of the Plym valley from its door.

As the valley narrowed and as the hill on each side steepened, they had to walk in single file, and later to cross the river to find a more practical route. Narrower and narrower became the valley, faster flowed the stream as it leapt down a succession of delightful cascades. At last they came to what almost amounted to a crevice in the rocky sides, hiding what lay beyond, though the sound of falling water told them that they had reached their destination. At a turn in the crevice they saw the fall, a ribbon of water tumbling from a rockface high above their heads into an almost circular cavern with a pool at its base. They were able to stand side by side, but for support Mary Ann put her arm round Tom's waist. They gazed in astonishment. Old Samuel was right, it was an eerie place. Instinctively Mary Ann clung closer to Tom. She was assailed by a sense of foreboding. It was not an evil place, it was a fairy dell, but to her it seemed to presage doom. Tom, being more practical, thought it a splendid sight, but in his male protectiveness put his arm around Mary Ann's shoulders. She looked up at him with a hint of fear in her eyes. They came away silent and subdued.

When they reached more open ground they sat beside the stream and ate the meal her mother had prepared for them.

"Tom, do you ever have presentiments?"

"I don't know. What do you mean?"

"Well, do you ever have a feeling of something that may happen?"

"No. What is worrying you, Mary Ann?"

"I'm not sure. That place frightened me, and I don't understand why."

Tom remembered his promise to Mrs Dawe to 'Take care of her'. When they resumed their walk he put his arm around her waist to comfort her. She responded by putting her arm around his. Thus they walked back to the ford.

He once more carried her across the river. If on the first occasion it had been a pleasurable experience, this time it was possessive. He did not want to let her go. He was forced to put her gently down because of the mundane necessity of donning his boots.

He held out both hands to help her to her feet. Almost subconsciously he drew her to him, put his arms around her and held her tightly. Her body was supple and unresisting. He put a hand behind her head and stroked her silky hair. Then bent down and kissed her forehead.

"Mary Ann," he whispered, "we are made for each other. Do you think you could ever marry me?"

She looked up at him with moist eyes. "Yes Tom. I love you."

Chapter Three

When Tom arrived at Ellisborough the following morning he was called immediately into Mr Deacon's office.

"Tom, I have a job for you. A twelve hours a day, seven days a week job."

Tom's heart sank. Was he to give up those precious Sundays?

"This mine has reached crisis point. We are in danger of closing down through lack of water. There is hardly enough coming from the Plym to keep the pumps going let alone the stamps. I've never known a drought like it; we must never allow a situation like this to arise again. I have engaged an expert to survey a route for a new leat from Langcombe to augment the supply from the Plym. He needs an assistant in the actual laying out of its course, and a gang of labourers to dig it. You will be his assistant, but when not required for the surveying you must be prepared to help with the digging. It may not help us this year, so in the meantime I am proposing to enlarge the reservoir here to give greater storage capacity. Some of the men normally employed on the stamps have already made a start on that. Mr Warne, the surveyor, arrives tomorrow. In the meantime you can help with the digging of the reservoir."

He gave Tom a piercing look. "I think I can trust you not to let me down."

At the reservoir Tom found that the water level was indeed low. The men were making a temporary bank to channel the water to the upper side of the reservoir so that deepening and widening of the main part of it could take place. Great activity was in progress with picks and shovels and buckets.

Tom knew most of the men by now and his help was welcomed. They worked with a will for they all knew that if the mine closed down they would all be out of a job. Not only was this part of the reservoir to be widened but the leat further back would be broadened, eventually to make a much longer reservoir.

At midday they had a break for a meal and a rest. For it was strenuous work and exhausting in the heat of the continuous sunshine. However other men off duty from underground work were called in so that the project went ahead continuously throughout the daylight hours.

While they sat and ate their meal, someone asked, "Where they goin' to find men to dig that there new leat then, bain't nobody round 'ere to call on?"

"Dunno, but they'll need a big gang if they's to do the job in two months, as Cap'n wants."

"Who's this bloke Warne comin' to survey the route, never 'eard of 'e?"

"They say 'e worked on that there Dock Leat; 'e must be getting on in years now."

"An' if they be goin' to 'ave this big gang of workers, where they goin' to sleep 'em? Bain't no room in the barracks 'ere."

"Plenty o' room up to Prince's Town now. Place be 'alf dead since the prison closed."

"Aye, that's true."

Tom did not contribute to the conversation but listened with interest. There were indeed some problems ahead. For him too. If he was to work throughout the daylight hours, when was he going to see Mary Ann? Since their secret betrothal she had been much in his mind. What did the future hold for them? He could not marry her without money. With overtime he would be making a nice little bit on this job, but it wasn't going to last. Where could they live? When should they tell her parents? When would he be able to introduce her to his mother?

The men continued to argue amongst themselves but Tom wasn't listening to them now. He could see no solution to his own problems.

At the end of the day, when the sun had gone down

and dimsey put a stop to the work, Mr Deacon came to inspect the progress. He expressed his thanks to the men for the great strides they had made. Though he had been praying for rain he hoped it would not come now. If it did and it was heavy, that would make work on the reservoir and the leat almost impossible. He *must* get the reservoir finished. He explained this to the men and urged them never to let up till the task was completed.

When Tom got back, in the dark, to Nillacombe, Nancy said, "Tom me dear, where 'as you been? Us 'ave been proper worrit about 'e. You'm lookin' proper done in. Come and get your supper."

He had to explain to the concerned old pair what was happening at the mine, how urgent the work was, how he would have to be up before dawn to get back to work as soon as it was light. Would they go and see Mary Ann tomorrow and tell her that he did not know when he would be able to see her again. How would she take it, he wondered. He longed to see her and explain.

Faithful old Nancy was up before he was in the morning and had not only got him his breakfast but had packed up some food for him to take with him. He had to be roused from his deep sleep, so exhausted had he been. But with the resilience of youth he was away again in good time to arrive at the mine and start digging before the sun was up.

At crib that morning, that is the mid-morning break for a bite of food and a drink (Tom knew it as crowst in Cornwall), he was called to the account house.

"Meet Mr Warne, Tom, he will explain to you what he wants. Then take this note to Jimmy at the Timber House and see that he gets what he needs."

Mr Warne was a smallish, thick-set man with a dark beard beginning to turn grey. He wore no hat and his long shaggy hair hung round his face like a sheep dog. It was difficult to tell his age, but his eyes were bright and intelligent. His walk was firm and purposeful. Perhaps he wasn't so old as he looked.

"Know anything about surveying, Tom?"

"No sir, but I look forward to learning."

"Never mind the 'sir', call me Daniel. 'Twill make it easier for us."

They soon reached the timber house just across the track from the account house, and Tom delivered the note to the foreman. Daniel inspected the timber with an expert eye and selected what he wanted.

"I need thirty pieces of this cut to six foot lengths. A hundred and fifty of this square stuff cut to eighteen inches long, ends to be pointed. And get the carpenter to plane this bit of three-by-one dead smooth and straight and exactly twenty feet long, with edges parallel. Then he's to firmly fix two pieces two feet long, one at each end, and at right angles to it. Got that?"

"Er, yes. I'd better write it down."

"When can you let me have say half the quantity plus the twenty foot long piece?"

"Day after tomorrow do?"

"You'd better think again. I want them tomorrow morning."

That was his method. Ask for the impossible and you'd get things quicker.

They went back to the account house where Daniel had been given a room for his own use. He began immediately to explain to Tom his method of surveying leats.

"This 'ere is me sights, mounted on a tripod with a level. And this yer is the staff what you got to hold."

Tom noticed two black bands near the top of the staff spaced about six inches apart.

"Now, what we do is this. We puts one of they six foot poles we'm 'avin' made into the ground where we wants the leat to come to, using this 'ere borer to make the 'ole for 'e, tamping it in firm like. Then I sets up me tripod beside it so that me sights are level and at the same height as the upper band on the staff that you'm holding upright, end of it firm on the ground. Then you goes away with the staff, pullin' the end of this tape with you until the tape is tight, t'other end being fastened to the pole my end. You'm then a hundred feet away. Now you goes sideways across the slope of the hill until me sights are on the lower band of your staff, then I shouts to you to stop. Since the bands are spaced six inches apart, the ground you'm standing on is six inches higher than what I'm standin' on. That's what we reckon is the best fall for the leat, water don't go too fast or too sluggish like.

"Then you puts up another pole where you are, using the tape to make sure 'tis exactly a hundred feet away. Then I come up to you and fixes up me sights again as before beside this pole, and we repeat what I just been telling 'e. We go on doin' that until we comes to the source of the water, so we get a line of poles marking the course of the leat.

"But that bain't much good to the gang what's diggin' the leat. That is where that twenty foot bit of wood comes in, 'e with the legs on. Now you got to remember that the difference in level between the poles is six inches in a hundred feet. Our twenty foot plank is one fifth of that. So the difference in level over twenty feet is one fifth of six inches, that is one point two inches. So we cut a bit off one of the legs of the plank so that it is exactly one point two inches shorter than the other. See what I mean?"

"Yes," said Tom, "I think so. But what do we do with this plank?"

"I'm just coming to that. We hammer one of they pointed stakes into the ground beside the first six foot pole, and another stake in line with the poles twenty feet away. We holds the longer leg of the plank on the first stake and adjust the height of the other one so that when we put the shorter leg on it, the plank is shown to be dead level by a spirit level on the centre of the plank. That is why the plank has to be accurately planed. That gives the same fall in level as that between the poles, but now the foreman of the diggers can line up the width and depth of the leat to the required amounts over a practical distance. We do that throughout the length of the leat. Now you got it, Tom?"

"Yes, I see now. When do we start?"

"Can't do much till we get that timber and some men to help with carrying it. I'm getting a gang of men from Tavistock and billeting them in the empty soldiers barracks at Prince's Town. Few years ago they was working on that tunnel that takes John Taylor's Canal from Tavistock to Morwellham. Clever bit o' work that was. 'Tis all finished now and there's been unemployment in Tavistock since.

They was only too glad to hear of a job. Meantime we'll go down to the weir on the Plym where the Engine Leat comes off it and plan what us 'ave to do for the start of the new leat."

A rough track led from the mine road, between the timber house and blacksmith's shop towards some old workings near Crane Lake, where Mr Deacon had plans for development. The source of the Engine Leat was a little upriver from there; so the track provided a direct route to it. To have followed the actual course of the leat would have taken them about three times the distance.

At Crane Lake they came across the leat as it looped around the little valley. It was possible to follow it for only a short distance before it entered the main valley of the Plym. It was here that the leat makers had their problems, cutting its channel along the very steep side of the valley up to the weir. The plan was that the new leat should enter the Plym just above the weir. Daniel saw that he was going to have similar problems on the opposite bank, which was just as steep and boulder strewn.

"You see, Tom, 'tis going to be a bit difficult 'ere, we'll 'ave to use a different method of levelling to what I've been telling 'e. But there bain't too much of it as I seen when I made a rough survey of the route. 'Tis all in the day's work."

This relaxed expedition with Daniel had been a pleasant interlude from his strenuous digging of the reservoir. But it was not just an enjoyable walk through new scenery for him, it was a chance to get to know this rugged character, a mixture of bluff efficiency and kindly patience in instructing his new assistant. He felt at ease with him but instinctively knew that he would get short shrift if he displeased him.

It was with some disappointment the next morning that Tom found he was not required on the new leat. When the gang of men had arrived from Prince's Town only a limited number were required on that difficult ground near the weir, there was not space for all. The surplus men were directed to the reservoir to work, Tom with them. With this extra labour great progress was made that day and Mr Deacon foresaw that within a few days it would be completed, and enough water stored soon after to resume normal working.

Tom's work with Daniel commenced the next day. The ground had been cleared of boulders from the river to the point where clean ground lay beyond, the course of the leat marked out and levelled to the correct gradient. Work could now commence on the sighting and erecting of the hundred foot marker poles. After a slow start the system of working became automatic and at the end of the day they had advanced to the head of a broad valley that led down to the Langcombe. The following day they had completed the course to the Langcombe itself, high up towards its source. Daniel eyed the small amount of water in the river at this dry season, and wondered if the new leat was going to be worthwhile. However, that was not his problem. He had been given a contract and he was fulfilling it.

Tom was revelling in the work. This wonderful open-air life suited him, the scenery thrilled him. The continuous exercise of either digging or walking hardened his muscles. The intoxicating air brought vigorous health. Tired he might be at the end of the day, but not exhausted now.

Work could now commence on the pegging of the stakes and their accurate alignment, height and twenty foot spacing. Apart from the very long grass it was easy country to work, being reasonably boulder free and with no awkward gradients. The workforce was efficient, the work on such a small leat being child's play compared with the width and depth of the Tavistock Canal and the Herculean task of cutting that tunnel through Morwell Down. There was one member of the workforce who stood out above all others. A black-haired, black-bearded giant of a man of enormous strength. When any heavy boulders required moving he was the man to do it, with obvious pride in his strength. At digging he was worth two of any of the others. Unfortunately his nature did not match his magnificent physique. He was uncouth, blasphemous, lewd and sarcastic. He was not liked, and for the most part the men avoided him, or if they could not, took care not to antagonise him. He was temperamental and aggressive at times, as a drunken man might be. On one occasion he had lashed out at someone who had annoyed him, striking him across the face with the back of his huge hand, sending him reeling.

When Tom's work with Daniel was not required he would assist with the digging. On the first occasion Jethro, for that was the big man's name, said, "Hullo sonny boy, left yer nice little cushy job, have you? The boss's favourite I suppose."

Tom had ignored him and got on with his work. However, next time, when Jethro purposely came up to work beside him, seeking confrontation, and after a few leering glances, he gave Tom a push and said, "Get back to your pimping, boy, it's man's work here," Tom's hackles rose. He came back and squared up to fight him, but the men quickly pulled him back saying, "leave him, he's drunk." It was harder still to swallow his anger as he saw the sneer on Jethro's face.

That ugly episode could not be forgotten, but fortunately all the survey work was now over. Work on the New Engine Leat, as it was to become known, was making such good progress that he was no longer needed there. Other work was found for him.

With the perversity of nature, as soon as the leat was completed the first rains came. All day and all night it rained, with tropical intensity. The rivers rose dramatically, water poured into the new leat and gave it a spectacular christening. The enlarged reservoir filled and overflowed. But, again perversely, so violent was the storm that no work could be carried out on the mine.

Meanwhile Mary Ann lived a life of frustration, not being able to see Tom and unable to tell her parents of her new relationship with him. She wanted Tom to break the news to them, and ask her father for her hand. She became a little moody and restless. To make a break from the daily chores and routine she asked her mother if she could take Nelson and ride over to Tavistock; she would like to buy a new dress. Mrs Dawe was a keen horsewoman, having been brought up with a stableful of horses. She had always kept a pony here. Periodically she would harness it to a gig and drive over to Ashburton to see her parents. She had encouraged Mary Ann to ride at an early age. They had named the pony Nelson as he had been born at the time of the famous admiral's victory at Trafalgar.

On the day of the storm they had been concerned about

Nancy and Samuel in their rickety cottage. When the following day Mary Ann looked out of her bedroom window to find that the rain had at last stopped, she decided that she would go and see if they needed any help. She hurriedly dressed and immediately after breakfast set off, carrying her mother's gift of a parcel of food, just in case they might need it.

On arrival at Nillacombe she was about to open the porch door when it was opened from within.

"Tom!"

"Mary Ann, oh my dear."

They were in each other's arms, hugging each other with joy, when they heard, "You two goin' steady, then?"

Nancy had come in from the kitchen when she heard the voices.

"Oh, Nancy, you weren't supposed to see that."

"Couldn't 'elp it me dear, and right glad I am to see it."

"Tom, what are you doing here, I expected you to be working?"

"The crisis at Ellisborough is over, Mary Ann. I've been told to take a day off and return on Monday. Oh, how glad I am to see you."

"I've missed you Tom, and been a bit worried for you when Nancy told me you only came home to sleep. Have you kept well?"

"Never felt better. I've had a very interesting time, I'll tell you about it later. Why have you come here?"

"Nancy, I've come to see if you need anything. Here's a little parcel from my mother. Have you had any rain damage?"

"Yes, a bit. Tom says he will have a look at it this morning. But he said he wanted to go over to see you first. Then 'e meets you on the doorstep. Is what I'm thinkin' true, me dears?"

They looked smilingly at each other.

"Yes, Nancy, I've asked Mary Ann to marry me."

"I be right glad to 'ear that. And does your mother approve Mary Ann?"

"She doesn't know yet."

"What, you tell me before 'er! You better go and tell 'er quick before she 'ears it from me."

Old Samuel heard their laughter as he came in from the courtyard. When he heard the news he shook Tom by the hand and kissed Mary Ann's forehead.

"An' now what'll us do without the pair of 'e?"

"Oh, it will be a long time yet. I still have to find a settled job."

When at last they left, it took them quite a bit longer than usual to walk the short distance to Classywell.

"Well Tom, this is a surprise," said Mrs Dawe as they entered the living-room. "We have missed you." She noticed the heightened colour in Mary Ann's cheeks and the increased sunburn in Tom's. Mr Dawe rose from his chair. "Welcome back Tom, me boy. You've had a hard time of it over to Ellisborough I hear."

"Yes. It has been a very interesting time though. But I have something more important to talk about than that. Mr Dawe, I have asked Mary Ann to marry me. I have nothing else yet to offer her but love. But I will find something, and in the meantime I would like to know that I have your consent."

"You have only known each other for a very short time, Tom. You've got to make sure. Only time will tell. If you prove yourself to be the man I think you are, you have my blessing. What do you say, Linnie?"

"It is no surprise to me, Will. I welcome Tom into our family."

She came over and kissed her daughter and then Tom. "Bless you both, I am very happy for you." She remembered her own whirlwind courtship and the parental opposition to it.

"I think this calls for a celebration, Will. Get that bottle of Burgundy, we must drink to their health and happiness."

The morning passed in festive mood. Never before had Tom felt such a friendly, homely, relaxed atmosphere. The warmth of their welcome touched him deeply. The comfort of their home was in such contrast to his spartan living at Nillacombe and the rough labour he had been experiencing at the mine. When generalities turned to the more serious subject of the recent storm, Tom suddenly remembered the damage to the roof at Nillacombe and his promise to repair it.

"I'd better go and get on with it," he said, "I reckon it'll take me quite a while, Samuel will be getting impatient."

"Come tomorrow for the usual Sunday dinner," called Mrs Dawe as he waved good-bye to them.

It was Sunday dinner-time before Tom had completed his repairs to the roof, it had been a bigger job than he had anticipated. He apologised for his late arrival, but they approved the reason for it, and of Tom's ever willingness to help.

Dinner was the usual substantial and delicious repast, by now a happy family get together. Conversation ranged from the crisis at Ellisborough to the state of affairs in Europe (Mrs Dawe kept herself well informed on that during her visits to Ashburton), the railway that Sir Thomas Tyrwhitt was proposing to build from Prince's Town to Plymouth, the folklore of Dartmoor, such as the legend of bottomless Classywell Pool, of Dewer the Wisht Huntsman and his spectral hounds, and so on.

When the meal was over, Mr Dawe said, "Where are you two going walking this afternoon?"

"I would like to go to Sheeps Tor," said Tom, "I haven't been there yet."

So to Sheeps Tor they went, and sat on the summit and gazed down at the valley of the Mew, with its meadows at one end, its gorge at the other; the farms of Longstone and Essworthy, and the lonely lane that led steeply up beyond it. The silver river threading its way through the fields, the white dots of sheep grazing beside it, and Drake's Leat making a straight line above it. The valley of peace.

In descending the slopes of the Tor, Mary Ann tripped and fell forward onto her hands and knees. Tom quickly put his hands under her arms to help her to her feet; then realised that his hands were on her breasts. She put her hands on his and held them there, just for a moment, before they resumed their walk, in silence awhile, for their thoughts dwelt on and relived that little episode. It became a treasured memory that Tom was never to forget.

Chapter Four

The following day Tom was once again called to Mr Deacon's office.

"Tom, I still have some work for you. The smelting house is nearing completion. After our recent experience it is quite obvious that the leat we have cut for it from Thrushelcombe stream is going to be inadequate. And anyway I have plans to build another and bigger stamping mill beyond it, its wheel to be operated by an extension of the smelting house leat. I have been told that there is an old leat that came off the Plym and goes to Thrushelcombe Ford. We may be able to make use of that; do you know of it?"

"No sir, I have never been to that part of the moor."

"I want you to go with Mr Warne and investigate it. Silas will show you where it comes to near the ford, but I can't spare him from the stamps for more than that. Whether or not it is of any use, Mr Warne has still to survey a route for another leat for the smelting house. He has asked for you. You will find him in his office."

They met Silas at the fourth stamping mill and he took them down to the ford.

"This is the crossing place," he said, "on the old Jobbers' Road from Sheepstor to Buckfastleigh."

"What are jobbers?" asked Tom.

"Oh, the old wool gatherers. Came to all the farms 'round 'ere they did, to collect their wool and take it to Buckfastleigh for the woollen mills there. You see the Longstone Leat coming round 'ere too? Comes off the Plym it do, near Plym Steps, and goes to Longstone Farm near Sheepstor.

Jobbers' Road goes round the hill above it, and also goes to Plym Steps. But you goes up that there gully to its left. You'll find the old leat at the top of 'e. Can't mistake it."

There *was* no mistaking it when Daniel and Tom reached the top of the gully, quite a substantial one. It took them up a steeper gradient than that which Daniel had explained was the ideal. It passed close to a small ancient pound, below which Tom saw the stone rows that he and Mary Ann had explored, and there was a fine view of the Shavercombe valley beyond them. When the gradient began to lessen they were leaving that scene behind them and the valley of the Plym lay ahead, and the next lateral valley appeared, Langcombe. The recent storm had heralded the beginning of unsettled weather, spells of sunshine being interspersed with showers. A leaden sky hung over Langcombe, sombre and menacing. Yet a shaft of sunlight lit up the crown of a tor on the hillside immediately ahead. When opposite the Langcombe valley the Jobbers' Road was plainly to be seen approaching the river, where presumably there was a ford, but no stepping stones were visible. Later the course of the leat lay alongside the upper wall of a large prehistoric pound, on the slopes below the sunlit tor. Beyond that their route took them ever nearer the river until they came to a wide shallow valley where the leat ended abruptly.

"Must 'ave crossed there somewhere," said Daniel, "and couldn't be all that far away before it reached the river."

But all attempts to trace it proved fruitless. The ground was wet and they were not suitably shod to explore it. Furthermore it began to drizzle; there was every indication that the weather was going to get worse. They donned their capes and returned along the same route, not knowing then of any better or shorter one.

"I reckon we can make use of this 'ere leat," said Daniel. "You remember where the leat made a less steep gradient as we turned into this valley. Seems to me we can start diverting it there and take it round the hill to cross Thrushelcombe higher up. We'll 'ave to bring me level out with us tomorrow and take a few sights, weather permitting. Don't look too good, do it?"

The next day, between showers, they made a rough

survey of the course around Thrushelcombe Hill and across the Thrushelcombe valley itself, about half way between the ford and where the Engine Leat crossed it, and from there to the fourth stamping mill.

Within a week they had the poles erected and twenty-foot spaced pegs hammered into place. The labour force had been reassembled at the barracks at Prince's Town. All was ready to start reconstructing the leat at its distant source.

This was the most difficult part of the project; not only the cutting of the leat in such wet ground, but the construction of a weir in the river. Despite everyone's dislike of the man, Jethro proved invaluable here. To give him his due, he worked with a will and seemed to take a perverse pride in proving himself superior to anyone else in his ability to overcome the difficulties.

It was at Mr Deacon's request, if it was possible, to take this new leat to stamping mill No. 4, from where the water would be channelled to the short leat already constructed to the smelting house. The water-wheel there could also drive a small set of stamps. If a lack of water now put the upper stamping mills out of action, this new leat would still keep No. 4, No. 5 at the smelting house, and the proposed No. 6, operating. There was every indication, Mr Deacon said, that the quantity and quality of the tin being extracted was going to make this mine a great success. This increase of stamping facilities was essential.

Tom was not required at the making of this leat, for which he was not a little thankful. He had no wish to have anything to do with Jethro. Instead work for him was found underground. A crosscourse had been discovered in the drive eastwards and was worth exploring. Two extra work faces were thus provided.

Those blessed interludes of Sunday dinners at Classywell and walks with Mary Ann were resumed. Fortune was smiling on him, all seemed well with the world.

August was well advanced and the weather more settled again when Tom asked Mary Ann if she would like to walk to Crane Lake. Being a Sunday no work was in operation either on the mine or on the new stamping mill leat, so they were not likely to meet anyone. The miners usually returned to their homes and the leat workforce to Prince's Town. He thought Mary Ann might like to see the new leat he had helped to survey flowing into the Plym. Even if she wasn't interested in that, it at least provided something different from their usual walks.

They walked up the valley, past Nillacombe, where all was quiet, "probably having their afternoon nap," said Tom; then across the little stream that flowed down from its source on Cramber Down, and up Drivage Bottom to the Ellisborough track. They did not take that track, though, but continued to a valley down which the South stream flowed on its way to Fox Tor Mire. This would lead them to Crane Lake without having to go anywhere near the mine.

"Tom," said Mary Ann as they climbed up this pleasant valley, "do you always want to be a miner?"

"I've never thought of doing anything else; why?"

"The thought of working down in the depths of the earth, in all that wet and darkness, makes me shudder. What do you like about it?"

"It isn't a question of liking. In Cornwall, apart from fishing, there is no other work available. My father had always been a miner. I was proud of him and his skills. I tried to equal, or even do better than he did."

"But isn't it very unhealthy down there?"

Tom gave that a bit of thought before answering.

"Yes, very few miners live a normal span of life. I am astonished when I see old Nancy and Samuel still working. They are over eighty aren't they? No miner lives to that age, usually not much over forty."

"And what sort of life do they have when they are not working?"

There was another pause before he replied.

"Mary Ann, if I was to describe to you the worst of the hovels many of the miners live in, you wouldn't believe me. Rarely are they any better than a roughly thatched cottage with two rooms, one for living, one for sleeping. Not only the miner, his wife and children, live there, there may be another family to share it, or else a number of lodgers. The beds are never empty, as soon as one miner rises to do his core, another coming off duty climbs into it. Most miners keep a pig for eventual eating. They usually have a small plot of ground in which they grow potatoes, the staple diet down there. That is what the average miner comes home to after an eight hour core, plus another hour or more descending and climbing ladders. By the time he has walked home and had a meal, there is little time left to do anything much except tend his vegetable plot."

"Did you live like that?"

"No. My father was a tributer. That is he was independent down below and could select where he wanted to work, as distinct from a tutworker who is paid so much per fathom worked, whether it is good ground or not. My father was very skilled at recognising where the best lodes were, and of course, the harder he worked the more he earned. He taught me those skills. We had a nice little cottage and did not have to share it with anyone. My mother worked at the mine too, the women are known as bal maidens. Their job is to break up the ore with hammers, working out in the open. They never go down a mine."

"What is it like here?"

"Very different. The mine is not a deep one and it is reasonably well ventilated by having a number of shafts. The men don't have to come home to a hovel; the barracks may be crowded but they are clean and comfortable. I am lucky to be able to come home to such a lovable old couple as Nancy and Samuel. And never in my wildest dreams did I think I would eat a meal such as we have had today. And now, above all that, I have you."

"I don't want you to die at forty. Please Tom, find some other job."

"I am no good at anything else. If I have to say it myself, I am expert at the job I do now. Perhaps one day I will be a mine captain. Then you are somebody. What would you rather I did?"

"Farming?"

"And where would I find a farm? Where would I find the money to buy a farm? Be practical, Mary Ann. Perhaps I can get a job on the stamps. I'll be in the open air then. And I'll promise to live longer than forty."

This brought a laugh to both of them.

"Let's change the subject. Tell me about your mother."

"What do you want to know?"

"I remember her telling us one dinner-time of the pranks she and her brothers got up to. It was a very different life for her then, wasn't it?"

"Yes. I used to be taken to that big house near Ashburton, with its servants, gardeners, grooms and carriages. I don't often go now but Mother likes to keep in touch, for her father's sake. Grandfather is a kindly old gent, that is his portrait in our living-room. He is still very fond of Mother, they had much in common. Grandmother ruled the house though, I was always afraid of her, Mother too, I think. She was always happier with the servants than she was when all dressed up for state occasions. It was at one of the fêtes in the village that she met my father. Grandmother was not amused when she was told that they wanted to marry. 'A common miner?' she had snorted. He wasn't a common miner of course. He had interests in many of the Dartmoor mines at one time or another. The trouble seems to be that these mines never last, successful one moment, collapse the next. Father says it wouldn't surprise him if Ellisborough goes the same way. And that is another reason, Tom, why you should look for another job."

By this time they had reached the head of the Crane Lake valley.

"Look at that heather," said Mary Ann. Indeed the whole valley was a mass of purple. "What a royal sight."

They walked along the edge of the steep scarp and feasted their eyes on the wild and colourful scene. When they reached a deep mining gert they scrambled down into it and followed it to the valley floor. Just as they reached its end, a figure appeared from a lateral gully.

"Oh no!" exclaimed Tom, and clutched Mary Ann's arm. "Jethro."

Mary Ann had not heard Tom speak of him but did not much like the look of the man.

There was no avoiding him as he came towards them.

"Hullo little man, got your fancy piece with you eh? Nice little thing."

Tom tried to brush past him, keeping Mary Ann away

from him.

"Oh no you don't," said Jethro, placing himself before them again.

"Perhaps the little lady would like to come for a walk with a real man," as he leered at her.

Tom tried to push him aside for them both to make a run for it. With a sweep of his great arm he brought the back of his hand across Tom's face, sending him reeling back a pace or two. Quickly recovering Tom came forward and hit Jethro a resounding blow on the chin. It was so swift that Jethro had not time to parry the blow. But it hurt Tom's hand more than it hurt Jethro, who now came forward, head down and both arms flailing. Tom had practised boxing in his days in Cornwall. He side-stepped nimbly, avoiding the blows and got in another punch to Jethro's head. In that moment he glimpsed Mary Ann with her hands to her face, terror in her eyes. His blows might just as well have been directed at a punch-bag for all the effect they had on Jethro, who now, enraged by these pin-pricks, came at Tom again. This time there was no avoiding his blows, a vicious punch catching Tom on his cheek-bone. He fell over backwards; the last he remembered was grazing his face on the side of a boulder as he hit the ground.

When consciousness began to return Tom thought he was on his hard bed at Nillacombe. He felt drowsy and did not want to wake up. But his face was hurting. He put his hand to his cheek. It felt sticky and wet. When he opened his eyes he found his hand was covered in blood. He looked round and was surprised to find himself in the open air. Realisation began to dawn; a fight. Oh God, Mary Ann. There was no one to be seen. Jethro; the terror in Mary Ann's eyes. He tried to get to his feet but fell back, his head swimming with pain. When he did manage to stand up he wondered where he was going to look for them. Then he realised he was in no condition to do anything if he did find them. He must get help. Ellisborough. Would anybody be there? He must try, it was the nearest source of help. He remembered the rough mine track that he and Daniel had walked. He staggered along it, strength gradually returning, but it was uphill and rough going, it took him a long time before he sighted the group of buildings; the timber house; the blacksmith's shop; they were both closed. The account house, would that be open? Yes it was, the door was ajar. "Is anyone there?" he called. Mr Deacon came to the door.

"Good God boy, whatever has happened to you?"

Tom blurted out his confrontation with Jethro and how he had gone off with Mary Ann.

"Who is Mary Ann?"

"My betrothed."

"Sit down here while I go and get some help." They would need a large gang to search such a wide area, there was no knowing what direction they had taken. There were a couple of miners in the barracks who had no real home to go to for the weekend. He sent one of them to Prince's Town to rouse the men in the barracks there, giving him a note to take so that they would know it was authentic and urgent. The other man he instructed to accompany Tom back to his home. "We'll find them, Tom, don't you worry; get yourself cleaned up."

All very well to be told not to worry. How could he help it? He was sick with worry. What awful fate was happening to Mary Ann? The possibilities filled his mind. He could not speak to his companion until they arrived at Nillacombe, where Tom thanked him and said he would be all right now. "Go back and help in the search."

Will Dawe was sitting on the seat at his front door, enjoying the warmth of the waning sun, the view of Down Tor that never ceased to give him such pleasure, the quiet of approaching evening, and counting his blessings. How lucky he was to have such a place, to have married a woman who had made it possible, to have a daughter whose beauty was blossoming since she had met Tom, for whom he was beginning to have a great affection.

It is time those two returned, he thought. He turned to look up the lane to Nillacombe. Ah, there's Tom. No, it can't be, he's alone; and swaying like a drunken man. That's not his face! Damme, it is though. He got up and walked towards him.

"Good God, Tom, whatever has happened to you?" He

saw one cheek black with bruises, the other scarred and streaked with dried blood.

"And where is Mary Ann?"

Tom was so tense and worried he could not find words to reply.

"Linnie, Linnie, come quickly."

"Oh Tom, my dear boy. What has happened, Will?"

"I don't know, get him inside and sit him down."

The nearest seat was a hard-backed chair at the refectory table. Tom slumped into it and hammered the table top with his fists in frustration.

"It's Mary Ann, Mary Ann, she's been taken by that monster Jethro. I couldn't protect her from him. We fought but I had no chance against a man like that. Now he's got her and I . . . Oh God, Oh God, what is happening to her?" He thumped the table again in his agony of thought.

"Will, bring a basin of warm water. Then make some tea please."

Mrs Dawe put a motherly arm around Tom's shoulder. She was now as worried and frightened as he was, but she controlled her feelings and said, "Come over here and sit in an easy chair." She could only hold his hand and try to soothe him as he fell back exhausted into the chair and she knelt before him. They remained silent until Will brought in the warm water. Mrs Dawe bathed the blood from his face. She was relieved to find there were no deep wounds, just lacerations, but so many of them it had drawn a lot of blood.

Whilst drinking the tea, and how he needed that drink, he was able to tell them of their meeting with Jethro. He had to explain who Jethro was and what sort of a man he was. Of the fight, and how he had lain unconscious, he did not know for how long. Of how he had managed to get to Ellisborough and how Mr Deacon was organising a search party.

"I must go and help," he said, and started to rise from the chair.

"Sit down, Tom. You could do no good in your state. Anyway by the time you get there it will be dark. The search will be over by then, whether they have been found or not. It will be impossible to search in the dark. Have you told Samuel and Nancy yet?"

Tom shook his head.

"Will, would you go up to them and explain what has happened, and tell them Tom will remain here for tonight."

No one thought of going to bed that night. They remained in their clothes. A meal was eaten but not enjoyed. The hours dragged. Soon after dark there was a knock at the door. With mixed feelings and hearts pounding they rushed to open it. It was a messenger from Mr Deacon. The search had been unsuccessful so far. The men would be kept at Ellisborough and the search resumed at first light.

Midnight came and went.

"We must have some sleep," said practical Mrs Dawe. "Tom, we will lie on our beds in our clothes. Try and get some sleep in this chair, you will hear if there is a knock on the door. Here's a blanket, cover yourself up."

It was a long time before Tom did get to sleep. Even then it was not a restful one, so full of unpleasant dreams was it. He was awakened by the sound of cups rattling. Mrs Dawe was pouring out a cup of tea for him. He noticed that it was now daylight but the dawn had not long broken. He hoped the search party had made an early start.

They drank their tea and ate, though Tom was not aware of what he was eating. Thoughts were sombre. What was happening?

There was a sudden leap to their feet as there came a banging on the door. A messenger?

Tom was first there to open it.

Mary Ann rushed into the room, her eyes wild, her hair hanging raggedly round her face, her wet clothes clinging to her, her hands clutching her water-laden skirts to stop them from encumbering her knees. She saw Tom and shouted, "Don't touch me, don't touch me." She rushed into her mother's arms, sobbing.

Tom could only stand and stare at this transformation. His lovely dainty, elegant companion of yesterday reduced to a wild, hysterical grief-torn apparition, covered in mud and filth. Uncontrollable fury filled his soul.

Mrs Dawe was the first to recover.

"Come my darling, we must get these wet clothes off you," and led her to the bedroom.

Will Dawe and Tom could only sit and wait, unable to speak, consumed with their thoughts. For a while there was no sound from the bedroom. Then sobbing was heard once more, increasing in intensity, ending in a wild hysterical shriek. Then silence again.

After what seemed an age Mrs Dawe returned, her face drawn and drained of colour. She looked at them both, and gave a nod, answering an unspoken question. She sank into a chair and put her head in her hands. It was her turn to lose control as she subsided into silent sobs. It was Will's turn to do the comforting.

With clenched fists, his injured face suffused with rage, Tom muttered in little more than a whisper, "I'll kill that man."

Chapter Five

Later that morning Mr Dawe accompanied Tom to Ellisborough, partly for moral support and partly to make sure that he did not do anything rash. It was essential to go to find out if the search parties had found Jethro. It was inconceivable that the man would have turned up for duty. He must know that there would be a man-hunt for him. He may have already escaped. Mr Deacon must be informed that Mary Ann had returned home, but how much to tell him was a problem that worried them; enquiries as to her safety were bound to be asked.

It was also necessary to call at Nillacombe and tell them that Mary Ann was back, but no more.

At Ellisborough the search parties were returning at irregular intervals, depending how far their search had taken them. They had covered a very wide area, in all the valleys, the gerts, the river banks, down to Ditsworthy Warren House. There was not a clue as to where he could be. When Mr Deacon was told of Mary Ann's return, they could not bring themselves to say more than that she had managed to escape and had been wandering about the moor, lost until daylight came. She was now sleeping off her ordeal.

And indeed that part was true. She was still asleep when they returned to Classywell. Tom wanted to know where Jethro had taken her. There had been no opportunity yet to ask her. She had been too hysterical and incoherent to tell her mother anything but the ordeal she had suffered. Sheer exhaustion, both mental and physical, had sent her into this deep sleep. Mrs Dawe blessed this and would not allow her to be disturbed, though Tom begged her to find out where she had been. If only he could speak to her.

It was mid-afternoon when Mrs Dawe eventually found her awake. She asked Mary Ann if she would see Tom. She shook her head vigorously. She would see no one. She felt too unclean and degraded. She knew that all must now be over with Tom. She didn't want to talk about it.

Then Tom begged Mrs Dawe to ask her a few simple questions. Could she remember how far Jethro had taken her? Did he take her to a building? If so what was it like? Why were her clothes so very wet when she got home? Had she fallen into a river? Tell her the safety of other women may depend on her answers. She must speak.

It was this last exhortation that persuaded Mary Ann to talk. When Mrs Dawe returned to the living-room she gave Tom what information she had been able to glean. Mary Ann couldn't remember much to begin with, she had struggled so much. But they had gone in the same direction as she and Tom had been walking, and she remembered seeing the river occasionally. Then she remembered crossing some wet ground and being carried across a ditch with some water in it. Then she saw the river again and soon came to a little hut, with a roof but no door. It was just after she escaped, when it was still dark, that she fell into that ditch and got wet. That is all she would say. The memories came flooding back and she had burst into tears again. "Poor child, I don't think she will ever get over this."

"That is something to go on," said Tom, "at least I know the direction in which they went."

"What are you going to do, Tom?"

"I don't know yet. But I'll never rest until I've rid the land of that . . . that beast."

Mrs Dawe looked anxiously after him as he took his leave.

Tom walked slowly up the lane to Nillacombe, turning over various plans in his mind. How could he hope to overcome that monster single-handed? Who would want to help him, knowing what his intentions were? He had still not solved the problem when he arrived at Nillacombe, where the warmth of welcome given him by Nancy and Samuel touched him deeply. For the last twenty-four hours he had been tense and belligerent, unable to rest. Now they were being a mother and father to him, concerned over the state of his face, wanting to do anything and everything to comfort him. He had to fight back the tears as their kindly ministrations helped him to relax. But he did not want to show weakness or to allow anything to lessen his resolve.

The following morning, when Tom had not appeared from his bedroom, Nancy said to Samuel, " 'E's sleeping well, 'e sure did need it, poor boy; 'tis wicked 'e should 'ave to suffer like this. Thank God Mary Ann's safe, 'e'll want to go down and see 'er, I 'spect. I'll take 'e a cup 'o tay."

But she came back still carrying it. " 'E's not there, 'em gawn!"

Tom *had* slept well, to begin with, but bad dreams woke him early and his resumed scheming then kept him awake. Suddenly he had a plan. He would have to get to Ellisborough early. He wasn't expected to report for duty for a day or two. But he had to get a weapon and that is where he would find one. So he had risen and dressed and crept out of the house just as day was breaking.

He did not use the mine track to Ellisborough, there was too much risk of meeting someone on it. He made a circuitous approach, eventually reaching the maze of pits and mounds through which he crept stealthily. He came to the back of the blacksmith's shop. He could hide here without being seen, but still able to look through a slit window and hope for a moment when it might be unoccupied.

The blacksmith arrived and unlocked the building. What work he was doing Tom could not see, but he had a view of the door and could see if he left. The waiting was agonising; he almost decided to go in boldly and ask for what he wanted. But that would arouse suspicion, he did not want anyone to know he was there, or to prevent him from carrying out his intentions.

At long last the blacksmith was seen to leave. Tom hurried round to the side of the house, opposite to the direction the blacksmith had gone, and waited for him to disappear into another building, the turf house. Quickly Tom entered the building and came away with a long-handled sledge-hammer, a tool he was expert at handling. He hurried away into the maze of mounds again.

At last he was far enough away to be out of sight of anyone at Ellisborough, and could walk in the clear towards Crane Lake. He arrived at the site of the fight. He must now walk towards the river, that is what Mary Ann had said, in the same direction as they had been walking. He crossed the Engine Leat and descended beside the stream towards the Plym, looking for any sign of footsteps. Perhaps a trained tracker might have seen some, but Tom did not. As he turned the corner into the Plym valley, leaving Crane Lake behind, he saw a hut in a sheltered position beside the rising ground. Clutching his hammer in both hands Tom approached cautiously. It was empty, roofless, and much too big to be what Mary Ann had described. He continued down river for some hundreds of yards until he came to that broad shallow valley where he and Daniel had tried to find the source of that ancient leat in the marshy ground. He had to choose his way carefully across the valley, so wet was it. This surely must be what Mary Ann had described. And she said that she had then been carried over a ditch. Perhaps that was the leat so recently made here, for the stamping mills. He reached it. Yes, there was water in it, no doubt seeping into it from all that wet ground higher up. But he could see now that it was temporarily dammed to allow the water to escape to the river until such time as the whole leat was completed.

Now which way to go? She said 'soon' they had reached that hut. It could not be far away. She said she had fallen into this ditch when she had escaped. There was only one direction where that could have happened. He walked beside the leat, looking for any sign of a small building. He could see the river. Surely it should be visible if there was a hut here?

Then he saw where the leat bank had been slightly damaged. Could that have been caused by Mary Ann as she fell into it? But she said that she had done so soon after her escape. There was no building to be seen. He descended from the leat bank beside a rounded hillock. And there, at the bottom of it, was an opening to a dark interior.

Once more he clutched his hammer in both hands and made a cautious approach. There was no sound. When he stood at the doorway he shut out what available light there was, and could see nothing. He crouched down and waited for his eyes to become accustomed to the gloom.

No one was in it. He saw a rough bed of bracken, a collection of bottles and a pewter mug. Then something white on the floor caught his eye, partially covered with earth. He picked it up but immediately dropped it with a sudden recoil of his arm and a gasp of breath. It was an intimate item of woman's clothing. He quickly backed out of the evil place, stood still in a paroxysm of rage and agony. Then like a madman he set about that hut with his sledge-hammer. Blow after blow he rained down on it, knocking stone after stone away from the doorway until the lintel came crashing down and half the corbelled roof with it. Tom leapt back to avoid the falling debris, but then attacked the rest of the roof until it had fallen in, together with its thick covering of earth and turf, and completely covered that infamous floor.

In utter despair and loathing for this evil place, exhausted though he was with his violent assault on it, he hurried away, stumbling over loose boulders, splashing regardless through the swamps, intent only on revenge. The thought of his cherished Mary Ann being ravished by that monster in that filthy black hole was driving him mad. He must get away from there. He must find that man, even if he was worsted or even died in the confrontation with him.

He found himself at Plym Steps. A horseman was crossing the ford. Controlling himself he asked the moorman if he had seen any sign of a very tall man.

"Yes," he said, "up Langcombe there, acting a bit strange 'e was, wandering about like. Never seen 'im before."

Without waiting to thank him Tom splashed across the ford, and quite oblivious of his sodden wet boots and feet, hastened up the valley. The moorman looked back at him, puzzled and surprised at the intensity of this man with the blotchy face. "Queer folk 'round 'ere this morning," he said to himself, "wonder what they two are goin' to get up to together?"

Tom could see no one as he ascended a path that led up the valley. He looked hard and long at the mass of low walling and loose stones that filled the valley floor to begin with. No sign of any life here.

He pressed on and came to a broad valley on the left. And there he saw him, staggering about as the moorman had said, going away from Tom. He had not been seen.

Stealthily and as quietly as possible he closed the gap between them, tantalisingly slowly.

Jethro came to a miry section of the valley and his feet sank into it. With a foul oath he extricated himself, taking some time to get himself freed and on to firm ground. When he turned he saw Tom and stood still. For what seemed an age they faced each other, weighing up the situation. Jethro saw that Tom had a huge hammer in his hand. Tom only saw Jethro as a man who had to be killed, but how?

It was Tom who started to move first. When within talking distance Jethro said, "Sho itsh the liddle man, ha, wash you doin' with that hammer, huh?"

Tom realised the man was hopelessly drunk. Now was his chance. Holding the handle of the hammer in both hands, near its butt end, and the heavy head facing towards Jethro, he rushed at him. Jethro's sluggish mind and body could not avoid the attack. The hammer head caught him in his jugular and he fell back choking. Without pause Tom brought the hammer down with all his might on to Jethro's head and smashed it in. He gazed down at him for some time, motionless. Then dropping the hammer, turned, and walked slowly away.

Reaction set in. He felt utterly weary and faint. At the sloping side of the valley he lay face down, his head resting on his arms. When all the tenseness that had filled his soul was suddenly released, there could only be one result. The tears could no longer be held back. They flooded out, his shoulders heaving with his sobs. There was no one to see this unmanliness. What did it matter. He could not help himself.

Gradually they subsided, he began to feel more at peace, more relaxed, more content. He fell asleep.

The sun was getting low in the west when he awoke, and the realisation of what he had done returned. With a glance back at the prostrate body to convince himself that the man really was dead, he left the scene and descended to Plym Steps. Once across the river he turned left. Nothing would have persuaded him to return the way he had come, across that evil combe. He never wanted to see it again.

The Longstone Leat provided a guide for him away from it. He followed it to Thrushelcombe Ford. He was not sure of his way from here. He was too close to the smelting house for his liking, he did not wish to meet anyone. So he continued along the leat, which was now flowing in the opposite direction. It seemed an interminable distance before he came to where it crossed the mine road that led from Ellisborough to Sheepstor. He looked anxiously along it but to his relief there was no one to be seen. He crossed quickly and followed the leat for a further half mile or so before turning away from it, for that was now heading in the wrong direction; he could see Down Tor and Combeshead Tor ahead. He arrived at the head of a steep little valley with a stream running down it. At the bottom he was able to cross the ensuing river on a small clapper bridge, beyond which a lane led up to a group of farm buildings. Dogs barked at his approach. A farmer came out of one of the buildings.

"Can I get up to Down Tor from here?" asked Tom.

"Yes you can; but you'm looking all done in, won't you come in and rest?"

"No, thank you. I want to get to Nillacombe, but if I get to Down Tor I shall know my way."

The farmer still eyed him doubtfully, at his scarred face and haggard appearance.

"Well, if you must, take that little lane up there, 't'will lead you to it. Steepish like and rough going. You sure you'll be all right?"

"Thank you, yes," said Tom.

Up the stony lane he climbed and was relieved to find it was not far to the tor when he reached the top. The memory of it hurt. He could not bear to look up at its top rocks. But he was familiar with the ground now and made good progress.

He must call in at Classywell to enquire of Mary Ann. Mrs Dawe came to the door, seeing his approach.

"Tom, where *have* you been all day? Samuel has been down, he's very concerned about you, for he says you were out of the house before they were up. What is it, Tom?"

Mr Dawe had joined them. They both looked anxiously

at him. The scars on his face seemed more inflamed and pronounced, his eyes were listless and dull, his whole appearance one of extreme exhaustion. He looked ten years older.

"How is Mary Ann?" he asked.

"She is more rested. She has been able to eat something. but . . ." She shook her head, unable to go on.

"Tell her she need no longer fear that man. He is dead."

Chapter Six

Tom did not wait to see what effect this bald statement had on Mr and Mrs Dawe. He turned away and ignored their calls for him to come back. Nothing seemed to matter now. A state of lethargy descended upon him. All was over between him and Mary Ann now, it must be so. No longer would there be those happy Sunday dinners. Those memorable walks. So dulled was his mind that he did not even contemplate what the result might be of his killing. Certainly there was no thought of escape.

At Nillacombe he could give no coherent replies to the old couple's enquiries of, "where had he been?" and, "what had kept him out so long?" No tendency now to give way to tears when they lovingly tried to console and comfort him. He ate the meal Nancy urged him to eat. He retired to his room, took his still wet boots and socks off, flung himself on his bed, still clothed, and lay for hours awake, all the events of the past few days turning over and over in his mind. There was no release from them.

And there Nancy found him the next morning, deeply asleep now, still clothed. She had understood that he was to be back at work this day, and had been worried as to whether to wake him or not. It was long past the time when he should have left when eventually she did so.

"You'm goin' to be very late for work, Tom."

"Yes Nancy, but it doesn't matter."

Some sanity had returned to him. He realised he must go back to Ellisborough. He had got to talk to someone. It would only be a question of time before Jethro's body would be found. He had come to have a great trust and liking for

Mr Deacon, and he had sensed that Mr Deacon had taken an almost fatherly interest in him. He just could not go back to the Dawes.

When he arrived at Ellisborough he was informed that Mr Deacon was engaged. When at last an angry looking miner left his office, Tom was called in.

"Tom, you look ill. Sit down. The rest doesn't appear to have done you much good. Sorry to have kept you waiting but I had to deal with that man. A sledge-hammer is missing from the blacksmith's shop. Suspicion has fallen on him. He has stolen before."

"He is innocent," said Tom, "I stole the hammer."

"*You* stole it? Are you out of your mind? What would you need a hammer like that for?"

"I have found Jethro, and killed him with it."

There was a silence of incredulity.

Tom unburdened himself of the dreadful events of yesterday, the hate he had for Jethro, for his insults, for having abducted his betrothed. But he just could not reveal the awful fate that Mary Ann had suffered. No one knew of that except Mr and Mrs Dawe. The story that she had managed to escape but had a terrible experience finding her way home was generally accepted. But nothing else was revealed.

"You realise what this means, don't you, Tom? I would be guilty of collaboration if I allowed you to go free after this confession. You will have to be confined here until such time as the authorities are informed. No one will be told where Jethro's body is until they have had a chance to examine it. There is no doubt that you will be arrested and tried for murder. This is a very sad day. I had such trust in you. How I wish I could help you."

The processes of the law took their course. The parish constable with his assistants arrived from Tavistock. The body was removed to a mortuary. The blood-stained hammer confiscated for evidence. Tom was taken away and confined in the clink at Tavistock.

A messenger had been despatched to Nillacombe and Classywell to inform them of his initial retention and again of his arrest. Poor Samuel and Nancy were heartbroken, they just could not believe it. Oh, how they were going to miss him.

For Mr and Mrs Dawe it was no more than they had suspected, but it was none-the-less hard to bear.

Mary Ann that morning had risen from her bed, had dressed, and had joined them in the living-room. So far they had only told her that Jethro was dead, not of their fear that Tom was responsible for it.

"What was all that?" asked Mary Ann when the messenger had departed.

Her mother took her hand and said, "Be brave, my dear, there is more bad news for you, it cannot be kept back any longer. When Tom heard of your ordeal he went in search of Jethro." Mary Ann put her other hand to her mouth, fear returned to her eyes. "He found him, and killed him. He has been arrested."

Mary Ann put both hands to her face and screamed, "Oh God, is there no end to this misery?" Once more she was shaking uncontrollably with her emotions.

"He has done it for you, to rid the world of that awful man, so that you may never fear him again. You should be proud of him."

When she had regained control of herself she said quietly, "Yes, I am. I still love him. I'll never want anyone else but him. What will happen to him?"

"We don't know; he will be tried. We can only wait and hope."

Some days later they heard that Tom had been transferred to Plymouth to await trial there. Early the next morning Mr Dawe came to a sudden decision to ride into Plymouth to see if it was possible to visit Tom, and to find out when the next assizes would be held there. He went to the stable and saddled Nelson, led him into the courtyard and tethered him whilst he went in for his long coat, cape and tricorn hat.

"Where are you going, Father?"

"Into Plymouth, my dear, I am going to try and see Tom."

"Wait a minute please." She ran back into her bedroom.

When he was all dressed and ready, and she still had not

appeared, he said, "What's the girl doing all this time, I am anxious to make a start?"

"Have patience with her, Will, I think I know what she is doing."

Mary Ann appeared, carrying a tiny little parcel.

"Please give this to Tom, Father. Tell him I am proud of him . . . for what he has done for my sake; and . . . "

"And what, my dear?"

"And that I will never forget him. I'll wait for him."

The day was well advanced before the sound of horse's hooves on the cobbled yard heralded his return. Mary Ann ran to the kitchen to bring in a meal that had been prepared for him. He came in after having unsaddled Nelson and given him his nose bag. He threw off his cape and coat. Mary Ann helped him off with his riding boots. As he sat down Mary Ann knelt at his side. "Well, Father?"

He patted her head.

"I was able to see your Tom. I gave him your gift and message. I wish you could have seen his face when he heard it. He had thought that all must be over between you. He now has hope. He would not open your little parcel until after I had gone. Whatever it was I am sure it will comfort him. He looked more relaxed when I left."

"And what about the assizes, Will?"

"Not until October. It is a long time to wait. Tom says he is being reasonably well treated. I was only allowed five minutes with him."

After Mr Dawe had left, Tom opened the little parcel. Wrapped in a small handkerchief was a lock of Mary Ann's golden hair, tied in the centre with a bow of narrow blue ribbon.

Life slowly returned to near normality at Classywell. Mary Ann resumed her benevolent visits to Nillacombe and Roundypark, but had to school herself to appear cheerful. Samuel and Nancy struggled on to keep the old farm going. At Ellisborough the Stamping Mill Leat was completed and the smelting house almost ready for its first firing.

It was on one of those mornings, when Mary Ann had gone up the lane to Nillacombe, when Mrs Dawe was in the kitchen preparing dinner, and Will was outside tending his vegetable plot, that Snap started barking. Will came round to the courtyard to see what it was all about. Standing at the gate were a roughly clothed elderly man and a middle-aged woman dressed in black.

"What can I do for you?" he asked.

"Is my son Thomas Tremain here?"

"Oh, you are Tom's mother; please come in."

"Linnie," he called as they entered the sitting-room.

Introductions were made. "This is my brother-in-law who has kindly shown me the way here."

When they were comfortably seated she went on, "Can you tell me where Tom is? He hasn't been to see me for some time, I have been getting anxious. The last time he came he told me of his engagement to your daughter."

Linnie and Will looked at each other, wondering who was to answer that question, and how to express it. Linnie was the first to recover.

"I am sorry, Mrs Tremain, we have some very bad news for you. Your son and my daughter were very much in love with each other. A few days ago my daughter was kidnapped by a villain of a man working at the mine here. Tom saved her from him. They had a great fight. He was a huge man and Tom was getting the worst of it when he managed to seize a heavy hammer and hit him on the head with it. It killed him. Your son has been arrested and is at present in Plymouth awaiting trial."

Still another woman was reduced to tears by these tragic events. To have so recently lost her husband and now apparently her son, was all unbearable.

"You may have the consolation of knowing," said Mrs Dawe as she laid a hand on the poor woman's shoulder, "that your son is looked upon as a hero here. He has rid the world of a man who was hated and feared by all. He may have to pay the penalty, but you should be proud of him. We are, and we love him as much as you do. Dry your eyes and be brave. Will you stay and have a bite of dinner with us?"

But she declined gratefully, "Albert has to get back to the farm," she explained.

It was on a blustery morning in early October when Mary Ann did not appear at breakfast.

Will came in from the stable, having given Nelson his feed.

"It's a horrid morning, beginning to rain now. Mary Ann not up yet?"

"No. Perhaps she doesn't like the look of the weather either. I'll go and see."

But Mary Ann had not bothered to look at the weather. She was still in bed, lying still and frowning.

"I don't want any breakfast, I feel sick."

It was a symptom of which Mary Ann was ignorant, but which her mother was so hoping would not appear, so afraid that it was almost inevitable.

When this sickness recurred for several days there could no longer be any doubt. She had to tell her daughter.

"My darling, do you know what this means?" Mary Ann looked up enquiringly. "You are going to have a baby."

All the horror of the recent past which she had so bravely been trying to suppress, now returned to her. That fear in her eyes again, that tenseness of body.

"I don't want his baby. I won't have his baby. Mother, what can I do?" as she flung her arms around her mother's neck and sobbed again those heart-rending sobs.

Her mother had no answer to that question. Mary Ann realised that there was none. In between sobs she said, "Tom won't want this baby. He won't want me either now . . . I have been so afraid that he wouldn't want me anyway after what that man has done to me . . . I can't stand it, I'll kill myself, I'll kill myself." And once more her whole body shook with the paroxysm of grief.

At last she calmed down and lay back exhausted on her pillows.

"I have more faith in your Tom than you seem to have. Don't you remember when your father came back from seeing Tom at Plymouth, he also had been afraid that all must be over between you. But when he got your message and your little gift he had said ‘now I have hope’. He would not have said that if he did not mean to be true to you, would he?”

These depressing bouts of sickness and the psychological trauma of having a baby she dreaded and hated, made Mary Ann listless and irritable. Her wan face and lacklustre eyes worried her mother. Would she do something desperate?”

The shortening days and a long spell of rain, fog, and then gales, only added to the low spirits that now prevailed in this little household of Classywell.

Two weeks later Tom’s trial was heard, with its almost inevitable result of ‘Guilty’.

It was Judge Buller who sat at the trial. Mr Dawe attended the sessions and brought back reports of its progress. Of the overwhelming evidence brought by the prosecution. Tom’s hatred of the victim; his theft of the sledge-hammer; the presence of the blood-stained hammer beside the body; of the accused’s own admission to Mr Deacon. The evidence of the defence weighed little against this. Mr Deacon, old Samuel, and Mr Dawe himself, were called to confirm the good character of the accused. Mr Dawe was able to confirm how the accused had been assaulted and knocked unconscious by the victim. And how his betrothed had been kidnapped; of how Mary Ann had managed to escape but had suffered a terrible experience wandering the moor in the dark before she had found the way home that night.

“That is something that must be deplored,” said the judge, in his summing up to the jury, “but it does not condone the killing of a man. Nor must it influence you in your deliberations.”

To save Mary Ann the stigma of her other ordeal that night, not a word was mentioned of it.

When Mr Dawe returned on that last day of the trial, mother and daughter looked anxiously at him when he entered the room. They knew by the look on his face that it was bad news. But they were not expecting, “He has been found guilty and sentenced to *life* imprisonment.”

Chapter Seven

Tom was led away from the courtroom after that harsh sentence, stunned at the thought that this was the end of his life as he had known it. He was taken back to the clink to await transport. Transport to where? Tom had no idea where prisoners were incarcerated.

His gaolers had some sympathy for him. Here was no ordinary criminal. They had taken a liking to him. Secretly they admired his defence of his girl; his battered face had shown proof of his courage. They were even more solicitous for him now.

Tom's mind was in a turmoil. What was life going to be like now, never to have freedom? What sort of a cell would he be put in? What work would he have to do? Would he ever be allowed to have visitors? Was he never to see Mary Ann again? Mary Ann. She was his life-line now. He must think only of her. He took the little handkerchief from his pocket and held the lock of hair between finger and thumb. Would he be allowed to keep it? Where could he hide it? He gazed at it for a long time, stroking its silky smoothness. Closed his eyes and tried to imagine it was the back of her head he was stroking. He put the treasure back into his pocket. Useless to ponder all these questions. He would know soon enough. In anguish he paced back and forth in his cell until he got sick and tired of that and lay still on his couch. How the hours dragged. And he had a lifetime of this ahead.

The following morning he was handcuffed to one of the parish constables and taken through the streets of Plymouth in a covered wagon. It seemed quite a long journey. Sounds of street noises gave way to silence, except for the rumble of their own cart wheels and the clop clop of the horse.

Then more street sounds, followed a little later by the clanking of chains, shouts of command, the creaking of wood against wood, and the slap slap of water against a quayside.

When they alighted, Tom found himself at a scene of great activity. Ships of all sizes were moored alongside the quay on which he stood; men hurried up gangways with heavy loads on their backs; carts rumbled back and forth between warehouse and ship. There were shouts from ship to shore. Flags flew from yardarms; sails flapped in the wind and halyards slapped against masts. This must be Plymouth Dock, the expanding Naval Dockyard that he had heard about, where that new leat he had seen coming out of the tunnel or adit at Nuns Cross was destined to flow. It was an amazing scene. Why had he been brought here? Was he to be transported? Now to be a world away from Mary Ann?

He was led away from the great bulk of a man-of-war that was hiding whatever lay beyond. Near the stern of the ship steps led down to water level. Down these they descended to a cutter moored alongside. They stepped aboard and sat in the stern. Orders were given to shove off. Men manned their oars and in splendid unison immersed their blades into the water and the boat surged away from the quay.

Tom now faced an open sheet of water, but with land beyond. Moored in mid-stream were more huge men-of-war.

Then Tom's heart sank. These were no active warships. their masts were stunted and their rigging minimal. They were hulks, possibly captured vessels. Mr Dawe had told him why the prison at Prince's Town had been built. To relieve the overcrowding of French prisoners-of-war in these hulks in the Hamoaze at Plymouth. Is that where they were going?

Indeed it was where they were going. The perfection of these Naval oarsmen took them there in a very short time, and skilfully they manoeuvred the cutter alongside the companionway. Tom and his gaoler climbed aboard, still manacled together.

The stench which met them as they passed through the

bulwarks was nauseating. They were led along a gangway towards the stern, where the atmosphere was somewhat better. The handcuffs were removed. Tom was handed over to a warder and signed for. The parish constable took his hand and shook it. Without a word he departed. No good wishing him luck here!

Tom was stripped of his clothing, examined, and given coarse prison garb. Whilst still naked the warder barked, "What have you got in your hand?"

With a heavy heart Tom had to show him. It was taken from him, the handkerchief opened, the lock of hair exposed. Even the hardest of hearts it seemed can be softened.

"All right, you can keep it."

Clad now in his repulsive outfit, Tom was led back into that stench, into a large gallery between decks, where hammocks were slung round the walls. He was led to one of them. "This will be yours, and don't forget where it is."

The gallery was full of men of all ages and appearances. All long haired and bearded. All dull-eyed and dejected. Some lying in their hammocks, some sprawling on the deck playing some sort of game. The smell of human sweat and stale clothing permeated the place. How can I live like this, thought Tom.

Within a few weeks he was as dull-eyed, dejected and as smelly as the rest.

At Classywell they were stunned by the savageness of the sentence, unable for a while to express their thoughts in words.

In Mary Ann's mind it was, 'Oh, my poor dear Tom, to be deprived of the open air life and the freedom of the moor he was loving so much, never to experience it again, it's wicked . . . he need never know about this baby now.'

In Mr Dawe's mind it was anger at the injustice of it.

Mrs Dawe had more practical thoughts. 'How are we going to get this wicked sentence reduced or annulled?'

At last Mary Ann spoke. "Where will he be imprisoned, Father?"

"In one of those prison hulks at Dock or Portsmouth, I

suppose, depends where there is room."

"Will he be allowed visitors?"

"I doubt it. If you have any thoughts of doing so, Mary Ann, you must banish them from your mind. From what I have heard of the conditions on these ships, it is no place for a woman to visit."

"Is that what they call justice?" almost shouted Mary Ann, "to deprive a man of his life because he has rid the world of a monster?"

"It happens to be the law of the land. The judge has to interpret that law."

"Law of the land or not," said Mrs Dawe, "I'm going to do something about this."

"Such as what?" asked Mr Dawe.

"I am going to see my father."

By the strangest of coincidences a messenger arrived the following morning with a missive for Mrs Dawe.

She opened it and read the short note. Then read it again.

"My mother has just died. I am summoned to the funeral. The groom has been instructed to wait and escort me. Will, would you harness the gig for me please."

She went to her bedroom and dressed for the journey, packing what was necessary for a few days stay at the family home.

The recently built turnpike road from Two Bridges to Ashburton meant that the journey would not be too difficult. They had first to take the lane past Kingsett to Nosworthy, then up the hill past Vennilake to Lowery, to join the Plymouth to Prince's Town road, and on to Two Bridges. They reached Ashburn Hall, the country seat of the Cockcroft family, by afternoon. Old Sir John met her under the portico of their ancient mansion.

"Welcome, my dear, good of you to come so quickly, come in."

They entered the great hall with its mahogany staircase, its high ceiling extending above the first floor; the panelled doors with fluted pilasters leading to the dining-room on one side and to the drawing-room on the other. Two suits of armour flanked the staircase, behind which was a magnificent stained glass window, for which the house was famed. They turned off into the drawing-room.

"Let Jane take your cloak and hat to your room. Come over here to the window recess. Jane, have some tea brought."

"Sorry to hear about Mother, Father, how long had she been ill?"

"I suppose I shouldn't say it, my dear, but she had been ailing for some time and had been cantankerous and not a little trying. It is a merciful relief really. I know I can speak frankly to you."

"Yes, there was little love lost between Mother and me. How are you keeping?"

"Reasonably well. Old Smithers runs the house, don't know what I'd do without her. She doesn't say so of course, but I think I can see the relief in her face now that she can get on with her job without interference. And how are you and your family?"

"That is something I want to speak to you about later, after the funeral. When is it?"

"Day after tomorrow. I want a simple funeral, at Ashburton Parish Church. Charles and his family will be coming from Exeter. Edward is in London at present, I still await his reply. He may not have time to send one and will just turn up. How is that lovely daughter of yours?"

"I have told you, Father, I will speak about it later."

"Oh yes, of course. Ah, here is Coaker with the tea."

"Very pleased to see you, madam."

"Hullo Coaker, my old conspirator, you were always on my side when I got into scrapes, weren't you?"

"I did my best, madam, you were always my favourite."

"Dear old Coaker. He must be nearly ninety, mustn't he?"

"Not much over eighty I think. The place wouldn't be the same without him."

"I haven't anything black to wear to the funeral, Father, there is no room at the farm to store much clothing."

"Jane will show you to your room shortly. Oh, of course, you know where your room is, don't you. Your mother never thought your marriage would last. She kept all your clothing, it is still there. Have a hunt through, there may be something suitable. Jane can make any alterations. See if you can find something pretty to wear to dinner tonight. You used to look so charming. Damme, you still do."

She leant over and kissed his forehead. "Bless you for that."

Linnie did find something pretty to wear that night. She was pleased to find that her figure had not changed all that much. She relished the experience of once more wearing an expensive gown, even if it was a little old-fashioned. Then again to be seated next to her father at that huge table, with its glittering silverware and Sèvres china, specially brought out for her benefit. To be waited on by Coaker and enjoy one of cook's specialities. The reason for her visit was forgotten in the nostalgia of this renewed contact with her father and reliving of an age long since past.

Linnie did not wish to mention the other purpose of her visit until after the funeral. The subject was too important to burden her father with it, whilst so many other distractions were taking place. They needed to be alone together.

The arrival of her brothers with so much family news to be exchanged, reminiscences to be laughed over, plans for the future to be hoped for, made the occasion a festive one, very much the reverse of what it should have been.

However, on the day of the funeral everyone adopted the decorum to be expected on such a solemn occasion, heads were bowed and prayers uttered. All went off with correct ceremony, and eulogies expressed for the departed.

Dinner that night though was another festive gathering.

When her brothers had departed the next morning, Linnie led her father back to the drawing-room, and to the window recess where they had sat on her arrival. Such a lovely view of the formal gardens was obtained from its window. After they had finished admiring it, Linnie said, "Father, sit down, I have something very important to tell you, and to ask of you."

"Are you in need of money, my dear?"

"No Father, it is more serious than that. Sometime during last spring a young Cornish miner came to our farm seeking employment on any of the Dartmoor mines. He had been told that Will might be able to advise him. He did get work on one of them and was well thought of. We liked the boy, he reminded us of our own son. It became the custom for him to spend Sunday dinners with us, the midday meal of course. He and Mary Ann have fallen in love with each other, they are now engaged to be married. In the course of Tom's work, that is his name, he came in contact with a labourer who was disliked by everybody, a huge man, uncouth and belligerent. By misfortune this man met them on one of their walks together and attempted to persuade Mary Ann to walk with him. This led to a fight between him and Tom. Though, as Mary Ann told us later, Tom put up a brave attack, he stood no chance against such a man and was knocked unconscious, suffering injuries to his face. When he recovered consciousness Mary Ann was nowhere to be seen. Though a search party was sent out neither she nor Jethro, that villain, could be found."

Linnie paused in her narration, finding it difficult to formulate her words now.

"Go on, my dear."

"Tom came to us to tell us what had happened, we were awake nearly all night with anxiety. In the early hours next morning Mary Ann arrived home, wild, filthy and hysterical, having walked for hours over the moor in the dark, after having been raped. Raped, Father, repeatedly."

Linnie wrung her hands in anguish at the remembrance of that awful night. She forced herself to use those words to make the biggest impact on her father.

"You will understand how Mary Ann has suffered since, and of the effect it had on Tom. The tragic outcome of this is that Tom hunted down Jethro and killed him. He has now been tried for murder, found guilty and sentenced to life imprisonment."

"Linnie, how terrible for you all."

"Father, you must help. You have influence. Do you know Judge Buller?"

"Not personally. I know of him."

"We must have that life sentence quashed. It cannot be justice."

"Did the judge not take into account the question of rape, to mitigate the crime?"

"That is the difficulty. To spare Mary Ann that has never been mentioned. No one but our family knows of it. Everyone else believes she managed to escape from Jethro."

"Let me think this over. When do you intend returning to Classywell?"

"Tomorrow morning, unless you particularly want me to stay longer."

On the morrow, when Linnie was ensconced in her gig and farewells had been said, her last words were, "Father, you *will* do something, won't you."

"All I can, I promise. I can't guarantee what other people will do. God bless you my dear."

A groom accompanied the gig. But Sir John did not mention to Linnie the instructions he had given him. It was a long shot that had only a small chance of success. He did not want to jeopardise that possibility by it being generally known.

When, after an uneventful journey, the groom had seen his charge safely restored to her home, he returned to Prince's Town, but after passing the Plume of Feathers Inn, he turned off on to a minor road to Tor Royal, where Sir Thomas Tyrwhitt resided when not away on his multifarious activities. He handed a note in at the door and said he would await a reply if Sir Thomas was at home. Fortunately he was. A note was handed back addressed to Sir John Cockcroft.

When Sir John opened it, he read, "I shall be here for a few weeks. Come Thursday if possible. Will be pleased to see you."

Thursday came and Sir John set off in his coach and pair, rehearsing in his mind how to express his request to Sir Thomas.

When the coach drew up at Tor Royal Sir Thomas was at the door to greet his guest. They had never met before but knew of each other's reputation.

The little house Sir John entered did not really live up to its rather grandiose name. He was surprised at its rather spartan accommodation but was careful not to show this, rather was he pleased with the warmth of his reception, and of the peat fire that was burning in the grate. He accepted a glass of wine as they sat themselves down before it.

"What can I do for you, Sir John?"

"I am well aware, Sir Thomas, of your activities here and of your long association with the Prince Regent. Do you have any influence with him now that he has ascended the throne?"

"I still have his ear, and am welcomed at the palace when occasion arises. Why?"

"I have a most unusual and rather embarrassing request to make. I am afraid it is rather a long story, but I beg of you to listen. A young man's life may depend on whether you can help or not."

Having given all the details of the tragic story as related to him by his daughter, Sir John ended, "Our only hope is that you may be able to persuade His Majesty to issue a Royal Pardon. Do you think there is any chance?"

"You probably know, Sir John, that as Prince Regent His Majesty was rather fond of the ladies. I expect he will be deeply affected by the story of the brutal ravishing of your niece, and the justifiable revenge taken by her betrothed. I am due in London shortly and will do my best to obtain an audience and put the case to him. A lot will depend upon his mood of the moment and how preoccupied he may be with state affairs. You have my word that I will do all I can."

After a third glass of wine and discussions of a more general nature, Sir John re-entered his coach and with mutual expressions of pleasure at their meeting, departed on his long ride home, pondering in his mind what other means of help it was possible to solicit if nothing came of this.

Chapter Eight

Days dragged into weeks on that prison hulk. Tom was now just one of a mass of dejected humanity that filled this foul place. If there was anything left of his scars they were now hidden by a stubble of developing beard. That did not however entirely hide his frank and intelligent face, as distinct from the criminal looking riff-raff around him.

To his surprise he was no longer aware of the stench that had initially so nauseated him. Continuous association seemed to have made him immune to it. What he could not abide was the filth. The lice that appeared in his hair. The bugs that bit him at night, their disgusting stink transcending the other odours. The dreadful food they were given, and the rats that came in the semi-dark in search of crumbs.

At the end of the day the dim light of an oil lamp mercifully hid most of the horrors surrounding him. In the quiet of the night, well almost quiet, for snores and other rude noises were never absent, he could lie in his hammock, close his eyes, and think of Mary Ann. He would take her little token in his hand and stroke it, it was part of her.

He would dwell on various incidents of their walks together. Of when he had carried her across the ford on their way to Shavercombe Falls. Of her fear of the place and her question about premonition. Did she then have some inkling of what was to befall them? Of his holding her in his arms on the recrossing of the ford, of his proposal, of her words, "Yes Tom, I love you."

On that never-to-be-forgotten moment when she had stumbled at Sheeps Tor, and he had held her breasts, and she had pressed her hands on his and held them there. Had it meant as much to her as it had to him?

And that vision on the topmost rocks of Down Tor, when the wind had pressed her clothing against her, and he had glimpsed the shape of her beautiful body. That body that he was now never to see.

Over and over again those scenes were to come back to him and keep him sane. Memories so secret, so cherished, so wonderful.

His hatred of the place was slowly turning to apathetic resignation when one morning a warder approached him and he was told to follow him. He was taken to a wash-house.

"Take your clothes off and get yourself cleaned up. You'll find a comb there, get the lice out of your hair. Then come out here and put your own clothes on."

What does all this mean, thought Tom. It can't be release. But how he relished and enjoyed the pouring of pail after pail of clean water over his body, sea water though it was.

When he had dressed the warder said, "The Governor wants to see you."

The Governor's office was at the stern of the old warship, what had been the Captain's cabin. As he entered, the fresh air that came in from the open window was balm. Tom took a deep breath of it as he approached the Governor's desk, the warder standing close behind him.

"What is your name?"

"Thomas Tremain, sir."

"Your case has been brought to the notice of His Majesty the King. He has ordained that your sentence be commuted to only three years detention, as distinct from imprisonment. You will remain here but under better conditions than hitherto. What sort of work can you do?"

"I have been a tin miner."

"That is not of much good here. Are you any good at carpentry?"

"I have used tools. I can learn."

"Take him to the carpenter. Get him fixed up with a hammock in the orlop. Report to me of his progress. You may go."

They descended a companion-way to the lowest deck

where a distinctly better atmosphere prevailed than on those prison decks. They passed the galley with its smell of cooking; some administrative offices, and finally, near the bows of the ship, they reached the carpenter's shop.

"Chippy, here is a new assistant for you. Try him out and see if he is any good to you."

"Hullo son, how come you got this job then?"

"I am finding it difficult to understand that myself. I have just been told that my life sentence has been reduced to three years. It is wonderful news. I do not know how this has come about."

"What were you sentenced for?"

"Murder. I killed a man who stole my girl."

"Probably served him bloody well right. Know anything about carpentry?"

"I am a miner, but I have seen some of the work the mine's carpenters did and admired their skills. I think I can learn."

"Good for you, lad. You watch what I'm doin' for a bit. Then I'll give you a bit of wood and see what you can do with it."

The friendship shown by this man was rather overwhelming for Tom after what he had been through. He was a stocky little man. His bare arms and gnarled hands looked powerful, as did his bull neck. To watch him work was a revelation. The way he handled a saw and made quick clean accurate cuts with it. Then chiselled a mortice in a table leg, with deft strokes of a mallet. In the piece of wood he had just sawn to length he marked out the dimensions of the tenon, sawed the waste wood away and then finished off with a chisel down to the marks. The rail fitted into the leg with a satisfactory click and stayed there, flush and true.

"Think you can make one like that?"

"No," said Tom. "How many years has it taken you to make one like it?"

"Good question, that. What's your name, son?"

"Call me Tom."

"Come on then Tom. Take these two bits of wood. Mark 'em out as you seen me do, cut a tenon in one and a mortice in t'other. If it falls apart when you've done it, it's no bloody good. You starts again until it's perfect."

And so Tom learnt to be an expert carpenter, just as he had learnt to be an expert miner, by example.

He loved the work, and he loved being taught by this bluff capable man. The days passed quickly, an additional blessing. He was allowed to sling his hammock in one corner of the shop, and so he lived in an atmosphere of friendship and the satisfying smell of freshly cut wood.

Alone in his hammock at night, he still dreamed those cherished dreams, and stroked that lock of hair. But there was hope now. Hope that one day he would be stroking that hair for real, on her lovely head.

Whilst Linnie was at Ashburn Hall pleading with her father, Mary Ann took charge at Classywell. To keep her mind from dwelling on that baby, on Tom's life sentence and any false hopes of any mitigation of it, she kept herself occupied with a variety of jobs throughout the day. She cooked and she sewed, she swept and she dusted. At school at Wakaton she had been taught cooking, needlework and knitting, as well as reading and writing. Sewing was an accomplishment that her mother lacked, it had never been necessary in her youth. Neither was cooking, but of necessity that had to be learnt the hard way when she got married. Any sewing work she was now delighted to hand over to her daughter. Mary Ann had loved these subjects. Arithmetic was her weak point, she couldn't see much need for it. The other subjects seemed to her to be the essentials of life. She had excelled at them. She received praise from her father for the meals she set before him. He was very pleased and relieved to see this activity. She was not moping over her misfortune, or did not appear to be.

Mary Ann decided that the bedrooms needed a thorough cleaning. A long passage at the back of the house led from the living-room to the bedrooms. Her parents' room was the first one. It had originally been the shippen. Even after the making of that passageway had cut off a part of it, it was still a large room. Her own room was at the end of the passage, where the house had been extended. Both rooms had windows facing onto the court and the fine view of the valley beyond.

Mary Ann now set about cleaning those windows, inside and out. All the furniture was then moved and the floors swept where all too long they had been neglected.

For respite from this manual work she retired to her room and resumed work on a capuchin she was making for herself. This was a new garment that had recently come into fashion in this country. It consisted of a combined cloak and hood. Mary Ann thought this a splendid idea and it would be so useful in the winter months, providing warmth and protection when she made her visits to Nillacombe and Roundypark.

The evening hours were those which dragged, when she and her father sat before the fire, now continuously kept alight, and she attempted to read by the light of an oil lamp. It was then that those thoughts would not be suppressed, and she found it difficult to concentrate on her book. More so when night came and she lay in her bed; they would not let her go to sleep.

When she could find no more that needed doing in the house, she asked her father if he would come with her to Nillacombe and Roundypark to make sure that both homes were well stocked for the winter months, both for the people and their animals.

They went to Roundypark first. There had never been quite the same warmth of affection for these neighbours as they had for the dear old pair at Nillacombe. Richard Crymes was a recluse, his wife a bit of a harridan. Yet they were always pleased to see Mary Ann, possibly because a gift nearly always accompanied her visits.

As they entered the kitchen, Beth was putting a leg of mutton into the cloam oven. Elizabeth was her real name of course, but always contracted to Beth, and more usually referred to by Richard as 'me missus'.

"How are you off for peat for the winter?" asked Mr Dawe, when they had seated themselves before the fire.

"Bit short like," said Richard, " 't'aint easy to get it round 'ere, and us can't afford to buy it."

"I'll arrange for Kingsett to send you up a load."

There were no peat ties within easy reach of the valley;

farm-hands at Kingsett would bring in peat from a site they knew of. It was then stored at Kingsett for sale as well as for their own use.

"And what about food?"

"Us 'ave got a good supply of 'taties. And meat of course."

"I have brought this for you, Beth," said Mary Ann as she handed an article of clothing to the old dame.

Beth unfolded it to reveal a warm woollen bodice.

"Aw, me dear, that be kind of 'e. Did 'e make 'un?"

"Yes. Call it a Christmas present in case we are unable to get to you nearer the time."

They made the same enquiries at Nillacombe with similar offers of help and a gift of warm clothing for Nancy. This had almost become a ritual by now and usually well before Christmas for one never knew what the weather might do on Dartmoor. But this visit to Nillacombe was marred with sadness when they heard of the terrible sentence imposed on Tom. They were missing him greatly, not only his presence but his help. They wondered how much longer they could keep the old farm going.

"Reck'n us'll finish up in Tavistock workhouse," said Samuel, "Can't say I fancies that."

They also needed their peat stock replenished and arrangements were made to have a cartload sent to them.

The following day Mrs Dawe returned from Ashburn Hall. When she had divested herself of hat and cloak, and warmed her hands before the fire, she related the details of her sojourn, the festive atmosphere that had prevailed in the old house in spite of the solemnity of the funeral. It was not until yesterday, she said, that a chance had occurred for her to speak in private with her father about the other purpose of her visit. "He said he would do his best, but he didn't sound too hopeful."

It was nearly a month later, towards the end of November, when the groom from Ashburn Hall arrived once more with a letter for Mrs Dawe. Will took the letter from him and realising its significance called, "Linnie, Mary Ann, come quickly."

The two ladies rushed in from the kitchen. Mrs Dawe opened the missive and read it first to herself. Then the important part of it aloud. "I am delighted to be able to tell you that the King has ordained that Tom's sentence be reduced to three years."

"Oh how wonderful. Father seems to have had some influence after all. Why Mary Ann, what is the matter child?"

Mary Ann's face had turned to stone. She sank into her chair and buried her face in her hands.

"What has come over you? Are you not well?"

Mary Ann lowered her hands. There were no tears, just that hard fearful look.

"Don't you see Mother; when Tom returns this damned baby is going to be three years old. How can he abide it when every time he sees it or touches it, it will remind him of Jethro, and everything else associated with that, that . . . " She could find no words bad enough for him.

Will went to the door and said to the groom. "Thank you, there is no reply."

When he came back Linnie was kneeling before her daughter holding her hand. Her thoughts were now those of Mary Ann. She is quite right. This baby could ruin their lives. Would Tom want to marry her now?

She pulled her daughter to her feet, put her arm round her and led her back to the kitchen. The mundane matters of life had to go on. But depression settled into that household at Classywell, as did a deep depression over England, heralding the worst winter that anyone could remember.

Day after day it rained, with a ferocity they had never known before. Soil was washed down into the rivers, their waters turned brown and overflowed their banks. Lanes and the approaches to fields were turned into quagmires. Sheep huddled in misery in the doubtful shelter of the dry stone walls, as the wind whipped the rain into near horizontal sheets.

In between recurring depressions there would be a fine day when Mary Ann or Will could struggle through the morass to Nillacombe to reassure themselves that all was well there. They were coping. They had lived all their lives on Dartmoor. If this weather was exceptional they knew how to protect themselves.

Christmas came and went without celebrations. In early

February there was a welcome break from the rain. On the first night of that welcome break, for the first time for weeks, there was not a cloud in the sky, resulting in a sudden and dramatic fall of temperature, and Dartmoor revealed one of its rarest and most beautiful phenomena, the ammil. Every branch and bough, every twig and sprig, every frond of bracken and blade of grass, was sheathed in ice, as if in a glass case. Icicles hung in fantastic ghost-like shapes. The weak morning sun highlighted the scene to give an ethereal, magical effect. The light breeze caused some of the fronds to knock together to produce tinkles of fairy bells.

It was Will who first saw it as he went out to attend to Nelson and Snap. He called Linnie and Mary Ann to come and see it. They gazed in astonishment. It is given to very few people to witness this rare sight. They certainly had never seen it before.

"Oh, if we could only capture that on canvas," said Mary Ann.

But alas, it was over all too quickly as the rising sun slowly melted those priceless gems.

That was the only thing that winter which was beautiful. But such a fine day was it that the opportunity could not be missed at Ashburn Hall to send a hamper of good things to Classywell, the traditional Christmas gift so unavoidably delayed this year. As usual Nillacombe must have its share of it. This time her mother accompanied Mary Ann with the basket of food, perforce rather late in the afternoon before they could set off. The old folk were delighted to see them and were profuse in their thanks, but scolded them for the risk they were taking in walking that frozen rutted lane. They did not delay their return, though Mary Ann could not resist showing Nancy her new capuchin, opening it out to reveal the lining and how it was made. Even so, such slow progress did they make over the difficult ground that dimsey was upon them before they had got little more than half way, with the leaden sky ahead threatening snow. Indeed it began to fall in large, slowly descending flakes before they had reached their destination, their capes now brilliantly white. Mary Ann blessed that capuchin.

After they had left Nancy remarked to Samuel, "Didun

she look pretty in that new cloak. And did 'e notice too, I be thinkin' a babby be on the way. It sure will be a 'ansome child, they'm both so good lookin'. 'Course they 'ad every opportunity, didun they, on them long walks together?"

Linnie was having similar thoughts. How else to explain this baby? Mary Ann isn't going to agree to that though. How can she ever love it, or even want to rear it? How complicated it was all getting; how impossible to find a solution.

They awoke the next morning to more flurries of snow and a gusting wind. The view of the valley was completely shut out, the falling flakes whirling crazily at one moment, rushing horizontally the next as the west wind hurled them up the valley. Drifts began to pile up against the walls.

Will had got most of the sheep into the pens; those he couldn't round up he hoped would find shelter somewhere. He could do no more now. Snap was brought into the house. Nelson had to endure the stable but had blankets thrown over him.

All day and all night it snowed, all the next day and all the next night, the wind increasing in fresh fury. The snow piled up in the court and drifted up to the window-sills. It found its way through the gap between edge of door and jamb and entered the living-room. A good stock of peat had been brought in and stacked each side of the fireplace. The fire glowed hot and kept the living-room warm. There was also a fireplace in the larger bedroom, it having been built into the end wall where originally the shippen doorway had been. This fire was now lit, but it only helped to warm Mary Ann's room in a very small way. All the doors to the bedrooms were left open to allow some of the heat from the living-room to filter through. They did not dare to undress fully at night, keeping their warm undergarments on. Mary Ann removed her dress before the fire in the living-room, wrapping a blanket around herself before retiring to her cold bed. How, they wondered, were their neighbours faring; at their age it could be serious.

On the third day the snow stopped at last, but there had been more heavy falls during the night. It was impossible to see through the windows, they were covered with snow.

There was an upstairs room over the living-room, access to it being by a spiral stone staircase in the corner near the fireplace. This had been their son's room, but it was now mostly used as a store. They climbed to it to find out what could be seen from the window there. It was incredible. It was now possible to see across the valley, but all was a wilderness of white, hiding all detail.

"I've got to get out somehow," said Will, "I must get feed to Nelson and some fodder to the sheep, if they are still alive. If I try to open the front door we'll get all that snow falling into the living-room. I doubt if I'll get out that way anyway. I think I have no choice but to jump from this window."

"Oh, Will, you can't do that. If you get hurt there is no one to help you."

"If anything happened to Nelson I'd never forgive myself for not trying. Mary Ann, fetch that long handled spade from the kitchen whilst I try to open this window." He blessed his bit of foresight in bringing that spade into the house.

The small window had not been opened for years, it took a bit of persuading before Will finally got it open.

It did not seem all that far to the snow. It would certainly break his fall, but would he disappear up to his neck in it?

He climbed out, lowered himself down, clutching the window-sill until he was hanging on by his hands alone. Then he let go. He landed up to his thighs in the snow.

Mary Ann dropped the spade to him, careful to hold it sideways so that if he missed it, it would not hurt him.

It took Will the rest of the morning to clear a way to the door, free the door, and then make a passageway through the snow to the stable. He came in periodically to warm his hands and have a hot drink.

To his relief Nelson was all right, but ravenously hungry and thirsty. But he could not see his sheep, they were buried in the snow.

After a midday meal of hot stew he resumed his seemingly hopeless task of clearing a way to the sheep pen. Linnie and Mary Ann donned their warmest clothes and came out to help. Linnie secretly hoped this strenuous exercise might rid Mary Ann of that unwanted baby. But the laws of perversity do not work that way. Mary Ann astonished her parents with the help she was able to render.

They reached the pen and one by one dragged the sheep out. They had all congregated near the gate and survived by their mutual bodily heat. More clearing had to be done in the courtyard to accommodate them, and fodder spread about. By nightfall they could do no more, though all the sheep had not been accounted for. Exhausted they returned to the blessed warmth and comfort of the house, but relieved that their efforts had not been in vain.

For weeks the snow lay on the ground. Slowly they improved the conditions in the courtyard for the sheep and kept them fed. There came a day when voices were heard. Two labourers from Kingsett had managed to clear a way through to them. They had experienced similar conditions but the trees surrounding their buildings had given some protection. They had managed to get through to Roundypark and given what help they could there. Old Crymes and his missus were all right. Now was the task of clearing a way to Nillacombe. The lane was solid with snow to wall height and above in places. Progress was painfully slow. The Dawes had so much to do on their farm they could only give limited help. The men reported what progress they had made as they returned each evening. It was some days before they finally got through.

When the Dawes heard them returning that afternoon it was to find they were carrying a roughly made stretcher. Their hearts sank. On it lay Nancy, still alive, but obviously suffering from the cold. They brought her into the warm room and persuaded her to drink some hot milk and take a little hot food. She looked very ill and could say little.

The men had gone back for Samuel who they said was in much the same condition. When they reached Classywell on their return they declared their intention of taking him direct to Kingsett, and to come back for Nancy. Although the Dawes were anxious to keep Nancy and look after her, the men said it would be better to have them both at Kingsett so that they could be taken to Tavistock as soon as the thaw came. They would be well looked after until then. Samuel's eyes were closed, he looked deathly pale.

That was the last they were to see of that lovable old couple. A few days later the thaw came, with its added problems of floods. It seemed an age before any news could get through to Classywell. When it did, it was to hear that Nancy and Samuel had been unable to survive their ordeal. They had died within a few days of each other. They had been buried at Tavistock.

Mary Ann felt the loss keenly. It seemed unbelievable that she would never be visiting Nillacombe again. A mere six months ago all was peace in this valley, romance was in the air and nothing but happy prospects ahead. Now tragedy seemed to fill every corner of it. Death prevailed, both human and animal, for many sheep were lost. The future seemed to hold nought but gloom. There was no incentive to do anything now. The growing baby was becoming painfully obvious both physically and mentally. She resented it, hated it for the inconvenience it was causing her as well as for its origin. The short respite of weather following the thaw turned to gales in March, which only added to the turmoil in her mind, and accentuated the burden of her body.

By April spring was in the air and unbelievably sheep gave birth to lambs. All traces of the snow, which had still remained in sheltered pockets on the hills, now disappeared. The days lengthened, the sun shone brighter and Down Tor took on its benign and noble appearance once more.

May came and so did the baby. Mothers had to be midwives on these remote farms. Mary Ann was thankful that no one else but her parents would see this baby, or would see her unnatural resentment of it. The physical pain of the birth was accompanied by the mental agony that its father was a monster. That it would know no father. That it could never have any motherly love.

The birth was difficult and prolonged. When at last the baby came Mary Ann lay back exhausted and indifferent to it. Linnie did all that was necessary. Will helped with the bringing of warm water and anything else required. When all was ready and the child crying lustily, Linnie put it to Mary Ann's breast, but had to persuade her to hold it there. She then covered them with the bedclothes and left them whilst she tidied up. With the baby comforted, they both fell asleep.

It was a girl.

The days that followed were unhappy ones for everybody. Mary Ann's neglect of her baby was understandable but worrying. She fed it to keep it quiet. Then put it in a makeshift cot that her father had made, and left it there, thankful that it had gone to sleep and she could forget it for a while. She could not bear to cuddle or comfort it. Her listless movements about the house and farm worried her parents, it looked as though *they* were going to have to bring up this child. Indeed much of the work of attending to it fell upon Linnie. It was a lovely, healthy baby and she could not bear to see it so neglected.

Will was irritated by the change that had come over his household. He was glad of the valid excuse to tend his farm. He had extra work to do now that he had taken over what was left of Samuel's flock of sheep. He had to make periodical visits to Nillacombe and ensure that all was safe and secure there, though who would want to occupy it now he did not know. It saddened him to see it so forlorn and neglected.

When his thoughts were not preoccupied with these matters they turned to his daughter, the daughter he loved so much and who had brought such life and sparkle to his home. She was now a different person. He found himself getting cross with her at times, and then chided himself for doing so. Was this a permanent change in her character? Was Tom going to want this girl now? She wasn't the girl he had courted. Damn that Jethro. Everything had stemmed from that dreadful night. He also became morose and silent during the evening hours.

It was Linnie who kept control of the household. Her strength of character showed to its best now. She understood both her daughter and her husband, made allowances for them, undertook all the extra work without complaint, cooked and comforted, washed and laundered, kissed them both goodnight to try and ease their troubled souls.

By the end of the third week since the birth a routine had settled into the house, and that is how it seemed it would go on, for a long time.

Linnie awoke one morning, at an hour that had become a habit because of the baby's cry for a feed. The child must be sleeping well, she thought dreamily, there was no sound this morning. She couldn't get to sleep again. With the coming of daylight she began to feel uneasy at the silence. She got up and went to investigate, opening Mary Ann's door quietly.

She came rushing back to wake her husband.

"Will, Will, Mary Ann has gone, and taken the baby with her. Oh God, what has happened now?"

They hastily dressed, having made sure that she was nowhere in the house. Will hurried to the stable. As he feared, Nelson also had gone. Now what desperate thing is our child doing?

He re-entered the house. "She has taken Nelson. Where do you suppose she has gone?"

"Will, I'm frightened. She has been so strange lately. But would she have taken Nelson if she had been contemplating . . . " She could not bring herself to say the word.

"No, I suppose not. And would she have taken the baby too . . . ?" The sentence was never finished. The sound of horse's hooves in the yard made them rush to the door.

Mary Ann had just dismounted, without the baby, and was tethering Nelson. She came in looking very tired, yet serene.

"My darling, where have you been? And where is the baby?"

There was no answer to those questions. She said, "Mother, I'm hungry and thirsty."

Linnie made some tea and came back with it and some bread and butter, all she could think of providing in her agitation. They all ate and drank in silence, waiting for Mary Ann to explain.

"Mary Ann, you must tell us what has happened to the baby."

"Never," said Mary Ann, "you must never ask me that question again. I will never tell you."

"You must, child," said her father.

"I will *not* Father."

Will and Linnie looked at each other, and back at Mary Ann. There was no gainsaying that determined look.

"You must be tired out, Mary Ann, go to your room and have a sleep."

"I'll stay here." She closed her eyes. In no time she was asleep. For the first time for months that face looked calm and relaxed.

Will went to stable Nelson and give him his nosebag. He noticed he had been sweating. He had been driven hard.

Linnie went to Mary Ann's room and removed the cot, and everything else associated with the baby, a bit of forethought for which Mary Ann was later to be very grateful.

When all had gone to bed that night, and a new atmosphere seemed to prevail in the house, Linnie whispered to Will, "Whatever has happened to that baby we may never know, but nobody else even knows of its existence. No one even knows that she was pregnant, except perhaps Nancy suspected. We have no need to register it, or even again talk about it. Only Mary Ann has got to live with the knowledge of what she has done with it. There is no guilt in her face. I just cannot imagine what she has done."

Chapter Nine

Life in the prison hulk had changed most dramatically for Tom. From being sunk to the depths of dirt, degradation and despondency, eking out a life both friendless and aimless, he was now almost happy. He was able to keep himself clean. If he could not shave he was able to trim his beard and keep it neat; and to cut his hair and keep it free of lice. The hours did not drag now, he was always busy, and had the satisfaction of producing something with his hands. But never too busy to forget that lock of hair, or cease to relive those precious memories. What is more, he had a friend.

Chippy was both father and guide to him. Not for some time did he learn his real name, Aaron Hardcastle. Everyone called him Chippy, it came naturally for him to do so too.

When work was over for the day, and they had eaten their evening meal, plain fare but more substantial and a little more appetising than he had been having hitherto, Tom listened with interest to the older man's ramblings.

He had spent all his life at sea, he said, until a few years ago when he had been taken ill with scurvy. He had been invalided home and then given this job on the prison hulk.

"I miss all the excitement of those sailing days," he said, "but perhaps I've had a bellyful of it, 'tis a nice snug little billet 'ere, I'm not complaining."

"Tell me something about your life at sea."

"Cor, what to begin with! I expect you 'ave 'eard about the battle of the Nile, eh?"

"No," said Tom, "where is the Nile?"

Chippy looked at him askance.

"Ain't you 'ad no edication, then?"

"Not much," said Tom, "my father taught me to read and write, but when I was ten I worked on the mine with my mother until I was fourteen. Then I went down the mine with my father. There was never any time for schooling."

"Well, I expect you 'ave 'eard of the Mediterranean, then?"

"Yes," lied Tom.

"We was chasing Bony, tryin' to stop 'im from invading Egypt. I was in the *Goliath*, in Nelson's fleet. One of Nelson's scouting vessels came back to say the Frenchies were at anchor near Alexandria, at a place called Aboukir Bay, where the Nile, that is Egypt's great river, comes into the sea. We found them there, anchored close inshore. Though we didn't know it then, it seems many of their crews was ashore. Their admiral thought that they were quite safe from attack on the shore side, being shallow water there. But Nelson, 'e knew better, 'e sent our ship and the *Zealous* and three others between their ships and the shore, whilst 'e in the *Vanguard* and the rest of 'is fleet sailed on the seaward side. We caught 'em proper unawares. Sunk 'em one after the other we did, or set 'em on fire. Their flagship, the *Orient*, blew up, amazing sight it was. We destroyed that fleet and saved Egypt. Bony never tried again."

That was the first of many seafaring tales with which Chippy was to keep Tom enthralled. He related how they had chased the French fleet right across the Atlantic to the West Indies and back again. The cat and mouse tactics to prevent the French from entering the Channel and invading England. Then chasing Villeneuve, the French admiral, back to Cadiz, and the final confrontation between the fleets at Cape Trafalgar, where many of the French ships surrendered and the rest were routed in disorder. Nelson's flagship there was the *Victory*. The tragedy of it was he lost his life in the battle.

Whilst listening to all these exciting tales Tom realised how ignorant he was of the world, its history and geography. He plied Chippy with questions. How was it possible to sail a ship against the wind? How were the sails hoisted? How were the guns fired? How did they find their way about the sea? What were the other countries like that he had visited?

There came a day when Chippy said, "Look 'ere, me lad, I been doin' all the talking. I dunno nothing about you, except that you was a Cornish miner and that you killed somebody. What was you doin' on Dartmoor, then?"

Tom related why he and his mother had come to Devon, how he had got a job on a Dartmoor mine. How he had been befriended by a family and how he had lived with a lovable old couple and been made so welcome. He explained something of his work and how he had fallen in love with Dartmoor, its scenery and its people.

"And you fell in love with that family's daughter," said Chippy, making a not too difficult guess.

"Yes," said Tom, wistfully, "I did. And when someone tried to take her from me I killed him. Well you know that already."

"Yes," said Chippy, "love is a strange thing. Can make men happy. Can make men mad. I don't hold that against you, Tom. I might 'ave done the same myself. I've 'ad me fancies."

The friendship grew. Tom's knowledge of the world grew. His carpentry improved. The time passed quickly, he would look forward to the next day instead of dreading it.

The winter months had been hard to bear, it had been so cold and there was little heating. Spring had come and gone and with it the fund of Chippy's stories. The evenings began to drag again. When August arrived he realised that it was now nearly a year since those dreadful happenings had changed his life. He suddenly had a vivid picture again of Mary Ann rushing into her mother's arms, filthy, bedraggled and hysterical. That was the last time he had seen her. What was she doing now? He hoped she had got over it. Then a thought suddenly struck him. How was it that it had never occurred to him before? Would a baby have resulted from that terrible ordeal? Oh, he hoped not. How awful it would be for Mary Ann, to have a baby she did not want and could not love. How could she cope with it? *He* could never love that baby, knowing its origin, if their marriage ever came about. If only he had some news of her. He had never been allowed to write or receive letters.

"What's come over you, Tom? You'm lookin' very glum."

"I was thinking about my girl, and wondering why I am not allowed to receive any letters."

"Part of the punishment I suppose. No accounting for some of their regulations. Is she goin' to wait for you, Tom?"

"She said she would. I always hope she will."

Autumn came and with it the thought that the first year of his incarceration was over, a third of his sentence served. He was surprised to be summoned to the Governor's office.

"Tom Tremain. I have received good reports of you. It is a pity that I cannot give you any remission of sentence for good behaviour; you will appreciate that, in a sense, you have had that already. What I can do is to give you some privileges. You will be allowed, weather permitting, ten minutes a day on the top deck for fresh air and exercise. This may be extended from time to time, depending upon your continued good behaviour. You will also be allowed to write and receive a letter once a month. Is there anything that you would like to ask me?"

"I would like the opportunity to improve my education, sir. Is it possible to have some books?"

"That is very commendable. The warders have a small collection of books. I will instruct them to let you have one at a time, when they can be spared." He went to a cabinet and selected a book. "You could do worse than make a start on that. You may keep it."

Tom looked at the title. *HOLY BIBLE.*

"Thank you, sir, thank you very much."

Tom could hardly believe his good fortune. All the hours of the day could now be filled in. Time would pass even quicker.

If Tom was finding life easier, so were Mr and Mrs Dawe at Classywell. They were delighted to see the change that the absence of that baby had made to Mary Ann. She seemed to have put the past behind her. She was now taking an interest in everything. Whilst not yet her old vivacious self, she was cheerful, active and helpful. As well as assisting her mother in the house, she took over part of her father's work on the farm. Old Samuel's chickens and the two goats had been brought to Classywell. They now became her responsibility. The goats soon got to know from where their livelihood came, and would come and nudge her as soon as she appeared. She milked the nanny-goat and learnt how to make cheese from the milk. She fed the chickens and collected their eggs. She took her fair share of the tillage of their vegetable plot. She encouraged some flowers to grow around the courtyard.

The old happy atmosphere returned to this household. Her parents soon came to the conclusion that it was no good speculating or worrying about what became of the baby. Nothing could be done about it. They mutually agreed that the subject should never be mentioned again.

The long summer days permitted Mary Ann, over and above these activities, to saddle Nelson and take him for long rides over the moors. But she kept to the moors to the north of Nillacombe. The southern moors brought too many unpleasant memories to her mind. Too much romantic nostalgia for an aching heart to bear.

All these activities had restored Mary Ann to vigorous health. Colour came back to her cheeks, sparkle to her eyes, lustre to her hair. Linnie had watched her dismount from those rides, with such grace and assurance, and lead Nelson to his stable and tend to his needs. She was proud of her daughter. Proud that she was overcoming her traumatic experience. Proud of her blossoming womanhood.

Meanwhile Will, shutting the door, so to speak, after the horse had bolted, had arranged for a porch to be built at his front door. Never again must he be caught out as he had been in that blizzard.

One day Linnie expressed a wish to see her father, to thank him for what he had done for Tom.

"Will you come with me, Mary Ann?"

"Yes, I would love to. I can't remember when I saw Grandfather last. I was always too afraid to go because of the old dragon! I expect he has aged, hasn't he?"

"He doesn't look much different from that portrait. I am sure he will be pleased to see you."

There was just about room enough for the two of them

in the gig. Having no hood they had to choose a day when the weather was settled and calm. June provided such a day. The long hours of daylight would allow them to start early and enable them to have several hours at Ashburn Hall.

The gardens were looking well-kept and colourful as they entered the drive; the old house just as stately and peaceful. It always had that welcoming look about it. At least Linnie thought so.

The large front door opened as they drew up under the portico.

"I saw you coming down the drive, madam," said Coaker, "the master will be pleased to see you. And Miss Mary Ann, too. I wondered who it could be coming with madam."

"Yes, Coaker, I suppose I have grown up a bit since last I was here."

"Master is in the drawing-room, madam."

They entered, and found him sitting in his favourite seat in the window recess.

"Ah, Linnie my dear, what a surprise. And who have we here with you?"

"Mary Ann, Grandfather, don't you remember me?"

"Good gracious me, so it is, bless my soul, quite a young lady now. Charming. Like your mother. Come and sit down beside me."

When they had seated themselves and exchanged the usual pleasantries, he said, "You will stay to lunch of course. Mary Ann, pull the bell cord. Pull it twice. That will mean I want Smithers."

"How are you keeping, Father?"

"Pretty well my dear, gout worries me a bit sometimes. But that's my own fault, isn't it? I believe you had a very bad winter."

In the middle of the narrative of their alarming experiences, Mrs Smithers knocked on the door and entered.

Dressed in voluminous black, her ample bosom surmounted by a white lace collar, her grey hair drawn severely back from her forehead and fashioned into a bun at the back, she looked every bit the reliable family housekeeper. When she spoke though it was with a soft friendly brogue. She had the rare ability of being able to exert her authority yet with an inborn kindness. Without waiting to hear why she had been called, she greeted Linnie and Mary Ann with genuine warmth. " 'Tis that good to see you again, madam; and Mary Ann here. Why the last time I seen you, you was romping about the garden in short skirts. Now look at you! You rang, master?"

"Yes, Smithers, they will be staying for lunch. I suppose cook can turn on something tasty?"

"I'll see that she does."

"Mary Ann, go with Smithers," said her mother, "she will show you round the house. I expect you have forgotten much of it."

When they had gone, Linnie said, "I have come to thank you, Father, for what you were able to do for Tom. I thought it best that Mary Ann should not hear anything that might bring back memories of her ordeal. She is getting over it very well. Tell me, how did you manage to get that sentence reduced?"

"I went to see Sir Thomas Tyrwhitt. I expect you know that he was the present King's private secretary when he was Prince Regent. It was a long shot, but I thought he might still have some influence with the King. I had to tell him all you told me as to what actually happened to Mary Ann. There wouldn't have been a chance otherwise. Sir Thomas is a courteous, kindly man and has great persuasive powers. They certainly had their effect on the King. I was able to see him again on his return to Tor Royal. He said the King was very moved and in sympathy with a man who could avenge that dastardly deed in the way he did. The outcome was very satisfactory, was it not?"

"Yes Father. I thank you from the bottom of my heart. Do you think I should go and see Sir Thomas and thank him?"

"No. With kindly forethought Sir Thomas said you need not consider that. He realised it might be an embarrassment for you."

They talked of many other things before lunch was ready. Mary Ann remained in the servants' hall, enjoying the fuss they all made of her.

After lunch they went into the garden. Her father saw the

gig in which they had travelled. "You must have something better than a gig," he said, "no protection in a thing like that. Come along to the stables and see what we have."

Amongst a variety of carriages he selected a cabriolet.

"What about that? It has a collapsible hood, a splash-board in front to protect you, and a waterproof sheet to cover your knees. It is still light enough for your Nelson to haul. By the way, he must be getting on in years, would you like a young filly?"

"The cabriolet will be fine, Father, thank you. But we wouldn't part with Nelson. He has a lot of life in him yet, he is the gentlest old stallion you could wish for, we love him."

"Right, my dear. Albert, harness Nelson to this cabriolet. You can then escort the ladies home in the gig, and return with the filly."

Autumn colours were fading; rainy, foggy or fine days alternating; the cooler weather of another winter approaching, when a letter was delivered at the new porch at Classywell. Mr Dawe took it and saw that it was addressed to "Miss Mary Ann Dawe, Classywell Farm, Walkhampton Parish, Dartmoor."

"Mary Ann, a letter for you."

"A letter for me?" Surprised, and with a quickening heart-beat, she took it, read the address, raised wide eyes to her father, then ran to her room to read it in private.

My dearest Mary Ann,

I am at last allowed to write to you, and also to receive letters. I long to have one from you.

I am being well treated here now. For some reason I do not know my sentence has been reduced to three years. My living conditions improved. I am working as a carpenter under a man who is being a second father to me. The prison Governor has given me a Bible. I am allowed to borrow other books. So you need not worry about me. I am keeping well, and I hope you are, and your mother and father. Give my love to Nancy and Samuel. And please, please write to me.

I still have your lock of hair. I dream of you and long for you.

I am only allowed to write and receive one letter a month.

I love you. I always will.

Tom.

She re-read it, then a third time, before returning to her parents for them to read it.

From then on, those cherished letters were exchanged monthly. Tom was deeply affected to hear of the tragic death of Nancy and Samuel, he could not believe that he would never see them again, or return to the old farm at Nillacombe. That prospect had been so frequently in his mind once he knew of his shortened sentence. Where would he live now? The narration of the blizzard, and Mary Ann's description of the ammil, brought Dartmoor that much closer to him. How he longed to walk those rolling hills again.

Another year went past, much quicker than the first one. The regular exchange of news helped so much. Tom's avid reading was a great factor in shortening those hours and days. Apart from the Bible, which he found he was able to read only a little at a time, he had been lent Cervantes' *Don Quixote*, Oliver Goldsmith's *Vicar of Wakefield*, Daniel Defoe's *Robinson Crusoe*, some of the plays of Shakespeare, *The Arabian Nights*, and old mariners' books of travel and discovery, which were a great help in furthering his knowledge of distant places, Chippy drawing maps on scraps of paper to explain where they were.

The third year brought sadness once again to Classywell. News came from Ashburn Hall that Linnie's father had suffered a stroke, and had not recovered from it. His death was peaceful, in the night, with as little trouble to anybody, as he had been in life. Such a considerate old gentleman, all the servants agreed.

The funeral was solemn and heartfelt by all. The family gathering was warm and close, far from being the festive event of the previous occasion. Furthermore it marked the end of an era, from the family's point of view.

Edward, now the head of the family, had business interests in London and had no wish to take over Ashburn Hall. Neither did Charles, who was settled happily in Exeter with his growing family. Linnie knew that Will would never leave Classywell, neither could she now see herself living the sort of life to be expected of her in that huge house.

They all agreed that the mansion must be put up for sale. What was so very hard to bear was to tell the loyal staff that their services would no longer be required. They were nearly all aged and due for retirement anyway. They received generous compensation.

When, months later, the will was read, they were all surprised to learn that the family fortune had been almost entirely dissipated. Maintenance of Ashburn Hall in its traditional manner; the wages of the excessively large staff; constant repairs to the fabric of the building; generous donations to charities, and all the other outgoings associated with the running of a large estate, had now largely resulted in debts, which would have to be paid off by the sale of the property.

When, in due course, that sale was effected, there was only a small legacy left to be distributed between the three recipients.

When Linnie received the documents giving details of the sale and the winding up of the estate, she could not restrain a few tears.

"What is it, Linnie?"

"Ashburn Hall. It has been difficult to find a buyer for it. Nobody wanted such a place in so remote a district; and now that the roof has been found to be infested with the death-watch beetle, it has had to be sold for a ridiculously low price. The debtors were clamouring for their money. It is not that we need any money from it, Will, it is the realisation that it has gone from the family. That beautiful place that held such memories, to feel that it is despised and unwanted. It is unbelievable. It makes me so sad to think that I shall never go there again."

She received a letter from her brother Edward later. He had been able to retrieve some of the family heirlooms and personal property of quite considerable value. He enclosed a list of them. Would she please choose what she would like.

"What on earth would we do with Sèvres china and silver goblets, Will? I'll pick out a few items of jewellery. They will make a nice wedding present for Mary Ann. I don't want trinkets and there is no room to hang expensive pictures in this place. I don't want it changed. I am happy with it as it is."

"Bless you for that, my Linnie. I have never ceased to wonder why I deserve such a wife."

Chapter Ten

"Good-bye, Tom. Look after yourself. I'm goin' to miss you. Best of luck," Chippy called after him as Tom descended the companion-way to the cutter.

They had given each other a hearty handshake at the gangway, with very mixed feelings on Tom's part. Elated at going to freedom, genuinely sorry to be leaving this man who had befriended him and taught him so much. They waved a last farewell as the cutter drew away.

The Governor, too, had given him a friendly handshake and wished him well. He had also given him a small amount of money to help him on his way.

At the quayside Tom looked about him, feeling lost and bewildered at so suddenly finding himself entirely dependent on his own initiative. He had to be directed to the dock gates. There, he asked how he could get to Plymouth. The guard at the gate, after having examined his pass, gave him some rather confusing directions.

That walk into Plymouth was a thrill. To be able to see the bustle of life in the busy streets of Dock. Then, after repeatedly having to ask his way, the green open countryside between Dock and a smaller settlement which, a passer-by informed him, was Stonehouse. There followed a long straight road between marshes, at the end of which he could see buildings. On one of them, when he reached there, he saw the name 'Union Street'. Presumably, he thought, so named because it united the new town of Dock to the old town of Plymouth. Then he was in Plymouth itself, with its cobbled streets, shops in fine buildings; costermongers selling fruit and fish; great cart-horses pulling drays; street criers; and people everywhere, all free to roam as they pleased.

"I want to get to Dartmoor, to Prince's Town or near there. How will I get there?" he asked a number of people, none of whom could help him.

He came to a large church with an imposing tower. Beside the railings surrounding it were a couple of traps. Perhaps he could hire one of them. He made enquiries of their drivers whether either of them would take him to Prince's Town. Neither was willing, but one of them said, "A friend of mine has got a job on the new Plymouth and Dartmoor Railway. Maybe you could get a ride on that. I'll take you as far as Crabtree where the line starts if you like."

Tom thanked him and climbed up beside him.

"Where do you actually want to go to on Dartmoor?" asked the driver.

"To a farm called Classywell, not far from Prince's Town."

"The railway don't go that far yet, just to some quarries. I expect they could drop you off somewhere handy though."

"How often do they make the journey?"

"That we will 'ave to find out."

They had been travelling east out of Plymouth, leaving the built-up area behind them. They came to a large estuary on their right.

"That is the River Plym coming out there, we 'aven't got far to go now."

The Plym? Oh yes, Plym Steps. He suddenly felt a bit tense. So this is where that river meets the sea. It happened to be full high tide, the river looked most imposing. Had it been low tide there would only have been a vast expanse of mud to be seen.

"Here we are." They drew up beside a long shed, on the far side of which were iron rails with a long line of small wagons on them. There was a strong smell of horse manure about the place. They walked around to the other side of the shed to find two doors, one securely locked, the other open, to reveal a stable. There was a man there attending to the horses.

"Is Harry here?"

"Not now; what can I do for you?"

"This fellow wants to get to Prince's Town, or somewhere

near it. Would he be able to travel on this railway?"

"P'raps. He'll have to wait till tomorrow, though. Come back first thing in the morning."

"I haven't anywhere to go," said Tom, "and I have very little money. Can I not stay here somewhere. I'm used to sleeping rough?"

"You off a ship, then?"

"Yes," said Tom, truthfully, but relieved that he didn't have to explain what sort of ship.

"You can doss down in one of the empty wagons if you like. I'll give you a couple of horse blankets to keep you warm."

And that is how Tom spent his first night of freedom, cold, lonely, hungry and uncomfortable. Would the hours never pass?

Fortunately, when morning came, activity commenced early. The man of yesterday, who was referred to as Bill, and his mate Harry, arrived and led the team of horses out, harnessing them to the traces. Bill thoughtfully brought a hunk of bread and some cheese for Tom, and a drink. How he needed that. The wagons were already loaded so there was no delay in starting. Tom sat with the two men in the first wagon on rough hard seats. Bill held the reins, but apart from the signal to start or stop, the horses needed little guidance; there was little alternative but to walk and pull between the rails.

The track ran inland from the end of the estuary, up a long valley which Harry said was called Forder. Where a fork occurred in the steepening side of the valley the line followed the right branch, into a deep cleft. Then to Tom's surprise and astonishment they entered a long tunnel, so straight that he could see the little circle of daylight at the far end. Only the straining of the horses indicated that the track was rising steeply. "We are under the Leigham Manor Estate," shouted Harry, to make himself heard above the rumble of the wagon wheels in this confined space. It was dark, dank and depressing as they penetrated its depths. Though Tom was no stranger to such conditions he was quite glad to emerge into daylight again, to find that they were beside a section of road.

Here Harry was informative again, he seemed to like to air his knowledge of the district, for which Tom was thankful. It was all so strange to him. "This road," he said, "goes down to a bridge over the River Plym. When the tide is high and it is not possible to cross the river at Ebb Ford, this bridge is the only way to get to Plympton and the Exeter road."

They now entered an area of steeply sloping woodland, the track following a tortuous route, penetrating deeply into a number of little valleys and curving sharply across their streamlets. Quite a deep cutting through solid rock preceded the first valley whose stream was crossed on a substantial embankment, built, no doubt, from the excavated material from the cutting. In between these indentations Tom felt almost apprehensive at the precipitousness of the hillside along which the track had been hewn. He expressed astonishment that anyone could have contemplated constructing a railway under such conditions. The thinning autumnal foliage enabled him to look down far into the depths of the valley of the Plym, but never able to see the river. Glimpses of the far side of the valley could be seen, and occasionally more extensive tracts of land beyond it. He lost count of the number of these little valleys that were penetrated, perhaps five or six, sometimes very deeply into them, where it would have been gloomy if it had not been for the sun, low in the sky, piercing through the trees in shafts of light and shadow that gave an enchanting effect.

At last they emerged from the woods into the open and a fine view of the Plym valley was obtained, the river far below. So gentle had been the gradient it came as a surprise to see the height that they had now attained. All too soon that view was lost as the track curved away from it, through cultivated country. Tom took the opportunity during this less interesting part of the journey to ask what freight they carried in the wagons. "Coal, sea sand and lime, timber, provisions, things like that;" said Harry, "coming back it will be granite from the quarries at Foggin Tor. That is as far as this line goes at present."

Then once more they were beside a road. "Where are we now," asked Tom.

"This is the new turnpike road from Plymouth to Dartmoor. This place is called Jump. Don't ask me why. Funny name isn't it?"

After following beside the road for a little while they turned away again in another long curve, still in cultivated country, eventually to come out onto open moorland. Then in the distance Tom saw the hills and tors of Dartmoor. Conspicuous amongst the tors was one that was unmistakable, the first one he had ever seen, one that looked like a crouching lion, Sheeps Tor. He could not restrain his excitement. It was like opening a door to freedom. He filled his lungs with the bracing air, looked long and ardently at the vast expanse of rolling hills. Somewhere over there was Classywell. Somewhere there his beloved was waiting for him. She knew he was coming, but not when.

More level ground followed now over grassy terrain, until they came to a shed with a peculiar broken-backed roof. Clearbrook Wharf, he was told, where a lengthy stop occurred whilst a change of horses was made, the old team rubbed down, watered and fed.

Soon after leaving the wharf Tom noticed that there was a leat on either side of the track. "That is Plymouth Leat below us," said Harry, "and that one above is Dock Leat."

If I was to follow Dock Leat, thought Tom, it would lead me so close to Classywell. Perhaps, though, there will be a better way.

The two leats were never very far away from the track for quite a distance, until they came once more to the turnpike road, this time crossing it near an outcrop of rock. "That is Ullestor Rock," said Harry, "strange isn't it, sticking up like that in flat country, not like most tors."

Near the rock the railway crossed Dock Leat on a little bridge, and parted company with the leats. Soon afterwards they stopped where a siding led away to a roofless, walled enclosure.

"This is North Devon Wharf," said Harry, "where we leave the lime and sand, fertilisers for the farms here, Elfordtown and the rest."

The two rearmost wagons of the train were uncoupled beside the points to the siding, and a horse led out to haul them to the wharf.

It was now about midday. A lengthy stay was made here whilst Bill and Harry ate a meal they had brought with them, sharing some of it with Tom. Parcels, letters and newspapers were handed to the man in charge, who stayed and exchanged news with Bill and Harry whilst they ate.

Tom was relieved when at last they resumed their journey, he was anxious now to get to his destination, not sure how much further there was to go before he could leave them.

Track and turnpike road followed the same route for a mile or so, the track re-crossing the road soon after leaving the wharf. Then, as the road ascended a steep hill, the track turned away at Dousland Barn and made a more gradual ascent around the slopes of a dome-shaped hill. Part way round it they made such an extraordinary extensive bend that they now faced about in the direction from which they had come, but gaining height all the time. The horses laboured as the gradient increased, still rounding the western side of that hill, until they were heading in the right direction again, to arrive once more at the turnpike road. When the track began to cross this road, Tom recognised where he was, he had passed here on that very first occasion when he had walked from Wakaton to Classywell. This was the ideal place to alight.

"Can we stop here?" called Tom, "I know my way now."

He thanked his two companions profusely. They would accept no money. "All in the day's work," they said. One day he hoped he might travel the rest of the way to the railway's destination, wherever that was, it had been such a fascinating experience.

But now he was nearing his own destination, and his destiny. What was to happen to him now? What had the future in store?

He followed that familiar road, past Lowery and Leathertor Farms; to the stepping stones across the river, where he had drunk its waters; where nearby he and Mary Ann had held hands for the very first time. Then up Raddick Lane and down past Roundypark. He was so near now.

* * * *

Mary Ann was feeding the chickens when she heard Snap bark. She turned to see a bearded man with tousled hair at the gate. Who could this be calling? Then the realisation that Tom had told her he had a beard, but her mental picture of him was always as she had known him.

"Tom!" she exclaimed. She dropped her basket of chicken feed and ran towards him. Tom had opened the gate and had made only a stride or two before they met, throwing themselves into each other's arms, hugging each other closely, heads side by side, Tom stroking those silken tresses that he had dreamed about for so long. Suddenly the world seemed to stand still. Snap looked up in wonder at them. Linnie and Will, hearing Mary Ann's cry, had come to the porch. They stood silently gazing at them, a half smile on their faces. The birds stopped their twittering, the chickens their clucking, or at least nobody heard them. For some time they could not release each other, such ecstasy was it to be together again. Mutually they drew their heads apart and gazed into each other's eyes. Then Tom bent down and kissed Mary Ann's forehead. That meant more to them both at that moment than a more passionate kiss would have meant, it held such tender memories. Tom drew his hands down her arms and held her hands, drawing them to his lips. It was then he saw her parents. Still holding each other closely, they walked towards them.

"Welcome home," said Linnie, giving him a motherly embrace. Will shook him warmly by the hand. Both were aware of the change in him. The beard, the unkempt appearance, those tired eyes and haggard bearing, all suggested a middle-aged man of the labouring class.

"You look hungry and tired, Tom," said Linnie, "when did you last eat?"

"I have had very little since yesterday morning, and no chance to wash or sleep much. I'm sorry about my appearance."

"We'll soon put that right. Come in."

The change in him made Mary Ann shy and speechless. This wasn't the Tom she remembered, but she felt tender compassion for him, longing to do something for him.

Linnie brought in a meal for him, and they all drank

tea whilst listening to Tom's description of his extraordinary travels since leaving the prison hulk. His voice had not changed, Mary Ann noted, that seemed to be the only link with the past.

When he had finished his meal, and what a luxury that was, Mary Ann at last found her voice and said, "Tom, I am sure you are longing for a wash and change of clothing. We have brought back your clothes from Nillacombe. You know where the wash-house is. When you are ready I'm going to cut your hair and you are going to shave that beard off. Then perhaps I'll be able to recognise you."

Whilst Tom was splashing water over himself, water from a branch of the potwater leat which had been led here to give a constant jet in the wash-house, Mary Ann and her mother ascended to that upstairs room which had now been cleared and restored as a bedroom, in anticipation of Tom's return. They made up the bed and laid out his clothes. Then Mary Ann remembered the cloth bundle that Tom had dropped at the gate, his meagre possessions, and her own basket of chicken feed. She went out to retrieve both, noting that the sun was just setting. Setting, she hoped, on an era so momentous and tragic, which must now be put behind them. From now on they could make plans for the future.

When Tom lay in his bed that night, he could hardly believe he was the same man who had lain awake the night before in such hard, cold, exposed and uncomfortable conditions. Now he was clean, snug and warm, his smooth cheeks caressed by an equally smooth and soft pillow. He was in the protection of a home he loved, amongst people who loved him. With such pleasant thoughts he was soon asleep. A long, dreamless sleep of weariness and contentment.

At breakfast the next morning Tom enquired about the progress of the mine at Aylesborough. He had to get a job somewhere.

"Mr Deacon has been paying us occasional visits to enquire after you, Tom. He says the mine is going well and that he will be pleased to find work for you when you are ready."

"Oh, that's good. Perhaps I'll be able to live at the barracks there."

"No you won't, Tom," said Mrs Dawe, "you are going to stay here. That room upstairs is yours for as long as you need it."

After thanking her for that kindness, he said, "I suppose I had better go and see my mother this morning. Have you ever heard anything from her?"

"Your mother came to see us twice, Tom. Once to enquire why you had not been to see her, at the time of your arrest. And again soon afterwards to say she was going to return to Cornwall. She was not happy in Wakaton, she wanted to be with her friends in Cornwall. She thought she had lost you for ever, there was no point in her staying here any longer. I am sorry, Tom, we should have told you. I suppose we were preoccupied with other things and forgot to do so. Will you miss her?"

"It all seems a long time ago now. I feel more relieved that she is with her friends. I knew she was not happy at Wakaton. You are more of a mother to me now. I can't call you Mother, yet; but may I call you Linnie? Mrs Dawe sounds so formal."

"Yes, of course; I am glad you feel that way."

Mary Ann came in from her bedroom, dressed in her capuchin, but with the hood thrown back behind her head; her hair neatly tied with a bow at the back.

"Oh, you do look lovely in that," said Tom.

Mary Ann smiled in pleasure at the compliment. "Come with me to Nillacombe, Tom. I go periodically to see that all is secure there. No one has yet taken it over; no one seems likely to, it needs a lot done to it."

They set off, Tom's arm around her waist. After they had gone for some distance, making only light conversation, Mary Ann looked up to his face and said, "You are looking more like my Tom today."

"Did I look so very terrible yesterday?"

"Yes, you did. I couldn't believe it was you. I felt disappointed, a bit angry that such a thing could happen to you. I couldn't speak. I just wanted to do something to bring you back to someone I knew."

"Well, you have, haven't you? I do feel a different person. Your mother has been very kind to me and told me I can continue to live at Classywell. Now I shall always be near you. You have changed too, Mary Ann."

"I have? How?"

"I am not quite sure. I have dreamed of you as I remembered you. I did not think there could be anyone more lovely. I suppose it is that you have changed from a girl to a woman. You are even more lovely for that change."

They stopped, facing each other. Mary Ann brought her arms from beneath her cloak and put them about his waist. She looked up to him with moist eyes. "Dear Tom." Then did they embrace with the passion that had been missing yesterday. He bent down, their lips met, and for the first time they knew what it was to be stirred to the very depths of their souls.

When at last they reached Nillacombe, Tom examined the old house more thoroughly than Mary Ann thought necessary. It was a pathetic sight. Rain had leaked through the damaged roof in places. What furniture there was had been packed into a corner away from the leaks. The roof had fallen in and lay a tangled mess on the floor of what had been Tom's room.

"How would you like to live here, Mary Ann?"

"You're joking, Tom."

"Then where would you like to live when we are married?"

There was quite a pause before Mary Ann answered.

"That prospect has always seemed so remote, I really haven't thought about it. But you can't be serious about this wreck of a place."

"I am, Mary Ann. I have got to provide a home for you. I've got to earn some money. If I can get work at Ellisborough, that will solve part of the problem. In my spare time I can repair this place. Maybe I can get wood from Ellisborough. We will have to get a thatcher to repair this roof, that is the first thing that needs doing and will be the greatest expense. We must do that at once if we are to save the place. My time in prison has not been wasted, I have learnt to be a carpenter. I'll make a home for you here you will be proud of. We both have an affection for this place, and its associations. How pleased Nancy and Samuel would be to know we are here. I'm sure we shall have their blessing."

Mary Ann stood wide eyed whilst he was expounding his plans, absorbing some of his enthusiasm, realising he was so serious about it; and then having belief in his ability to do this for her. Already plans were forming in her own mind of what she might be able to do to help.

"I am waiting for your answer, Mary Ann."

"A little while ago you said I had changed into a woman. I am feeling the same about you. You have changed into a man, a very capable man I think. I have faith in you, that you can do this for me. Our own home, planned by ourselves. What a wonderful idea."

Their plans were sealed with another loving embrace.

Tom did get work at Ellisborough. He was received with genuine warmth by Mr Deacon, and by those men who remembered him. He was forgiven by the blacksmith for the theft of his hammer, in fact at times they worked together. Mr Deacon was to recognise his skills in various trades. He assisted the carpenter too when necessary. He maintained the flat-rods, effected repairs to the stamps. He sometimes relieved miners underground when any were off sick or injured. There was always work for him in some department. Far from being considered a gaol-bird, he received sympathy for having been punished for doing something from which they had all benefited. The man Jethro had been a menace, even though he had only been employed on the leat making.

Mr Deacon was intrigued at Tom's plans to renovate Nillacombe. He had seen the state it was in when he had visited Classywell. He allowed Tom to have timber from their store at cost price, and to take free any abandoned timber from previous use.

Tom sought Mr Dawe's advice on the repairs to the thatched roof.

"I believe Nosworthy have recently employed a thatcher for their roof," he said, "I will make enquiries."

With the shortening winter days there was little opportunity for Tom to do much work on the house during the week. But on Sundays he made good progress on the clearing of his old bedroom and replacing the broken beams of its roof. Meanwhile Mr Dawe's enquiries had led him to Sheepstor where he engaged a thatcher who was only too glad of the prospect of work.

Amos Gray had a good reputation as a thatcher. It takes years of apprenticeship and more years of experience to be an expert at the work. To know where to find the best and most suitable reeds. How they should be stooked to dry and for how long before they are put to use. All this information was being imparted to Mr Dawe as the two of them rode to Nillacombe to inspect what had to be done. "Some reeds last longer than others," he was saying, "water reeds and wheat straw be good, but expensive and not easy to come by on Dartymoor. Us grows rye 'ere and there, 'tis best suited for the soil and climate; it serves our purpose purty well."

In due course, when weather permitted, he made good progress on the repairing of the roof at Nillacombe, removing damaged and deteriorated straw from where the leaks had occurred. Completely re-roofing where Tom had repaired the beams. Adding more thatch over the whole roof to give it a more uniform colour and shape, patting it flat with a square board fitted with a handle by which to hold it. Shaping it expertly over the upstairs windows and sealing it securely around the chimney stack.

Tom was thrilled as he returned home each evening to see the progress being made. How wonderful it looked when at last it was completed. He was apprehensive, though, as to how much it was going to cost him. When he made enquiries about this, Amos said that had all been settled between Mr Dawe and himself. He hoped Tom was satisfied with his work.

"More than satisfied, it's perfect. I can hardly believe it is the same cottage!"

When, at Sunday dinner, Tom broached the subject of its cost, Mr Dawe said that he and Linnie were only too pleased to offer that as their contribution to their daughter's future home. They had approved whole-heartedly of the renovation of the cottage, and of Tom's enterprise in tackling such an undertaking.

"How long do you think it is going to take you to finish it, Tom?" asked Linnie.

"Longer than I could wish. I have little spare time to work on it at present. But with the spring and longer evenings I'll be able to make much better progress. It will be a few months even then, I should think. Some of the flooring needs renewing and the window frames re-making; there is a lot of rotten wood there. I hope to make some new furniture, too."

"I am wondering about your wedding day, have you a date in mind?"

Tom looked across the table. "Have you thought about that, Mary Ann?"

"Yes, of course I have. I would like it to be in the summer, June or July. Do you think that is possible?"

"Oh, yes. Now that we have a sound roof I can work there. I'll have it ready for you."

For a present that Christmas Tom received a set of wood-working tools from the family. Mary Ann received from Tom a jewellery casket he had made during the last days in prison. Beautifully made of teak, a tray inside with fitted compartments, all expertly finished. Only one thing marred the happiness of that day. There was no hamper from Ashburn Hall that year.

With the coming of spring Tom was able to make good progress at Nillacombe. Unlike Classywell, the old house had seen little change in its structure over the centuries. It still retained its central passageway between living quarters and shippen. A porch, in need of some repairs now, protected the front entrance. A doorway, central in the passage, led to the shippen. Another on the right, near the end of the passage, led to the combined living-room and kitchen. A fourth door at the end of the passage gave access to the rear courtyard, and to the stone steps that led to the tallet over the shippen.

Immediately to the right as one entered the living-room was the fireplace and cloam oven. Thus the chimney was central to the house and it helped to warm the bedroom above. Access to the upper floor was by a semicircular stone stairway, built out from the rear wall. There was a small window on each side of the stairway, and a long, low mullion window in the front wall, which faced south, looking down into the valley.

At the top of the stairway a landing gave entrance to the two bedrooms, the larger on the right, the smaller one, which had been Tom's room, at the end of the building. Each had a small window facing south.

The shippen was still as it had always been, with its drain running down the centre of the floor to the end wall, and since the animal quarters were always located on the lower slopes of the ground, good drainage was assured. There were several small splayed slit windows high up in the walls, unglazed, of course. Tom had plans for that shippen, but it would be quite a major undertaking and would have to wait for the years to come.

Meanwhile it was all those windows in the living quarters that needed renewing. They were the first of the repairs that Tom undertook. The kitchen became Tom's workshop, Nancy's kitchen table providing him with a workbench. Now were Chippy's early lessons of such benefit to him; the making of all those mortice and tenon joints. They were second nature to him now. Mary Ann looked on in wonder on the occasions when she came to watch him work. The precious glass was carefully saved from the old windows and used in the new. Glass cutting was not one of Tom's accomplishments, so he was very careful not to break any panes. The mullion window of stonework did not require anything done to it.

Much of the flooring in the bedrooms needed renewing, as did some of the wainscoting throughout the house. Little by little Mary Ann began to see her home taking shape. What pleasure it was to give assistance when Tom needed something held whilst he fixed it. To sweep the floor of its shavings and chippings at the end of the working day. To make him cups of tea and sit on the rickety chairs whilst he drank them, and discuss the next job to be tackled. Then, when the time was ripe, to measure the windows and make curtains for them.

The potwater leat was in need of attention too, it was not

giving its proper flow of water. It came from the river below Willabeam. On a fine day in April the two of them set out with spades to examine the leat throughout its length. As happens so often with old leats, if they are not maintained, the turf had grown inwards almost to cover the channel in places. Elsewhere the banks had broken down and the water was escaping from them. At the river, work was needed to improve the diversion of the water into the channel. Apart from banking up the channel where the leaks were occurring, little more could be done that day. But on the next few Sundays the two of them worked on that leat and restored the channel throughout its length. This was a labour of love, doing something from which they would ultimately benefit. They revelled in the open air life on these warm spring days. The joy of just being together, alone together, a little meal together on the banks of the river. Walking home together, dirty, tired and happy.

There came a morning when Tom removed his tools and work-bench to the shippen. The living-room floor was swept and washed. Mary Ann had hung her curtains. Tom had made a new table, and repaired the rickety chairs. The room at last looked what it was supposed to be, a room to live in.

After dinner at Classywell that day, Linnie and Will accompanied them back to Nillacombe. They immediately noted the repaired porch. The front door which now opened and shut without jamming. The shining flagstones in the passageway. They inspected the rest of the house and praised Tom's handiwork and Mary Ann's curtains. When all was seen and approved, they sat around the new table and Mary Ann served tea, a little christening ceremony for their future home.

The wedding was fixed for the second week in June. The banns were called in the Parish Church of Sheepstor. Invitations were sent out to their neighbours and to Mr Deacon.

Mary Ann made her own wedding dress from material she had bought in Tavistock. Tom was fitted for a new suit.

When the great day came, Linnie and Tom drove to the church in the gig, pulled by a pony borrowed from Kingsett. Mary Ann and her father followed in the cabriolet, Nelson prancing proudly as though aware of the importance of the occasion.

Whilst waiting for the bride to arrive, Tom, from his place in the front pew, had time to study the beautiful carving on the pulpit and on the pew ends. More particularly was he interested in the delicate tracery of the ancient rood-screen, now so sadly broken in so many places. How he wished he could do work like that, and repair that screen.

Then the sound of the organ proclaimed the entrance of the bride. This was his first sight of her in her wedding gown. How elegant and stately she looked as she walked slowly up the aisle on her father's arm. How proud he was as he accompanied her to the altar rails.

And again, after the ceremony, as she now clung to his arm, past all those carved pew ends, to receive smiles from so many of his friends from the mine in those pews. Then out into the bright June sunshine as the church bells rang out a joyous peal. They turned right to the lichgate, beyond which was the waiting cabriolet. Chivalrously he helped her to her seat, then climbed beside her. Laughingly she took the reins. This was something she could do better than Tom. Quite a procession followed as they drove back to Classywell for the reception. Not for a long time had the old house heard such chatter and laughter.

That night, as they lay in bed together, by the light of the oil lamp, Tom looked down at his lovely bride, her face encircled by her golden hair. She looked up at him, and in those eyes he saw fear. The fear he had seen at Shavercombe Falls. The fear he had glimpsed during his fight with Jethro. And to his mind came the sight of her rushing into the room at Classywell shouting, "Don't touch me, don't touch me." He knew then what was in Mary Ann's thoughts. He stroked her hair and whispered, "Not tonight, dear heart. Just when you are ready. Go to sleep."

The tears welled up in her eyes. She put her hand to his face and stroked his cheek. It was a touch which said what she could not put into words. "Thank you for that understanding."

Tom wondered if they were ever going to be rid of the memory of that dreadful night.

Chapter Eleven

Late in October, in the year 1831, Tom returned from Ellisborough at an earlier hour than usual. The tempo of his walk was a little slower, the expression on his face more thoughtful than was customary.

Arriving at Nillacombe he sank into an armchair and looked around at this room on which he had spent so many hours and so much labour in the making of it; changing it from a cow byre to a comfortable sitting-room. The slit windows had been filled in. In their place were a large wide window facing the valley, and two smaller ones in the rear wall. On them hung pretty curtains. A new floor covered the old drain. A fireplace in the end wall warmed the room and made a focal point about which to sit and relax after the day's work was done. He had made it to please his beloved wife. She had covered him with kisses to show her delight at the result.

Mary Ann had not yet returned from fetching their son from school at Wakaton; the same school that she had attended and where she had learnt to sew and to cook. John sat astride Nelson in front of her as they made that journey twice a day. Weather permitting they enjoyed that ride, their close proximity bringing such comfort to them both.

Nelson had been given to Mary Ann as part of her wedding present. Her parents knew how much she loved that horse. She had grown up with it, they had a perfect understanding of each other. The Dawes had obtained a Dartmoor filly and had trained it, as a replacement.

Tom loved his son. He was their only child and it seemed

that he was likely to remain so. He was a lively, intelligent boy, always asking questions, always trying to emulate his father, helping, or more likely hindering, when Tom was doing any woodwork. Now that they had this sitting-room, the kitchen served a dual purpose, cooking and dining at one end, a workshop at the other. There was always something to make or to mend.

Tom cast his mind back to the birth of that son, conceived in such great love and compassion and submission to his caresses. Linnie had been a perfect midwife. The labour had been mercifully short; the baby suckled with such tender love. He could still see the joy on Mary Ann's face, how serene and beautiful she had looked, as he bent down to kiss her.

It was Linnie who had suggested the name John for the child. After her father's name, the father who had been so understanding of her own choice of life, and who had made that choice possible. He had been so kind to her own children. Mary Ann, what she remembered of him, had thought him a dear old man. She readily agreed to the name.

Those early years of their married life had been happy in spite of their poverty. Their home, this house, had meant so much to them. It was their own creation, yet associated with the affection they had had for its previous occupiers, whose aura was never far away.

Their fortune had improved as Tom had progressed to a more responsible position at Ellisborough. The mine had been a phenomenal success, producing high grade tin, reaching a peak of production in 1825, and reaping profit from the smelting of the ore from other Dartmoor mines. His wages had correspondingly increased. But since that peak there had been a steady decline in production. This year had been disastrous, necessitating a reduction of their workforce.

Tom's reverie was interrupted by the sound of Nelson's hooves on the cobbles. He got up and went to the porch.

They had dismounted. Mary Ann was leading Nelson to his stable. John saw his father and came bounding towards him, arms outstretched. Tom caught him and lifted him on high, then into his arms, John flinging his arms around his father's neck.

"Have you had a nice ride home, son?"

"Yes, Father, I held the reins, and Nelson did what I told him to."

He put him down as Mary Ann came towards him, her cheeks high coloured with the exertions of the ride and the cool autumn breeze. She looks so graceful, Tom thought, whatever she wears. Under her close-fitting jacket she wore a divided skirt and riding boots. The divided skirt was her own idea. Ever since childhood she had ridden astride, side saddle seemed so impractical to her. The divided skirt made this possible whilst still appearing feminine.

"You are home early, Tom."

"Yes, dear. I'll tell you why when you have seen to John's tea." In fact they all had tea together in the kitchen.

Later she joined him before the fire in the sitting-room, leaving John to draw on his slate at the table.

"What's on your mind, Tom, you look worried?"

"Yes, I am. I believe Ellisborough Mine is finished. You know that things have not been going too well lately. Captain Treweek and I have been examining the underground workings today. The lodes are practically worked out. The shareholders have been concerned at the falling off in production over the past few years and are reluctant to put up any more money to find new ground, especially with the falling price of tin. It has been my unpleasant duty over the past few months to pay off about three-quarters of the men, many of whom are my friends. Today the smelting house has been closed down for the winter. Perhaps for good. And now we have had a complaint from a local farmer that three of his bullocks have been lost down our shafts. We shall have to fence them in, or fill them in; I don't know what will happen yet, but the site is very dangerous if left unattended."

"I thought Mr Deacon was developing Wheal Katharine at Crane Lake; isn't that a success?"

"Yes, there is a good stamping mill there now. He has asked me to join him there. But I can't do that, Mary Ann. I don't want anything to do with Crane Lake. I hate the place."

"Yes, I understand that only too well. I wouldn't want you to go there. But what is to happen to you? What about Whiteworks, could you get work there?"

"I do not think prospects are any better there. It is always the same in tin mining. Periods of prosperity and boom are followed by depressions and closures. It is unpredictable. There could be a revival somewhere on Dartmoor, but how long do we have to wait for it? And even then, there would probably be too many miners chasing too few jobs."

"What are you going to do then, Tom?"

"The only successful industry on Dartmoor at present is the quarrying of granite. I believe there is some future in that. I could apply there for work. I don't know anything about it, but I would soon learn."

"It will be a lot further for you to walk to Foggin Tor than to Ellisborough."

"If they have any accommodation there, would you be prepared to move?"

"Oh, no Tom. Give up this place after we have put so much work into it, where we have been so happy? I couldn't. Don't ask me to."

Tom took her hand and kissed it. "I was teasing you. I just wanted to hear you say that. I would walk twice that distance to work, just to be able to continue to live here. But I am serious about getting a job at the quarries. There is nothing else. You know what I feel about farming. I would never make a good farmer. Anyway, it can wait until after Christmas. I think there is enough work for me at Ellisborough until then. It is sad to see the place being run down, though."

John came excitedly into the room, putting an end to this conversation.

"Look what I've drawn, Father." He showed his slate with its pictures of a house, a cow and a face on it, things he had been told to draw at school, just outlines, but recognisable as such. He sat on his father's knee and prattled on about what had happened at school that day, about his friends and his teacher. Then suddenly changing the subject, said "Are we going for a walk tomorrow, Father?" For tomorrow would be Sunday, and they nearly always did go for a walk on Sunday mornings before going to Classywell for dinner.

That tradition had been kept up.

"If it is a fine day, yes we will."

"Where, Father?"

Tom liked to encourage the boy to have initiative.

"Where would you like to go?"

A pause whilst he pondered that.

"Up to the top of a tor." He loved climbing the rocks of a tor.

So the next morning the two of them set off. Mary Ann said she wouldn't go with them this time, she had promised her mother to help her with some sewing.

It was cold and windy as they descended to the river, but otherwise it was a fine exhilarating day. John leapt the boulders across the river, refusing to be helped. They climbed the steep hill on the far side to reach the ancient leat that Tom had seen all those years ago when he first came to this valley. It provided a good and level path to the foot of Down Tor. John ran ahead, searching out any group of rocks that might provide a bit of adventure. Tom was delighted to see the boy's enthusiasm for this land that he himself had come to love so much. They had been here many times since that memorable first occasion, but as always when they came to the summit, he was overcome with nostalgia at the memory of Mary Ann on that topmost rock. John, after scrambling over all the surrounding rocks, wanted to be lifted up to it. "No, son, not today, it is too windy, you will be blown off it. Let's eat our apples here, out of the wind. Then we can start going home."

Half way through his apple John said, "Can't we go to that stone row?" He remembered having gone there once before, it had obviously made an impression on him.

"We'll have to run all the way if we do, otherwise we will be late for dinner."

"All right," said John, "I'll race you there."

That brought another poignant memory of Mary Ann saying, "I'll race you to the top." All the tragic events that had intervened since then made it seem so very long ago.

They did run all the way to the stone row, and once again Tom allowed his competitor to win. Then John played a game of his own, making a zig-zag course between all the stones of the row.

They *were* a little late when they arrived back at Classywell, but easily forgiven by Linnie when she saw the boy's rosy cheeks and listened to his excited chatter about his adventures. A warm glow filled Mary Ann's breast as she saw the two of them enter the room, so strong, so healthy, so lovable.

Tom's fears about the closure of the mine proved all too correct. In December the last remaining stocks of tin had been sent off to Tavistock for coining. A small remnant of the workforce had been retained to dismantle the headgear of the shafts, and to fill in those shafts. The flat-rods had been dismantled and all material collected together in readiness for their sale. When that sale was over, and the waterwheels and the whims and all the stores had gone, the last act was to fill in all those wheel-pits in an endeavour to make the site safe. The leats ran dry as their sources were blocked. All the buildings were locked up, to remain silent sentinels over what had been one of the most successful mines on Dartmoor.

On a bitterly cold day in early January of 1832, Tom walked home from it for the very last time.

Mary Ann knew it was his last day there. She knew he would be coming home cold, depressed and worried. She had baked his favourite cake for him. She had put a good quantity of peat on the fire in the sitting-room and made it glow hot and welcoming. She had left John with her parents on the way back from school. She just wanted to be alone with her Tom and to comfort him.

When Tom saw the preparations that had been made for him, his sombre mood melted. He drew a very willing wife into his arms and hugged her closely. He was deeply moved by the warmth of her embrace. How well she understood his need for her love at this time.

They sat close together before the fire whilst they drank their tea. Tom praised her cake whilst recounting the events of the day. The subject then turned naturally to their problems of the future.

"What is my quickest way to Foggin Tor?" asked Tom, for Mary Ann knew that part of the moor so well.

"If the weather is suitable, go first to Classywell Pool. You remember that there is a footbridge over Dock Leat above it. From there you go round the slopes of Cramber Tor, more or less on the level, until you see Hart Tor ahead. If you walk towards it you should come to a ford on the Hart Tor Brook. It is a convenient place to cross if you are riding, but if you are walking it is better to find a place above the ford where the river narrows. Then keeping Hart Tor on your left, and still keeping on fairly level ground, you should come to the Mew at Devil's Bridge, where the turnpike road crosses the river. Then you turn left from there on the lower slopes of North Hisworthy Tor, and in about a mile you will reach the quarries. When are you contemplating going?"

"Tomorrow, I can't rest until I find a job."

Tom got up to light the oil lamp, at the same moment as John's voice was heard. The door opened to admit him and his granny and grandad.

All cares were cast aside for the next half hour as they enjoyed the pleasure of their company. John as usual was excited and rumbustious, wanting his grandfather to play games with him and climbing on his lap, until Mary Ann realised that her father was beginning to show some distress at such boisterousness. She took John by the hand and gave him a mild reprimand.

"It is time we left," said Linnie, "it will be too dark to see our way presently."

As Mary Ann kissed her father good-bye, she said, "You are looking tired, Father, are you all right?"

"Yes, my dear, but I think I need a rest after all that excitement."

When they had gone Mary Ann took John to the kitchen to give him his supper, whilst Tom cleared the tea things away and tidied up the sitting-room. He was about to go to his bedroom when there was a violent knocking on the porch door. He and Mary Ann ran to open it, to see Linnie looking distraught. "Your father has collapsed in the lane, I can't move him. Come and help please."

"You look after John," said Tom, "I will go with your

mother."

"Get your coat, Tom," said Linnie, "it is freezing."

Indeed it was freezing, the puddles in the lane had a thin crust of ice on them and crackled underfoot as they hurried as fast as they could in the semi-dark. They were nearly at Classywell when at last they reached Will, he was lying on his back as Linnie had left him. Tom put his hands under his shoulders and armpits as Linnie took his feet. Fortunately he was not a heavy man and they managed to carry him without pause to the house and to his bed.

Tom was no stranger to death, he had seen it all too often in those Cornish mines. He had very little hope as he felt for Will's pulse and looked for any sign of breathing.

"He is dead, Linnie."

Linnie knelt beside the bed, gazing unbelievingly at her husband. Tears trickled down her cheeks as she also felt for his hand and pulse. Tom went round the bed and helped her to her feet, and then to the living-room.

It was a long time before either of them could speak.

"You must come back with me, Linnie, you can sleep with Mary Ann. I'll be all right in the sitting-room."

"No, Tom. I can't leave him alone here, I just can't, even though there is nothing I can do for him. I'll sleep in Mary Ann's room. You go home and comfort her."

Tom was torn between conflicting desires. It was awful to leave this woman alone with her dead husband. Yet if he didn't go back to Mary Ann there was a danger that she would come out in the cold to see what had happened and to help. But she wouldn't leave John alone. No, she couldn't do that. He had to go back to her. She would be getting worried.

He took Linnie's hand and kissed it. "God be with you this night, Mother. Come to us tomorrow morning, we will work out what has to be done."

Linnie looked her thanks, she could not trust herself to speak. It was the first time he had called her 'Mother'. That had given her a little comfort. All she could do was to nod her agreement at his last instruction. With a heavy heart Tom left her.

Now he had to face Mary Ann's grief. How would she take

the news?

The temperature was still falling on this cloudless night as, hatless and gloveless, he wended his way back to Nillacombe, the burden of his worries weighing heavily upon him.

Mary Ann came towards him as he entered. "How is he, Tom?"

Tom put his arms around her shoulders and led her back to the warmth of the kitchen fire. *How* to tell her?

She took his coat from him. Then looked up to his face. His silence answered her fears. "He's dead, isn't he?"

"Yes, Mary Ann, he died of a heart attack, in the bitterly cold walk home. It must have been so sudden, he would not have suffered. Be brave, dear heart."

"I'll make you a hot drink, you look frozen."

"You are comforting *me*. I thought I was going to have to console you."

"I have shed my tears. I was so sure of it. How has Mother taken it?"

"She is very brave. She would not come back with me, she would not leave him. She will be here in the morning."

But later, in bed, there were more tears to be shed. Tom did have to do some consoling. Sleep would not come. The future looked even more uncertain. What would her mother want to do now? Mary Ann could not envisage her living alone at Classywell. There was little enough room for her to stay here on a permanent basis. Round and round went her thoughts until, with exhaustion, she did finally fall into a restless sleep.

In the morning, though, she showed some of her mother's qualities. She knew what had to be done. She got breakfast for them all. Then she sent Tom down to fetch her mother, meanwhile cooking a stew that could easily be warmed up later. There would be no school for John today so she set him something to do to keep him quiet.

When Tom returned with her mother she said she was going to ride into Tavistock to make arrangements with an undertaker. She was all dressed for the journey, Nelson already saddled. As she set off Tom looked after her in wonder at this new wife of his, so capable, so forthright, so self-assured, so calm.

It was mid-afternoon before she returned. Linnie and Tom and John had already partaken of their stew. Linnie now warmed some up for her daughter.

Whilst she ate she said she had arranged for her father's body to be taken to a mortuary, and had fixed the date for the funeral in four days time at Wakaton Church. The undertaker would be calling later on to explain the details of the funeral procession.

"I hope that is all right, Mother. I just wanted to save you having to deal with such matters."

"Yes, of course, my dear. I am so grateful to you. I would not have been able to cope with all that today."

"You are going to stay here for as long as is necessary. I'll make up a bed for you in John's room, he can sleep on the floor in our room, unless Tom can fix up some sort of bed for him. What about the animals at Classywell?"

"Perhaps Tom would come there with me tomorrow. You have quite enough to do without worrying about them."

John was taken daily to school as before, but all thought of Foggin Tor was set aside for the moment. The family was content to be together and gradually to overcome their grief. The January weather remained cold but mercifully fine.

Mary Ann was the rock on which they all depended now. She proved herself capable of coping with every situation and taking all the worry off her mother's shoulders.

The day after the funeral Tom at last set off for Foggin Tor. John had been taken to school. Over their midday meal Mary Ann asked her mother if she had formed any plans for the future.

"I have been thinking a lot about it, dear. I cannot see myself living alone at Classywell. I couldn't manage it as a farm anyway. And obviously I cannot continue to stay here. I know it is a stupid thought, but I would so loved to have gone back to Ashburn Hall and looked after my father. It doesn't seem like nine years since he died. He has been much in my thoughts these last few days. But to be practical, I am going to write to my brother Edward in Exeter. He has never married, he is too tied up with his business interests. We were always good friends. I just wonder if he would welcome me to his house as a sort of hostess for his entertaining."

"We would miss you terribly, Mother. I can't imagine this valley without you. If you go to Uncle Edward I hope you will visit us frequently."

"Yes, of course I would. It has been a great joy to me to see how happy you and Tom are together. How well you are coping with life. There is something of the Cockcroft spirit in you."

"What will happen to Classywell?"

"Would you like to go there to live, instead of here?"

"No. There are too many unhappy memories about my bedroom there. I have been able to forget them here, where there are nothing but happy memories."

"Yes, of course. I had almost forgotten too. Then we shall have to sell the place."

Tom returned with encouraging news of Foggin Tor. The quarry superintendant had said that he had taken on many of the redundant miners from Ellisborough; they had enough men working on the quarry face, but they were short of masons to work the granite.

"I admitted," said Tom, "that I had no experience of that, but that it would be the sort of work I felt I could do after some tuition. That is the kind of work I want, I could enjoy doing that. I have been taken on as a sort of apprentice, and start work on Monday."

Chapter Twelve

Two years later a settled pattern of life had returned to the Nillacombe valley. It had not been possible to sell Classywell, but it had been let to Henry Giles, who, by arrangement with and as a gift from Linnie, paid the rent for it to Mary Ann and Tom, which happily covered their own rent to the Duchy for Nillacombe. Henry and his wife Elizabeth farmed the property. Their son Richard, aged eleven, attended Wakaton school. He was a likeable, sensible lad; Mary Ann had no qualms in entrusting him to take John to school with him; only two years separated their ages. The two boys got on well together. Richard often came with them on their Sunday morning walks. Mary Ann, with more time to spare now that she did not have to take John to school, had started her own chicken farm. A very friendly atmosphere existed between the two households.

With little difficulty Tom had mastered the skills of a stone mason, his natural ability with his hands standing him in good stead. He enjoyed the work, and was well thought of at Foggin Tor.

Linnie's hopes of living with her brother in Exeter also had a satisfactory outcome. Edward welcomed her to his home. What a different life style she now lived, entertaining the elite of Exeter, though often hankering after the peace and simple life of the valley. She made a point of paying frequent visits to Nillacombe. Because of the difficulty of communication these visits had to be arranged on a regular basis, on the first weekend of every month, except for the winter months when travelling was too unreliable if not hazardous over the moors. She would take the stage-coach to Tavistock on a Saturday, where Mary Ann met her in the cabriolet, returning in similar fashion on the Monday. At Nillacombe she shared a bed with Mary Ann, whilst Tom fixed up a bed in the kitchen. It was a small price to pay for the pleasure of seeing the happy reunion between mother and daughter.

During school holidays John and Richard frequently went on exploratory walks over the moors. As they became familiar with its topography, so the lengths of their walks increased, always seeking new places. This caused occasional concern to their parents when they were more than usually late home. However, their enthusiasm and self-confidence in their ability to find their way, and to take sensible precautions, was reassuring. Tom was pleased to see this developing maturity in his son. But he was more than a little disconcerted one day, when they had walked the length of the Langcombe valley, to be asked, "Why is that valley up there called Dead Man's Bottom, Father?"

Recovering himself from that unpleasant memory, Tom tried to make a joke of it.

"That has nothing to do with a man's backside, John. Many broad shallow valleys on Dartmoor I understand are called bottoms. It distinguishes them from deep valleys which are usually called gorges or cleaves. I suppose someone lost their life in that valley, perhaps in a snow-storm or something like that."

"Richard has been telling me, well he said an old farmer told him, that the Jobbers' Road goes that way, and then goes down the River Erme. We have never been there, have we? Do you know it? Where is the River Erme? Who were the jobbers?"

"So many questions all at once, son. I don't know the River Erme, but I believe the jobbers were wool merchants, collecting wool from the Dartmoor farms and taking it to the border towns for it to be made into cloth."

John was only partially satisfied with that. A few days later he said, "Richard has asked the farmer to take us on the Jobbers' Road and to the River Erme. Can I go, Father? He says it will be an all day walk."

Tom looked at Mary Ann for her reaction to this.

"Who is this farmer, John?" she asked.

"I don't know, someone at Kingsett, Richard said."

"Go and ask Richard to come up and see us."

When he had gone Mary Ann said, "I'm not letting those boys go with any old character around here. They are not all to be trusted."

When the boys returned, Mary Ann asked Richard if he knew the name of this farmer.

"Yes, everybody knows him, he has worked at Kingsett for years. Elias Caunter."

"Oh, dear old Elias. Yes, I know him well."

She looked at Tom. "Why don't we all go on that walk?" Then to Richard, "Would you mind if we came too?"

"Of course not. It would be lovely."

Elias Caunter was not all that old, though his long beard may have given that impression. He was a moorman, who had tended sheep for many years on that part of the moore to which he proposed to take the boys. He was not really a farmer, but he had been assisting at Kingsett for some years now.

Dartmoor weather can be most unpredictable, even in summer. But there are occasions when settled weather can be assured. It was on such a day that the party set off from Kingsett, where they had assembled. They crossed Nillacombe Lake at Kingsett Ford. The first part of the walk was by now very familiar to them all, past Down Tor and Combeshead Tor, across Combeshead Brook and on to Thrushelcombe Ford, a place now fraught with conflicting memories for Tom. Here Elias showed them the track that the jobbers took. They followed it, but only for a short distance before all trace of it disappeared. However they took a reasonably level route all the way to Plym Steps, where again the track was well marked on both sides of the river. The ford itself did not present a good place to cross the river on foot. Elias took them a short distance upstream where the river narrowed and suitable boulders enabled them to cross easily. As they ascended the Langcombe valley Tom was beginning to feel decidedly uneasy. Even more so when they turned into the lateral valley and John exclaimed, "This is Dead Man's Bottom, Father." Thank goodness Mary Ann had never been told where Jethro had died. She was so enjoying this walk and was a little surprised at Tom's lack of enthusiasm. They actually passed the place where Jethro had walked into the mire; Tom remembered only too well his blasphemous oath.

"What's the matter with you, Tom, aren't you enjoying the walk?"

"Yes, of course I am. I was . . . my mind was elsewhere . . . I was dreaming of another walk, up Shavercombe." It was the best excuse he could think of to explain his mood. It had the desired effect. Mary Ann put her arm through his. Her physical contact restored his mind; he banished those unpleasant thoughts, as they found a dry place above the mire to cross the valley.

From there Elias took them unerringly to Broad Rock. It was indeed a broad, flat rock, not very high so that it could not easily be seen from a distance. Yet it was an important landmark, Elias explained, for not only was it a bond stone, but it indicated the point where the jobbers had to change their course, depending whether they were bound for the Sheepstor area or for Tavistock.

Not many yards from here they found themselves standing near the source of the River Erme.

"Oh, Elias, what a wonderful view," exclaimed Mary Ann.

"Yes, ma'am, it is one that always pleases me."

"It isn't often, is it Elias," said Tom, "that one can stand at the very source of a river and see so much of it stretched out before you?"

It was Dartmoor displayed at its best, and under the most perfect conditions. The rolling green hills, bereft of trees, but all the better for that in this wild part of the moor, were highlighted here and there by the bright summer sun; darkened elsewhere when the shadows of the cumulus clouds made them appear sombre and mysterious; all offset by the immediate foreground of desolate waste, the womb of the waters of the river. No scene could be more inviting for exploration, no day more ideal to do so.

They were standing, as they gazed, beside another low rounded rock, on which, Elias now pointed out, were the weather-worn incisions of some letters, so faint now that they could easily be missed unless one knew of their existence.

"This stone marks the head of the river," said Elias, "can you see the letters 'A Head'?"

Yes, they could just decipher them.

"But why 'A' head?" asked Tom.

"The old name of the river was Arme," explained Elias.

From here they had to make quite a detour around the mire, and then to cross a stream at a little ford, another source of the river. Beyond here the main valley became a wild jumble of stone mounds where, Elias said, the old tinners had turned over the river bed in their search for the valuable tin stone. He then led them to the hillside where deep gerts had been excavated, once more in the search for tin. John and Richard were in their element here, exploring the depths of these astonishingly deep gullies. They found the remains of two small buildings. They were reluctant to leave this fascinating place, but Elias said they had better get on, they had some way to go yet.

Below that jumble of stony hillocks, where more level ground existed, they crossed the river at a ford to its left bank. A most pleasant walk then ensued, between the hill on their left and the reed-covered ground that separated them from the river.

They arrived at another river, coming in to join the Erme from their left. "I always think this should be a part of the Erme," said Elias, "it is a much longer river and carries more water than what we have been following. But it is always known as the Wollake for some reason. We'll be coming to another one presently, called Hux Lake, but that has so little water in it, it is sometimes known as Dry Lake."

"Will you take us up this river one day, Elias?" asked John, "it looks exciting."

Beyond Hux Lake they came to a section of a stone row, which thrilled the boys. "Can we walk to the end of it?" exclaimed John.

"Not today we can't. It is a very long one. Goes up the hill 'ere, to a cairn at the very top of the hill. And in that direction, you see it going towards the river, it continues beyond the river to a stone circle nearly two miles away.

Some people calls the circle 'The Dancers', because they was supposed to be maidens dancing on a Sunday, who were turned to stone because that was a bad thing to do."

Soon after that they reached the limit of their walk at Red Lake. Here they could see that the Erme changed its course to flow south, and a high hill faced them beyond Red Lake.

"The jobbers crossed that hill to reach the River Avon," said Elias, "then they followed beside that river. But if it is all right with you, we will stop here and have our meal."

They sat beside the banks of that little stream, whose waters certainly had a tinge of red about them, as they splashed and gurgled their way to join the Erme at the bend of that river.

What could be more wonderful than this, thought Tom, such peace, such beauty, such remoteness, such mystery. He wanted to go on and on, to see what lay beyond those hills; where this or that valley led. He wanted to explore the land, preferably with just Mary Ann for company. He looked round at her, at the two boys, and old Elias, all now munching their pasties. A great contentment filled his soul. He bit into his own pasty. He had introduced this delicacy to his household. What a success Mary Ann had made of these today. How satisfying they were.

"Which way do we go back, Elias?" enquired Mary Ann, when they had all eaten.

"Over Green Hill, where I used to pasture my sheep. Good ground there. Then we re-cross Hux Lake, where the valley is broad and dry; and then on to Wollake and Ducks' Pool. If that be all right with you, ma'am?"

They had not gone far over Green Hill before they once more came across the stone row. They followed it uphill for a little way, not very large stones and getting fewer or perhaps buried as they ascended, but so mysterious on this lonely hill. They turned away from the row and continued on their previous course, the two boys, one on either side of Elias, plying him with questions, whilst Tom and Mary Ann, arm in arm when the uneven ground permitted, followed a little way behind.

"I am glad to see John taking such an interest in everything, he really is enjoying this walk."

'Yes," said Mary Ann, "I only hope his enthusiasm doesn't lead him one day into difficulties. We are having such perfect conditions today, it couldn't be better. But there are so many hazards on Dartmoor which he hasn't experienced yet, treacherous ground and bad weather, fog, snow and gales, the conditions can change so very quickly. I feel apprehensive sometimes that he will venture off on his own and get hurt or lost."

Tom remembered her 'presentiments', as she had called them, at Shavercombe Falls. Was she foreseeing more doom ahead? Surely that couldn't be possible now. Their lives seemed so settled and straightfoward, they were all so happy. He must not allow the thought of such possibilities to spoil this day.

They caught up with Elias and the boys as they were examining two small huts where Wollake is joined by a small tributary from the west. Obviously they were associated with the old tinners, for the ground above them, between the two streams, was a maze of tinners' debris, some of the stones arranged in shallow walls. It was a desolate scene as they walked up this subsidiary valley beside the barren waste, up to the source of the stream, a shallow bowl in the hills which was Ducks' Pool. It was easy to visualise that it could once have been a small lake, but it was now only a mire.

They skirted the reed-filled area and climbed the hill beyond it. After walking along its crest for a while, through a sea of waving bog cotton, they came in sight of the Plym valley, scenery which they could now recognise, though they had never viewed it from this direction before. They crossed the head of the river above its miry source, on good firm pasture land, to follow the northern side of the valley, well away from the river, where there looked to be treacherous ground.

Mary Ann found herself walking with Elias, well ahead of Tom and the boys who had stopped to examine something on the ground.

"What do you think they are looking at, Elias?"

"Perhaps a caterpillar, or more likely a frog near that wet ground."

As they walked on she began to sense something familiar about the land ahead. Surely she and Tom had walked near here years ago. Oh, God, yes. That is Crane Lake. A sudden panic filled her breast. A picture of Tom fighting Jethro came to mind. She saw that awful back-handed swipe that had nearly knocked Tom off his feet. Tom's brave attempt to hit back. She remembered feeling petrified with horror, of having a faint hope that Tom could do something miraculous when he caught Jethro a blow on the head. But then that awful punch that had sent Tom to the ground, where he lay so still. Of Jethro coming towards her and her attempt to run away. Hopeless, of course, in no time he had caught her and held her in his powerful arms. How she had fought and screamed, but to no avail. He had put his filthy hand over her mouth and said if she screamed again he would choke the life out of her. Then he had lifted her bodily off her feet, his arm around her waist. She had lashed out with her fists in fury, hopelessly she had thought, but presumably she had hurt him for with an oath he had dropped her, then caught both her wrists in one hand and with the other arm round her thighs he had lifted her across his shoulders like a sack of potatoes. She was completely powerless now, kicking her legs did no good at all, it only brought a lascivious chuckle from him. That is how he had carried her to his horrible hide-out. The memory of those libidinous happenings that followed there made her feel quite sick. She stopped walking and said, "Where are you taking us, Elias?"

"I thought you would like to see a deep and narrow gully at Crane Lake, 'tis a strange, uncanny sort of place, ending in a cliff with a dark pool at the base of it."

"Please, can we go over the hill to Nuns Cross instead?"

Elias noticed her distress.

"Are you not feeling well, ma'am?"

"I think I am over tired, we have been far enough for one day."

"I am sorry if I have taken you too far, ma'am."

"Not really, Elias. It has been a wonderful walk. We are very grateful to you."

When Tom saw the direction Elias was now taking, he also was glad to avoid Crane Lake, though his dislike of the place did not hold quite the same horror as it did for Mary Ann.

This walk indeed had been a memorable one, for its length, for its scenery, for its interest and for the perfection of the weather.

But the weather wasn't always so kind to them, as John and Richard were to find out a few days later.

It had been an established custom for the two boys, during the summer holidays, to go out occasionally with the whortleberry gatherers. These were mostly women and children from the border villages who, if they were asked where they were going in such large numbers, would have said, "Gwain to moor, to pick hurts." Many of them did so for the sole purpose of earning a few coppers, or even shillings, by selling the produce later at the local markets. Nevertheless, if the weather was fine, a holiday atmosphere prevailed and everyone enjoyed themselves in spite of the back-aching task of bending to pick the fruit. But on this particular occasion a thunderstorm accompanied by heavy rain sent the pickers hurrying home. John and Richard arrived back at Nillacombe soaked to the skin, and not a little scared at the closeness of the lightning and shattering sound of the thunder immediately following the flash. The rumbles of the receding storm followed them all the way home. Their mothers had been equally frightened for their safety. But later that day, when they sat down to a meal which ended with a plateful of whortleberry tart and cream, they were able to laugh at the incident and declare, "Cor, it was worth it, wasn't it?"

On those days when persistent rain put paid to any hope of such expeditions, John would busy himself with his woodwork. He had, of course, been taught by his father, and had come to love the work.

Tom had bought quite a stock of wood at a reasonable price at the sale when Ellisborough closed down. The small offcuts from the various articles he had made he gave to John to practise making joints. His first effort he proudly brought to his father to see. Tom had criticised it severely; it was not truly at right-angles; the faces did not meet properly; it was too loose a fit. John had gone away crestfallen and nearly in tears.

"You were a bit hard on the boy, weren't you Tom?" Mary Ann had said.

"Perhaps, but I remember my own first joint being thrown into the waste box and being told to make it again. He will thank me one day."

John had now progressed to some reasonably good work. At the end of the day he was always careful to put all the tools away carefully, where they belonged, and to clean up after his work and collect all the shavings for use later to light the fires. His father had insisted on this.

On the morning that John went back to school, Mary Ann took a basket of eggs to Classywell. There was a sudden heavy shower of rain as she arrived there. When Elizabeth opened the door to her and saw the rain she said, "Come in, my dear, quick, let me take your cloak." She admired Mary Ann's slim figure as she did so. She herself was becoming rather buxom, but she was tall and carried herself well, her movements denoting plenty of energy, even athleticism. Her dark hair set off a full cheerful face, her eyes held humour when she was not overburdened with work, her mouth could so easily break into a charming smile when occasion occurred.

It was not often that Mary Ann was invited into the house, Elizabeth was usually too busy, cooking or helping on the farm. Those early days on the farm had been rather hectic. She came from a seafaring family from Plymouth and knew nothing about farming when she met Henry, a farmer's son, at Tavistock Goosey Fair. He was a tall, sturdily built man. If not exactly handsome, he had that attractive weatherbeaten countenance of one accustomed to day-long exposure to the open air. He was some years older than she was, she had found out, but his compelling, persuasive manner had swept her off her feet, both mentally and physically, as he had almost carried her away from an unpleasant brawl amongst some hooligans in the crowd. It had been a whirlwind romance. They were well suited to each other.

Their early life together had been at a cottage on Henry's father's farm, just outside Tavistock. Henry had helped his father on the farm since he had left school. But to Elizabeth farming was a new experience. She had lent a hand when necessary, but for the most part she had not been expected to take any more than a minor interest in it. When Henry heard of Classywell Farm being available, he had jumped at the chance of having a farm of his own. But it had placed quite a burden on Elizabeth's shoulders.

This day she was rather glad of the opportunity of having Mary in for a chat. Mary Ann had only told her of her first name, the double name had always been exclusive to the family, at least after she had left school, and only her mother and Tom used it now. That was precious to her.

"You must be lonely up to Nillacombe, Mary, with your husband away all day to Foggin Tor and John now back at school."

"Yes, it is a long day until they come home, but I usually find something to do. I love sewing, and I sometimes take Nelson out for some exercise. Are you happy in the valley, Elizabeth, it is a new life for you, isn't it?"

"It was strange at first. But everyone has been so friendly round here, and helpful. I am getting used to it now. I am beginning to realise why people love this valley. It has been a relief to me to see Richard and your John such good friends."

"Yes, I am grateful for that too. Is there anything I can do for you?"

"Not really, my dear, we are coping pretty well. Henry is now milking our two cows, you shall have some to take home with you. How is Tom liking his work at Foggin Tor?"

"He has taken to it like a duck to water. He was a miner, you know, and always said he couldn't do anything else. It just shows you can when you have to. He was telling me recently that the Reverend Edward Bray from Tavistock, you probably know him, has been complaining to the superintendent of the quarries about the destruction of Foggin Tor, and that Swell Tor is going the same way. He is right of course, but men have to earn a living, there are hundreds working there now, many of them miners who are out of a job now that so many of the mines are having a bad time."

"What sort of work does your husband do there?"

"He is a mason, he shapes the stones to exact sizes for

building purposes, and supervises them being lowered down the incline to the railway, for transport to Plymouth. He is on the new quarry at Swell Tor now."

There was an awkward pause in the conversation, when neither could think of anything to say, until Elizabeth plucked up courage to mention what she had been wanting to ask for some time.

"Mary, I hope you won't mind my saying this, but Richard has been saying that . . . well people have told him that your husband has been in prison. I can't believe it. That can't be true. Tell me that it isn't true."

Another silence whilst Mary Ann recovered her poise.

"I suppose there are people who will always gossip about that, but this is the first time that I have heard it mentioned. Yes, Elizabeth, it is true. What would you think of your husband if, in defending your honour, he killed someone in doing do?"

"Is that what happened to you?"

"Yes, before Tom and I were married, Tom was working at Ellisborough Mine. A beast of a man tried to kidnap me. I managed to escape from him, but it was a dreadful experience. Tom hunted that man down and killed him. That was the measure of his love for me. I waited three years for him, until he came out of prison. That was the measure of my love for him. Can you understand that, Elizabeth?"

"Yes, my dear. I am so glad you have told me. It worried me that people could say such things about your Tom, he is such a fine man, I admire him so much. I couldn't believe that he could do anything wrong."

That conversation was a bond of friendship between these two women and their families that ripened throughout the ensuing years. A friendship that culminated in another tragedy that was to strike this valley five years later.

Chapter Thirteen

It was half term holiday for John, on an autumn day in the year 1839. The morning had been overcast and windy, there was no incentive to go walking in such weather. Rather was John more interested in the making of a step-ladder. Their old one was getting decidedly rickety; he thought his father would be pleased to have a new one.

However, by afternoon, shafts of sunlight began to appear through the clouds. Mary Ann decided to take Nelson for a canter over Cramber Down, he had not had much exercise for some days. John was quite happy to be left alone with his woodwork; he had made good progress and was now thoroughly absorbed in what he was doing.

Mary Ann let Nelson make his own pace as they climbed the slopes of Cramber. She patted his neck and talked to him. "You are beginning to feel your age, aren't you, old friend. You are thirty-four years old this month; did you know that? Take it easy then, it's your day out, not mine." How well Nelson knew that soothing voice. He seemed to nod agreement as he plodded up the hill. "You've had enough, haven't you? We won't go to the top of the hill. We'll go along the level to Cramber Pool."

Cramber Pool is a lonely little tarn tucked away out of sight at the top of some 'old men's' workings, one of Dartmoor's secrets known to few. Mary Ann dismounted and led Nelson to the water to drink. They were out of the wind here, all was silent and mysterious. She found a rock on which to sit, whilst Nelson grazed the nearby luscious grass.

Nelson can't live much longer, she thought. How I shall miss him. No other horse can mean the same to me. "We have some secrets, haven't we Nelson, you and I? . . . One in particular, that no one else will ever know about . . . I wonder what has happened to that baby . . . Did it die on that doorstep? If so I am a murderess. If it lived, she will be grown up now . . . What sort of a girl is she? . . . I cannot feel guilty about that, I could never have loved that child . . . I hope perhaps somebody else does. Why am I thinking about this now? I thought I had put all that behind me. Thank God Tom doesn't know anything about it. Only mother knows, and she has never mentioned it since . . . If that girl is alive, I wonder what she is called? . . . Will she have fair hair or dark? Will she take after me, or after him? Oh, God forbid that."

"Come Nelson, I'm getting morbid, let's go home."

She mounted and they climbed out of the hollow. Nelson picked his way carefully beside the edge of the gert that led down from the tarn until they came to Classywell clapper bridge over Dock Leat. Nelson needed no guiding from here to find his way to Classywell Farm.

"Come in and have a cup of tea, Mary," called Elizabeth, as she came to the door at the sound of Nelson's hooves.

"Thank you, Elizabeth, but I think I had better get back; this wind is getting up again, I don't want to leave Nelson standing about in the cold. I'll bring you some eggs in the morning."

Having stabled Nelson and patted the old boy good night, Mary Ann entered her home. "Time to tidy up, John," she called, "your father will be home soon."

She went up to her room to change her clothes. She was some time there, tidying her room, and she was about to do the same to John's when she heard a strange rushing sound overhead. Then a crackling. "Oh, no," she exclaimed, and rushed down the stairs to see John throwing shavings on the fire. "Stop, John, I believe the roof is on fire." They rushed outside to see blazing shavings falling from the chimney stack onto the roof, which was now well alight. The strong wind had caused such an updraught in the chimney that the burning resinous wood shavings had been carried up with it. They gazed terror-struck at it, helpless to do anything to prevent the fire spreading. They both rushed inside to bring out any articles that were portable. The strong wind fanned the flames and in no time the whole roof was ablaze. The chickens scampered and fluttered about in panic, clucking and cackling in their haste to flee from this unknown danger. A pitiful equine scream came from the stable as Nelson saw the flames. Mary Ann rushed to him to set him free. There was terror in the animal's eyes as he reared up trying to escape. Suddenly it was all over, he collapsed on to the floor. Mary Ann knew that his poor old heart had given out, that he was dead. She turned to see the roof of the house cave in, sending sparks high into the air as the inferno took fresh hold of the upper floor. Burning material was falling about them as she clutched John's arm, stopping him from going into the house again and drawing him to a safer place. In the distance she saw Elizabeth and Henry rushing up the lane. They could only stand and stare as the flames gutted the building. "It can't be true, it can't be true. Oh, John, our home, our home, all gone." John was speechless, terror-struck with awe and guilt that he had caused this. The window-panes cracked and flames leaped through the openings. There was another roar from inside the building as the bedroom floors collapsed into the kitchen. Just then Elizabeth and Henry arrived, breathless. Words were useless. Elizabeth took Mary Ann into her arms. That motherly embrace, in spite of the little difference in their ages, brought the tears flooding into Mary Ann's eyes, her shoulders shook with her sobs. Henry put his arm around John to comfort him. There was nothing more anyone could do. Yet they couldn't leave until the fire had burnt itself out, leaving only blackened smouldering debris inside stark barren walls.

It was then that Tom arrived, also breathless. He had seen the flames from afar and had run all the way. But too late. He couldn't have done anything anyway.

John ran to him. "Father, Father, it was my fault. I put shavings on the fire. I didn't know it could do this. The shavings bin was full, I thought I was doing the right thing to burn the rest."

Tom sat on one of the chairs that had been salvaged, panting and horror struck. That beautiful roof that Amos had made; all the years of work that he had put into the making of their home. All gone in a matter of minutes. he lowered his head on his hands in disbelief.

"Go to him, Mary, he needs you. Henry and I will take John. You come down to us as soon as you can. We will look after you all."

Mary Ann knew she was right. She mastered her own grief and went to Tom, took his hands and drew him to her. He put his hand behind her head, stroking her hair. That accustomed habit of his, the physical contact of their bodies, helped to release their pent up feelings. "Thank God you are both safe. I see you have managed to save some furniture. We had better put it in the outhouse here for the time being. What about Nelson?"

The memory brought more tears to Mary Ann's eyes. "He has gone, Tom, his heart gave out with fright. He had not long to live, but it was terrible to see him go like that; I'll never forget that look in his eyes."

"Come, let us store this furniture." Some physical action was necessary to ease their troubled souls. When all was stored, and little enough there was, they looked back at the ruins.

"The old shippen part doesn't seem to have suffered so much," said Tom.

Cautiously they approached the building. The heat from the ashes was intense, the acrid smell of smoke horrid to breathe. The light was failing, but they could see enough to give some hope that all was not lost in there. "Stay clear, Mary Ann, I will see if it is possible to get to the door of the room."

Tom entered the porch, but the passage was covered in hot ashes.

"It is not possible," he said as he returned, "but I have a feeling that that room is untouched. The roof has gone but I think the westerly wind blew the flames away. It is possible that the tallet floor did not catch alight. We can do no more now. Let's go; here comes the rain, that will damp down the ashes. Oh, if only the rain had come sooner, this might never have happened."

The rain rapidly increased in intensity and added to their

misery as they hurried along the lane to Classywell. Before they had got half way they were soaked through.

In spite of all his troubles, the thought came to Tom's mind that it was here, or near here, that he and Mary Ann had experienced their first passionate kiss, all those years ago.

Suddenly he stopped, held Mary Ann's shoulders at arm's length, looked into her eyes and said, "My darling, we will survive this day. My love for you is only strengthened by this tragedy, as it had been once before. I am going to kiss you now as I kissed you then."

He pulled her almost violently to him, and kissed her long and ardently. The unexpectedness of it, the sheer incongruity of the situation with the rain pouring down upon them, alleviated some of the pain in their hearts. They still had each other, that was everything.

When at last he released her, she was almost smiling, as she grabbed his arm and urged him on their way. "You dear man, that was absurd but lovely."

Henry opened the door to them when at last they reached Classywell. "Good gracious, you poor things. Elizabeth, quick, take Mary to the bedroom and change her clothes. Come, Tom, I'll find something for you."

They were indeed a bedraggled pair. Mary Ann's usually immaculate hair was flattened to her head and face, water dripping off her nose and chin, her clothes sodden about her figure. Yet to Elizabeth's surprise her face looked composed, it had lost that wild distress that she had seen so short a time ago.

"Come, dear, never mind your dripping clothes on the floor." Henry went with them to the bedroom and grabbed some clothing for Tom.

When at last they were all reassembled in the living-room, Tom and Mary Ann looked a comic pair in clothes that did not fit and were so different from their own. That, the cheerful fire, and the warm affection shown by these genuine friends, all helped to ease the stress and trauma of their loss. Elizabeth busied herself making hot drinks for them. Henry reassured them that they could stay with them as long as was necessary, they would arrange things somehow. John sat with Richard, silent and dismayed by this sudden upheaval in his normally tranquil life, awaiting his father's anger. Tom became aware of him at last, and called him over.

"I know how you are feeling, son. When I was your age I worked down the mine with my father. I incurred his wrath one day when I had done something stupid. I have never forgotten that. You will never forget this day, but it will make you think before you take action in the future. It will make a man of you." He ruffled the boy's hair, a little action which meant love and forgiveness. John looked his gratitude and relief. Mary Ann, too, looked her approval.

Elizabeth returned from the kitchen with the hot drinks. Whilst they were sipping them, she said, "I have been wondering how to sleep you whilst you are here. We have two single beds in the end room, will that be all right for you and Tom, Mary? We can easily move Richard's things into the room upstairs, but there is only one bed there. Someone is going to have to sleep on the floor."

"I'll do that," said Richard and John simultaneously.

"No you won't, Richard, I will. I'd rather, really."

It was John's guilty conscience coming to the fore again, he still felt responsible for the situation and that this was a small penance to pay.

"That settles it," said Tom, "I think I know how John feels. You are being very kind, Elizabeth. We do appreciate what you are doing for us."

"You would do the same for us, I am sure of that. I've got some mutton stew warming up, we will have that presently. Then Mary and I will make the beds. I hope you will all get a good night's rest. You need it, poor dears."

It was strange for Mary Ann to be back in her old bedroom again. It looked very different now. Tom had never seen the room before, but was acutely aware that this was the room from which he had heard her anguished cries on that terrible dawn. How that haunted him. He could never forget that climactic scream.

It was a long time before they could get to sleep that night, their thoughts were so preoccupied by memories of the past, the events of the day, and the prospects for the future. Where were they going to live now? They could not stay here for long. Where was new furniture to come from? New clothes? They had nothing left but what they had worn here. Alone together all the tragedy of their loss returned. Mary Anne thought of all those articles that Tom had made so beautifully, now just ashes. And Nelson. Never to ride Nelson again. That was unbearable. His body was still up there in a heap on the stable floor, I mustn't, I mustn't think of that. I must think of Tom, and do what I can to help him.

Tom was wondering if there was anything more that could be salvaged from Nillacombe. What else needed doing there? He would have to go to Foggin Tor to see if there was any accommodation available there. Some houses were being built but it was unlikely that there would be anything available for him, there were too many other employees waiting for houses. What were the prospects in Prince's Town? Would it be possible to stay in the Inn there for a time? They would have to go to Tavistock as soon as possible to buy some clothes.

"What are you thinking about, Mary Ann?"

"My mind's in a whirl. I keep hoping that I'm only having a bad dream; that this can't really have happened to us. It seems unbelievable that Nillacombe is no more. That everything we possess has gone. I can't see any solution to it. What about you, what are you thinking?"

"Everything that I have got to do tomorrow, how to fit it all in. Try not to worry, darling, I'll find a way out of it. Go to sleep now. We are all safe, and with good friends. Let's count our blessings, that will send us to sleep."

She put her arm across the beds and touched his face. Tom took her hand and kissed it. "Goodnight, dear heart."

When Elizabeth went to their room the next morning there was no answer to her knock. She opened the door quietly and looked in. They were both deeply asleep. She put their dried clothes at the foot of their beds and left them.

It was a relief to her later to see them dressed in their own clothes and looking refreshed.

"We have had our breakfast, my dears. The boys have gone out walking. Henry has gone to Kingsett to get some help. They will go to Nillacombe and deal with Nelson, you don't have to worry about that. They'll know what to do. It was Henry's idea, he knew how painful it would be for you."

"Oh, Elizabeth, I'm so grateful for that. It has been on my mind, I couldn't sleep for thinking about it."

"You are not to go up there until they come back, it will be all over then. Now I'll get your breakfast."

"Isn't she a dear, Tom, how can we ever thank her?"

"Yes, indeed she is. I don't think there is much point in us going to Nillacombe just yet, though. It is more important that I go to Foggin Tor and tell the superintendent of our predicament. Then I'll go to Prince's Town and enquire about accommodation there. You stay here and see what you can do to help Elizabeth."

"I'll be quite content to do that."

Fortunately the overnight rain had given way to a more settled looking morning. The sun shone warm and invitingly as Tom set off on that now so familiar walk to Foggin Tor. The sight of the distant hills, clear cut against an azure sky, cheered his spirits. Having passed the slopes of Cramber the square knob of South Hessary Tor stood out bold against the blue. Black Tor nestled dark and rugged in a sea of browns and greens, speckled with the white dots of granite boulders. Hart Tor, nearer at hand, was grey and serene in its simplicity. The air was crisp and pure; the silence awesome. The regular pace of his plodding footsteps numbed his mind, lulling him into a state of hypnosis. This was normality, perfection. Yesterday's events were too awful to be real; surely they could not have happened. Oh, that it could be so. Alas, that it could not.

His interviews at Foggin Tor and Prince's Town over, Tom returned along the ridge of land due south of the village, past South Hessary Tor, the watershed of the valleys of Swincombe and Mew, a path that could be unpleasant in the depths of winter, exposed to all the winds that blow, wet and rugged underfoot, barren of interest, bleak of outlook. But in fine weather, as today, it provided a welcome shorter route than that via the road to Tor Royal and the track to Whiteworks. Before reaching Nuns Cross Tom turned onto the Whiteworks to Nosworthy track that crossed Dock Leat at Older Bridge. From there he made his way to Nillacombe, his mood now changing to sadness and heartache. He could not bear to look at the blackened shell of the main part of the building, he only wanted to find out what was left of that sitting-room. There was more light to see now. He peered through the window. What he saw made him even more dejected. He continued on his way, shaking his head in sorrow.

Mary Ann had spent a busy morning with her offer to cook the midday meal, whilst Elizabeth took over some of the farm work until Henry's return. She was glad the two boys had gone for a walk, on this only fine day of their short holiday. They had taken some food with them. She was thankful to have something to occupy her mind, and pleased to have only Elizabeth for company, she found her gentle disposition so soothing. When Henry arrived and took over the farm work, they sat together and exchanged reminiscences of their early lives. Their upbringing had been so very different, they became quite absorbed in each other's stories until Henry came in and enquired if it was not time for dinner.

It was mid-afternoon before Tom arrived, tired and hungry. Whilst he ate he recounted the result of his enquiries. The superintendent at Foggin Tor had been sympathetic and allowed Tom time off to find accommodation. He was sorry he could not help in that respect, they were building houses but there was a long waiting list for them.

He had then gone to the Plume of Feathers Inn at Prince's Town. "Mr John Leger is the proprietor there now," said Tom, "He was shocked to hear of the disaster at Nillacombe. He had known the place when Samuel and Nancy were there, and had been saddened to hear of their deaths. He also knew of my restoration of the place; these landlords, of course, get to know all the news in the district. He said he would be very pleased to put us up until we could find a house, at a special rate in consideration of our loss, he was very understanding and kind. It is rather a grim old place, one of the first buildings to be erected in the village. After this valley, Mary Ann, you are not going to like it. It will be only temporary, but anywhere in that village is going to be depressing, the whole place looks run down and squalid. I'm sorry, dear, I don't know what else I can do."

"I know what the place looks like, Tom, I have seen it many times. I never expected to have to live there though. There is one consolation, you won't have to walk so far to get to work. When do we go to the Plume of Feathers?"

"We could go there tomorrow, but John is due back at school tomorrow. What are we going to do about his schooling? It is a bleak walk for him over the exposed road from that Inn to Wakaton, all by himself, and frequently in fog."

"Leave him here with us, Tom," said Elizabeth, "at least for the rest of this term, until you have settled down and found out what alternative there is. We would love to have him."

"Would you really, Elizabeth?" said Mary Ann, "that would solve a problem. What do you think about that, Henry?"

"I am all in favour. The two boys get on very well together. It is Richard's last term, it seems a pity to separate them. You will always be welcome here when you want to visit him."

"I hope you will come often," said Elizabeth, "we are going to miss you."

"Will you look after my chickens, Elizabeth? I have only just thought of them, poor things."

"They were pecking around quite happily when I passed them just now," said Tom, "Which reminds me; I have a bit more bad news for you. The tallet floor has fallen in onto our sitting-room there. It is an indescribable mess. It will have to stay like it. I cannot bring myself to salvage anything. I doubt if it will be worth trying anyway."

"Tom, that ceiling could have come down on you if you had gone in there yesterday. Thank goodness you didn't."

The two boys returned from their walk at that moment. John came straight to his father. "Are you feeling better, Father?"

"I didn't know I had been ill. What made you think so?"

"Well, you looked a bit funny last night, and when you

didn't come to breakfast I thought you must be ill."

"Your mother and I didn't sleep very well last night, and we overslept this morning. We are all right now. Where have you been today?"

"To Fox Tor. We ate our pasties there. Then we went to Fox Tor Farm and a Mr Eden gave us a drink of milk there. He told us where there was a little bridge over the river, and to keep well clear of the mire."

"How did you know the man's name?"

"Someone at school knows him," said Richard, "he took the farm over from a Mr Windeatt who built the house about thirty years ago. That's why we went there, I wanted to see the farm."

"John, it looks as though we are going to have to live at Prince's Town. But for the rest of this term, how would you like to stay here with Richard, whilst we look for a house there?"

"Oh, yes please, Mother, that would be lovely."

The weather was still fine and mild the following morning. Since they had no capes, Tom was anxious not to tempt fate by delaying their departure. The boys had already said their good-byes and set off for school. Mary Ann hugged Elizabeth, thanking her profusely for her kindness. Then, to Henry's surprise, she kissed him on the cheek, having to go on tiptoe to do so, and said, "I'll never forget your thoughtfulness in dealing with Nelson, it took a great load off my mind. Thank you, Henry."

They climbed through the fields to the Whiteworks track, avoiding the lane to Nillacombe. Would they ever want to walk it again? They turned when they reached the track to give a last wave to their two friends. With heavy hearts they were about to leave this valley for a new life. They knew it could never be the same again.

They entered Prince's Town where the Plymouth and Dartmoor Railway now terminated, the line crossing the turnpike road to a wharf behind the Railway Inn. Turning left onto the road they came immediately to the Plume of Feathers Inn.

The landlord, John Leger, was at the door to greet them, he had seen them coming down the track from South Hessary Tor.

"Where is your baggage?" he asked.

"We haven't any," said Tom, "all we have we are wearing."

"I didn't realise things were as bad as that," he said. "Come on into the bar by the fire, we've no customers at this time of day. I'll have some coffee brought in and we'll have a chat. Have we met before, ma'am, I seem to recognise you?"

"I have often ridden my horse through Prince's Town, perhaps you saw me then."

"Ah, yes, that will be it. We call the place Princetown now, 'tis easier on the tongue. Now make yourselves comfortable whilst I order the coffee."

"Well, that was a warm welcome," said Mary Ann. "It is nice and cosy in here, too. Perhaps it won't be so bad as we feared."

The landlord returned.

"Would you like to see the room I have prepared for you while we're waiting? Come this way."

They ascended to the first floor to a room facing the street. What took the eye immediately on entering was a large double bed complete with tester. Beside it was a cabinet on which stood a brass oil lamp. Against the walls on one side was a chest of drawers, and on the other a marble-topped washhand-stand with basin and ewer, a soap dish, a carafe with inverted tumbler over its neck, and towels hanging from rails at the sides. A table and two chairs completed the furnishings.

"I think this will suit us very well, Mr Leger."

Tom, having made a quick look round, was gazing out of the window.

"What is that round house on the far side of the road, Mr Leger?"

"That is the toll-house. Mr Lee lives there and collects the tolls."

Returning to the bar they found that the coffee had arrived. As Mary Ann began to pour, she thought she had better set the landlord's mind at rest that they were not the complete paupers they appeared to be.

"We must get to Tavistock at the earliest opportunity, Mr Leger, there is much that we need to buy, and we need some money of course to pay for it. We have an account with Gill, Rundle and Company, where I am well known. Is there any conveyance we can hire to get there?"

"George Challacombe still keeps a pony and trap, ma'am. I expect he will be pleased to take you there. When would you wish to go?"

"Could we have an early meal here, and go immediately afterwards?"

"You may have forgotten, ma'am, that this is Wednesday. Most of the shops in Tavistock will be closed this afternoon. May I suggest you go first thing tomorrow, it will give you more time there and will allow you to come back in daylight."

"Yes, I had forgotten, that is the sensible thing to do. Will you make the necessary arrangements with Mr Challacombe?"

"I will, ma'am, leave it to me."

"Have you made any enquiries about a house for us?" asked Tom.

"There is a house further down the road which has been empty for some time. It requires quite a bit of work done on it. Perhaps you would like to see it presently?"

"I wish to get a letter to my mother in Exeter, to tell her of our misfortune. When does the next stage-coach go?" said Mary Ann.

"Saturday afternoon, from Tavistock. We'll have to intercept it at the Rundlestone Inn."

When they had finished their coffee Tom asked if they might have a look at that house now.

They turned right on leaving the Inn and crossed the railway line. Not far beyond the Railway Inn was a terrace of small two-storey cottages. Mr Leger took them to one, more or less in the middle of the row, which had a rather attractive bay window with three lights.

"This is the one. It is locked at present, but you can look through the window. It is Duchy property. If you are interested I will get the key from the bailiff this afternoon, and you can have a good look round."

After a meal at the Inn, which they were pleased to find was tastefully served, substantial and appetising, they were given the key of the house and they were able to explore it at their leisure.

The front door, to the right of the bay window, led to a short passage ending in a flight of stairs. A doorway opened on to the front room.

"I could make something of this room," said Mary Ann. "That window gives it so much light and space. Now where does this door go?"

They opened a door opposite the window and found themselves in a small kitchen, with a window and door facing a long narrow garden, now overgrown and neglected. There was a sink and small worktop beneath the window, a cast-iron range in the left wall, a cupboard beneath the stairs. Outside was a dilapidated shed with two doors. One hid a toilet, the other a coal bin.

"This is grim, isn't it?" said Tom.

"Well, let's see what it's like upstairs."

A small landing at the top of the stairs gave on to two bedrooms. Both rooms had a fireplace. All the walls needed attention and redecorating. The only item in the whole house which was not a fixture was a hip-bath in the back room. There was not much of a view from the windows, which were small and dismally dirty.

They returned to the front room downstairs.

"Are you as depressed as I am?" asked Tom.

"What is the alternative, Tom? You once made a home for me out of a ruin. I believe you could do the same here. It is small and cramped, but if you imagine it furnished, with a fire glowing in the grate, I think it has possibilities. At least it seems dry, one advantage of it being in a terrace. Can you suggest anything else?"

"We don't have to decide now. We haven't had a proper look round yet. There may be something more suitable."

"With so many families at Foggin Tor looking for homes? I doubt it."

They had a light meal served in their room that evening. On the tray were two glasses of white wine.

"With the landlord's compliments," said the serving maid,

"he hopes you will have a good night."

While they were sipping their wine, Mary Ann said, "What with this wine and the sight of that bed, I'm beginning to feel like a bride in her bridal suite."

"Well, let's pretend you are. We haven't got any night clothes anyway!"

For the first time since the tragedy they were able to laugh.

True to his word, Mr Leger had arranged with George Challacombe to take them into Tavistock the following day, returning in the afternoon with many parcels of new clothing, and a quantity of material for Mary Ann's sewing projects, something to keep her busy whilst Tom was at work. On the Friday he did return to work, a relatively short walk now, along the railway-track.

Mary Ann had further talks with Mr Leger about accommodation. He assured her that there was nothing else available in Princetown. Even the old barrack buildings, he said, that had housed the soldiers when the prison had been in use, had been turned into units of accommodation for the quarry workers. He went on to tell her about the school there, that had been set up for their children, over thirty boys and twenty or more girls. They were taught the scriptures and arithmetic; they were all supplied with slates. The girls were taught to knit and sew.

She made another visit to the cottage, trying to visualise what it would be like when furnished. She also visited the Duchy Steward and persuaded him to effect some repairs to the building. Her charm won him over where others had apparently failed. He promised to do something if they decided to take it.

She wrote a letter to her mother, ready for it to be taken with others and some parcels by the carter to Rundlestone the following day.

She discovered that the landlord of the Railway Inn, James Rowe, kept a store at the back of the Inn, opposite the railway wharf, where most of the necessities for daily living could be purchased, goods such as coal, flour, tea, salt, and some vegetables, all coming from Plymouth and district on the railway.

She met and talked with some of the other wives who lived in that terrace of cottages. Someone assured her that Mr Rowe was a most versatile man. He had been a blacksmith in his time, and had been known to extract a tooth if necessity arose. Mary Ann squirmed at the thought of a blacksmith extracting one of her teeth. What sort of tools did he use, she wondered!

Mean and run down the village might look. Cold, windy or foggy it often was at this time of the year. But there was no doubt about the warmth and camaraderie of its inhabitants. They had to pull together to make life worth living here. When the husbands returned from the quarries, there was laughter and chatter in the bars of the two inns.

When Tom listened to her account of the day's happenings, he was more than a little proud of this wife of his, who could see light and hope where all had seemed to him dark and depressing; who had the ineffable attribute of making friends with all and sundry; who was so bravely overcoming their loss and was prepared now to put up with a period of hardship without complaint.

But he also had some cheering news to bring to her. The quarry had been supplying granite for the Plymouth Breakwater construction. Over the last decade or more many thousands of tons of stone had been conveyed to Plymouth on this railway. He had been told that it was as long ago as 1812 when that astonishing project had been started. It was nearly a mile in length, three miles out from Plymouth Hoe, and intended to provide shelter for the many ships that used the harbour. It had now reached the stage when it was appearing above sea level. Foggin Tor Quarries now had the contract to supply dressed granite for surfacing it. He would be working on that stone and was assured of employment there for many years to come.

Then he asked, "What are your thoughts, Mary Ann, about John's schooling? At the end of this term he will be nearly fifteen. Is he likely to learn much more at that school?"

"Perhaps not. What are you suggesting?"

"That he learns a useful trade. There is work for apprentices of his age at the quarry. As a mason he could earn a good wage eventually. It is interesting, fascinating work. I believe he is capable of making a good mason."

"Yes, Tom, you are right. He is no longer a child. He must have older boys to mix with. Did you say that there were boys of his age at the quarry?"

"Yes, and I am sure I can get him work there. Hopefully near me, and I can keep an eye on him."

The following week a reply came from Linnie on the mail-coach. She was shocked to hear of their calamity and of the death of Nelson. She and Uncle Edward would be coming in their own coach this weekend, arriving Sunday afternoon. "Please fix up accommodation for us at the Plume of Feathers if possible, or failing that somewhere in Tavistock. We will stay for a few days and make sure you are properly housed. My love to you both."

It was not often that Princetown witnessed the arrival of a private carriage and the alighting of such fashionable occupants. The gentleman stepped out first, wearing a fawn-coloured redingote with a short cape. Under it could be seen narrow fitting trousers and highly polished brown shoes. His hat was a kind of flattened topper with a brim curled up at the sides, though straight and slightly depressed at front and back. He helped the lady to alight. She was elegant in a long dark green cloak and a matching hat not dissimilar to his, but of a softer material and adorned with an ostrich feather that lay along its brim on one side, and drooped down the back. The hat was tilted slightly forward over her right eye in a most becoming manner.

Mary Ann and Tom were waiting for them at the door of the Inn. Mother and daughter greeted each other affectionately. Then almost shyly Mary Ann turned to her uncle.

"I haven't seen you, my dear, since you were a child, but I have heard so much about you. I am delighted at this chance to renew our acquaintance. And this is your Tom, I presume." The two men shook hands. Tom then greeted Linnie. Could this stylish lady really be the same person who had befriended him at Classywell?

During these preliminaries the landlord had been hovering in the background. He now came forward and welcomed his guests, escorting them into the Inn. An ostler directed the coachman to the stables.

Mr Leger showed them to a front room on the opposite side of the house to the bar. "This is our sitting-room, ma'am; your rooms are immediately above it. I am sure your daughter would like to show you there first, so that you may divest yourselves of your cloaks. Then, if you will return here, I will have some tea served."

Tom remained in the sitting-room whilst Mary Ann took her mother and uncle upstairs. He felt not a little uncomfortable at this rather unexpected display of wealth. He was feeling rather shabby in contrast. Here was a new Linnie, and he felt he would have little in common with her man-of-the-world brother.

Mary Ann took her mother's cloak and hung it in a wardrobe. When she turned she exclaimed, "Mother, you look perfectly wonderful." She eyed her up and down. Her velvet dress was of a lighter green than the cloak. The close-fitting bodice tapered to a full ankle-length skirt. Down the front of the bodice and the skirt was a series of little white rosettes. The sleeves ended in white lace frills. Round the neck was a white collar trimmed with similar lace. Her hair was immaculately set. Her face still held some of the beauty of her youth, especially now as she smiled at her daughter's compliment.

"I'm glad you think so, dear. You must blame your uncle for that. He is fussy about what I wear."

Her brother was equally as fussy about his dress. When he came in from his adjoining room, he was wearing a brown frock-coat with high collar and wide lapels. The points of an inner white collar almost reached to his chin. Below it a cream silk cravat was held in place by a pearl-headed pin. His trousers were the colour of pale sherry.

Over their tea Tom expressed the hope that they had had a good journey from Exeter.

"Yes," said Edward, "the roads were better than I had expected. It was a long slow climb up those steep hills to the moor. It is my first experience of Dartmoor. What a bleak place it is. I just can't understand why people want to live here."

"It grows on you, Uncle," said Mary Ann, "you have not seen it at its best today. When you have lived here, and learnt something of its history, explored its hills and valleys, and met some of its simple, kindly inhabitants, you get to love it. Tom and I wouldn't want to live anywhere else now."

"Have you found anywhere to live yet, Mary Ann?"

"Not definitely, Mother. At the moment there is only one cottage available, but it needs some repairs. I'll show you tomorrow."

On the morrow, before visiting the cottage, Mary Ann took her mother and uncle for a short walk along the road that led to Rundlestone. Her uncle had expressed the wish to see the prison.

It was a grey, overcast morning, windy but fortunately dry. Uncle Edward was interested to hear about the railway, he was amazed to think that such an enterprise would have been built for such a small and insignificant place. Where the line turned away from the road it followed beside an area of swamp and reeds which he thought the most depressing sight he had ever seen. His revulsion was not lessened by being told that the isolated building on the other side of the road, beside the stream that emanated from that swamp, was the butchery.

They came to the church that had been built by the French and American prisoners-of-war, lonely and pathetic in a field of unkempt graves. Beyond a bend in the road they came to the entrance to the prison, the gates in the portal closed and locked. A short distance beyond it they could view the great grey stone buildings of the prison itself, surrounded by its perimeter wall, silent, dead.

"So this was Sir Thomas Tyrwhitt's wonderful achievement, was it? What a misguided man. What a monument to failure. But surely something ought to be done with these buildings. Make a civil prison of them. That should deter the most hardened of criminals. What a dreadful place."

They walked as far as the quarry, where some of the prisoners used to work.

"I think that is far enough," said Uncle Edward, "I don't like this cold north wind." That wasn't the only thing he didn't like about the place. He could see no merit in any of it. "Show us this cottage of yours, Mary Ann."

"It isn't ours yet, Uncle, but there seems to be little alternative."

But Uncle Edward was even less impressed with the cottage than anything else he had seen in this benighted place. Linnie, who had been a little critical of her brother's disparagement of the village and of the country in general, was now forced to agree with him.

"Mary Ann, I don't see how you can live here, I can't see anything to recommend it. If there is nothing else, why don't you go to Tavistock and get Tom to find work there?"

"Or come to Exeter," said Uncle Edward, "I could find a job for Tom I am sure."

"Mother, I have to do what Tom wants. The only work for him in Tavistock would be to go down the mines again. I have already begged him not to do that. In Exeter there would only be clerical work, or something similar, he could never do that. Anyway, he has fallen in love with this Dartmoor, he wouldn't leave it. He is happy with the work he is doing now, and he is good at it. I must do as he wishes. I'll give up everything for him. If only this place was properly repaired, we could be happy here."

"Who is the landlord?" asked Uncle Edward.

"The Duchy. I have already seen the Duchy Steward; he has promised to do some repairs."

"Does he live in Princetown?"

"Yes, at Tor Royal, Sir Thomas Tyrwhitt's old house."

"Then take me to him."

The drive to Tor Royal commenced at a lodge and gateway between the terrace of cottages and the Railway Inn. When they reached there the grey skies of the early morning had lowered and were depositing their burden as a miserable misty rain.

"How far is it?"

"About fifteen minutes walk, Uncle."

"Then we can't go now, we will have to have the coach prepared."

They returned to the Inn whilst waiting for the coach, and tried to cheer themselves up by ordering coffee to be served in the sitting-room, where they proceeded to warm themselves before the fire.

"Uncle, you are seeing this land under the worst possible conditions. It isn't always like this. If you will come and visit us in the spring or summer we will show you a different Dartmoor, with sparkling skies, colourful hills and gentle streams in lovely valleys. Do not judge it by what you have seen today. We learn to take the rough with the smooth here. You have got to see the smooth part of it before you condemn the place out of hand. Isn't that so, Mother?"

"Yes, Edward, she is right, I beg you to be patient. You will remember I was a stranger here once, and wondered what I had let myself in for. I came to love the land. Mary Ann has been born to it and has a fierce love for it. You cannot understand the effect Dartmoor has on you until you have experienced it in all its moods."

"I am beginning to understand this daughter of yours. I like her fighting spirit. A bit of the Cockcroft in her, I'll be bound."

"Your carriage is at the door, sir."

"Come, let us see what we can do with this Duchy Steward."

The outcome of that interview was highly satisfactory. When the Steward realised that some of the cost of repairs to the cottage would be met by this forceful man, he was more than willing to do everything that was necessary there, even to rebuilding the toilet shed with a proper stone-built extension, accessible from the kitchen. He would put the matter in hand immediately.

There was a festive dinner party at the Plume of Feathers that night. Uncle Edward was mellowed by the excellently cooked meal, a bottle of wine whose quality was far above his expectations, and by the comely serving wench who waited upon them so cheerfully. He showed the other side of his nature. He was affable and jovial. Tom found it easier to talk to him. Mary Ann began to realise why he and her mother had always been such good friends.

There was nothing more to keep them in Princetown now. They left early the next morning. When Uncle Edward kissed Mary Ann good-bye, he pressed an envelope into her hand. "Something towards furnishing your new home, my dear. I have a great admiration for you, and for your loyalty to your husband. He is a splendid fellow."

When the carriage had disappeared from sight, Mary Ann opened the envelope. In it was a cheque for £100.

Work commenced on the cottage almost immediately. It gave Mary Ann a lot of pleasure to see each room in turn being renovated. The chimneys being swept. The new toilet block taking shape. On the days when the weather permitted, she spent happy hours clearing the garden of its weeds and preparing the ground for the eventual production of vegetables.

There was no privacy in the garden, it was separated from the adjacent ones by low stone walls only. Thus she soon made the acquaintance of her neighbours. On the side nearest to the Railway Inn was Suzannah Hutchings. She was a painfully thin, petite woman, of about her own age. Her face was pale and drawn, which marred what once must have been a pretty one. Her brown hair hung rather untidily about her cheeks. Her shabby clothing denoted hardship and poverty. The reason for all this was accounted for when she revealed that her husband had been killed in an accident at the quarry, and she feared for the safety of her son William, who was only fourteen but was now working there to earn a few shillings. Mary Ann felt desperately sorry for her. She brought her little gifts of tea and sugar so that they could sit together and enjoy a brew of this beverage whilst Suzannah unburdened herself of her troubles. She was able to give her a little financial assistance by suggesting that Suzannah helped her to weed her garden. She did not really need that help, but it created a bond of friendship that was beneficial to them both.

Her other neighbours were elderly, in their sixties. Harriet was a neatly dressed, prim and stately woman, her iron grey straight hair drawn back from her forehead. More usually, though, it was covered by a mob-cap. Her husband, James Pascoe, was a senior mason at the quarry. He was a kindly man who had been instrumental in finding work for Suzannah's son at the quarry, and always accompanied him there and back. They had come from east Cornwall after their children had got married.

All this news was imparted to Tom as they sat over their

evening meal. It was a relief to Tom to know that Mary Ann was fitting in with this new way of life here, she seemed to be reasonably happy in the role was was playing; it augured well for the future. He made a point of seeking out James Pascoe and young William, and walking with them to the quarry.

Every Sunday, however, was spent at Classywell, where they always received such a warm welcome. All too often, it rained, but they had good capes now, and it was worth a little discomfort to be with their good friends and with John again. John was given a note to take to school informing them that this would be his last term.

By the end of November the cottage was ready for occupation. George Challacombe was hired to fetch their few belongings from Nillacombe. The new furniture they had ordered was delivered from Tavistock. Mary Ann made curtains for the windows. It was difficult to believe that this was the same house that had so depressed Tom when he had first seen it. All the more credit to his wife that she had foreseen its possibilities. Small it might be, but how cosy and comfortable it looked now, on the day that they moved in, with a log fire burning in the grate.

Mr Leger was sorry to see them go, but wished them every happiness in their new home.

A few days before Christmas John joined them. The family was reunited again.

Mary Ann, in her mind, had been making plans for this Christmas. Something had to be done, she decided, to dispel the impression that, to use an expression she didn't like very much, they had come down in the world. It was going to be a Christmas to remember. Suzannah and William must share it with them. They must have a goose, with all its trimmings. No, it had better be a chicken. She remembered how thin Suzannah was. She was probably half starving herself so that William should not suffer. A goose might be too rich for her. To make her ill would ruin the whole day. Yes, a chicken would be better, and roast potatoes. And whatever vegetables Mr Rowe could supply from his store. She would go there and buy everything she felt she would need, plus whatever luxuries he might stock for the festive season.

She hoped she had learnt enough about the vagaries of her kitchen range not to make a disaster of her cooking. A great responsibility lay on her shoulders. It just *had* to come right.

She sent John out to scour the countryside for holly and ivy, and mistletoe if he could find some; even if he had to trespass in the Tor Royal plantation!

On Christmas eve John and his father hung the ivy and the holly, with some bright red berries on it, around the walls of the sitting-room. Pity there was no mistletoe to be found.

On Christmas morning, having got all the food prepared and in the oven, Mary Ann found time to go next door to Suzannah. She had persuaded her the day before to wash her hair. She now trimmed it and set it about her head in the most attractive way she could think of. She was pleased to find it had a little curl in it.

Then she dressed her in one of her own frocks. It had to be gathered in around her waist, and kept in place by a colourful sash. Oh, dear. The bodice drooped rather pathetically beneath her emaciated bosom. "Well, we'll just have to pad it out with something. And we are going to feed you properly in the future so that this will never be necessary again."

"Mary, why are you doing all this for me, you hardly know me?"

"Because I am one of the lucky ones, and you are one of the unlucky ones. And I can't bear to see you depriving yourself of everything."

"You weren't lucky when your house burnt down."

"Well, no. But there are varying degrees of luck. You have had more than your fair share of the bad. I have received help from my mother to overcome our bad luck. You must let me help you to overcome yours. Come now, I must get back to my cooking. We shall have the house to ourselves until Tom and the boys come back from church. Perhaps you would like to set the table whilst I put on the vegetables."

Suzannah was sufficiently familiar with the house now to know where to find the cutlery and the plates. All was ready by the time the church-goers returned, with the tune of 'O Come all ye Faithful' still ringing in their ears. As they entered the sitting-room John exclaimed, "Oh, what a gorgeous smell."

And William said, "Good heavens, Mother, is that really you?"

"A merry Christmas to you, Suzannah," came from Tom, with a smile as he recognised the frock she was wearing. Suzannah was quick to interpret that smile and his glance, it brought a blush to her cheeks, the first bit of colour there for many a long time. What with that and her little laugh at her son's remark, she really was a new person.

Tom went immediately to the kitchen. "Can I help you, dear?"

"Yes, take the chicken in and start carving. I will bring in the vegetables."

Mary Ann was pleased to find that the chicken was tender and cooked to perfection. William was ecstatic at the taste of the crispy roast potatoes, he had never known them cooked this way before. They all came back for second helpings. There was nothing left of that chicken at the end of the course.

Then came the plum pudding and the mince pies, which the boys consumed with relish. But Suzannah could only manage a very small portion of the pudding, her stomach was not accustomed to such quantities of food. "Thank you, Mary dear, for a wonderful meal, I don't remember when I have enjoyed one so much."

She was not allowed to help with any of the chores of clearing away the remains of the meal, or the washing of the dishes. Tom and Mary Ann insisted on doing it all. Tom was glad of the opportunity, when they were alone in the kitchen, of showing how much he appreciated what this dear wife of his was doing for them all. He nearly squeezed the breath out of her as he hugged her so closely.

Harriet and James were invited in to tea and to sample Mary Ann's cake. To receive congratulations from Harriet on the quality of her cake was indeed something to be relished. She also showed that she had a lighter side to her character. Some of the stories of her children's escapades in Cornwall caused a lot of laughter.

There were games to be played in the evening, and more

tasty things to eat, oranges and dates, and chestnuts to be roasted at the fire. Everybody went to bed happy that night.

Two days later, John set off with his father, and with William and old James Pascoe, for his first day of work, to learn the art of shaping stone.

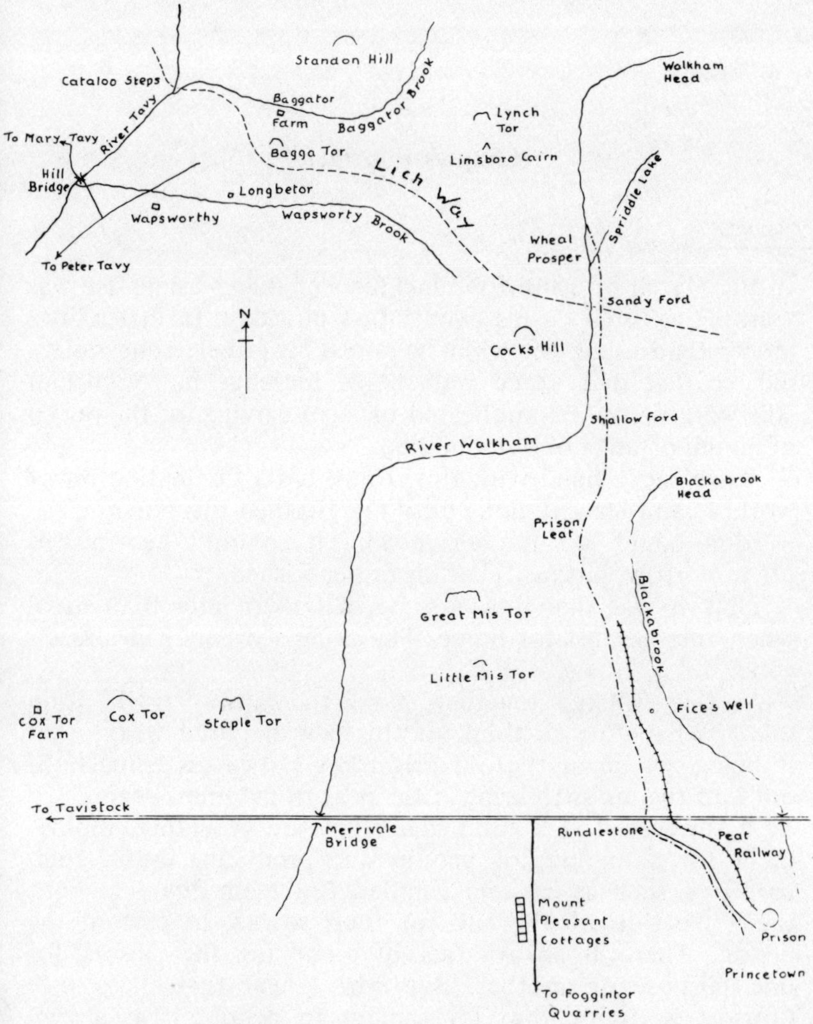

Reference map covering the story from Chapter 14.

Chapter Fourteen

In the March of 1846 John had reached man's estate. He was working as usual on his twenty-first birthday. In fact a little longer than usual, for when he joined his father, as he always did, so that they could walk home together, he found him still working on a complicated piece of carving for the portal of an important London building.

"Give me a hand with this, John. It's a fascinating bit of work, I can't leave it alone until I've finished this portion."

John could see no reason why it couldn't be finished off tomorrow, but he did as his father wished.

Thus it was that it was some half hour later than usual when they set off for home. The other workers had already gone.

As they walked together, along the railway track, John said, "What do you think of this new naphtha works that is being set up at the old prison? A railway is being built out into the moor to bring in the peat from Omen Beam."

"I suppose it is a good idea, they are providing employment for a number of people, and producing useful commodities, such as gas and candles. But I am dubious about their selection of the site for their works, in part of the prison. There is always talk of reopening the prison, for one purpose or another. But now I hear that the Prince Consort is urging the Government to restore it as a civil prison. That, to my mind, is the logical use for it. We can't expect to go on deporting our criminals to Australia and Canada. It is not surprising that those countries are objecting to it."

"That will make a big difference to Princetown if they

do, won't it."

"It certainly will. A vast amount of new housing will be built. Something Sir Thomas Tyrwhitt had always hoped for, but never achieved in his lifetime. What an extraordinary man he was. He lost his fortune in trying to develop the area, yet all his schemes failed. Even this wonderful railway would have been a failure if it hadn't been for our quarries."

At this point in their conversation they had reached the head waters of the little Yes Tor Brook, the track making a semicircular penetration into the shallow valley to cross the stream. There was still another mile to walk before another more gentle curve in the line would take them around the mire that cradled the source of the River Mew, and then into Princetown. The strong March winds were fortunately behind them and helped them on their way.

"You had a ride on this railway soon after it was opened, didn't you, Father? How did that come about?"

"Yes, John. We have always been frank with you about the fact that I killed a man in defending your mother, once you were old enough to understand, and that I went to prison for it. I might have been one of those unfortunates who were deported to Australia. You would not have been born if I had. But instead I was imprisoned in a hulk on the Hamoaze at Plymouth. When I was released, after three years, I managed to find my way to the terminus of this railway, and rode on it to freedom. I will never forget that part of the journey when I first saw the hills of Dartmoor again, and knew that I would soon be with the girl who was waiting for me, that lovely girl who was to become your mother."

There was a long silence between them as their thoughts travelled different avenues.

"Doesn't the line go through a long tunnel somewhere?"

"Yes. I didn't realise it at the time, of course, but that tunnel represents for me a dark period of my life that is best forgotten."

"I'm sorry, Father, I shouldn't have mentioned it."

"That's all right, son. But let's think of the future instead, which I believe has every promise of being a bright one. There is plenty of work for us ahead."

They reached the end of the line, which now terminated before it reached the road. The crossing of the roads and the negotiation of the sharp bends involved had been found to be not very practical.

When they entered their home his father said, "Let's change our clothes first," and hustled him up the stairs.

I wonder why, thought John, we usually have our tea first.

Gathered in the sitting-room was a group of people who were admonished to silence by Mary Ann's finger to her lips, when she heard her husband and son open the front door. There was Suzannah and her husband George Cole. A Suzannah who was almost unrecognisable from the waif who had first entered this room; who, with Mary Ann's help and feeding, had recovered her figure and good looks. No wonder George had fallen in love with her. They had been married for three years. Then there were Henry and Martha Perkins. They had taken over the cottage vacated by James and Harriet, who had returned to Cornwall after James' retirement from the quarry. Henry and Martha were a young and lively pair, there was always fun and laughter when they were present. And, of course, there was William, who would be celebrating his twenty-first birthday before long.

The table in the centre of the room was laden with food. There were beef sandwiches and chicken sandwiches, mince pies, plates of fruit, two different kinds of cake, and some small buns. The hungry men were finding it difficult to keep their hands off the food. They had been home in plenty of time to change into their best clothes. The women looked charming in theirs. The long wait in silence was becoming unbearable. Martha had her hand over her mouth to restrain her laughter, her bright eyes expressing her mirth. Mary Ann was hoping against hope that no one would spoil the surprise.

At last the door opened, and John stood there in astonishment.

"Happy birthday, John," they all shouted.

The men shook him by the hand; Suzannah and Martha, much to John's embarrassment, planted a kiss on his cheek. Now he realised why his father had delayed their departure from the quarry, and why he had been ushered up the stairs to change his clothes. It was a plot. He joined in the laughter. Then he went to his mother. "I know who is responsible for this. You do think up some lovely ideas, Mother, it was a complete surprise." He bent down and kissed her.

Tom then went to the chiffonier and produced another surprise as he poured out glasses of claret for them all to drink John's health, happiness and good fortune.

The evening was well advanced before the guests departed, in merry mood and with expressions of thanks.

"Mother, that was a party to remember. How you managed to arrange it and prepare all that food without my knowing, I just don't know. It was perfect."

"I'm glad you enjoyed it, dear. Suzannah has been a great help, she has been with me all day. Now I have a little gift for you." She took from her pocket a tiny jewel case. "This was your great-grandfather's signet ring. I still remember him as a dear kindly man. I'll tell you more about him, and his great house Ashburn Hall, one day. Your grandmother has kept it all these years. On her last visit here she gave it to me to give to you on this day. See if it fits you. It should go on your little finger on your left hand."

"Yes, it does fit. What a marvellous present. A bit of family history. I shall be afraid to wear it in case I lose it."

"Well, you won't wear it to work, of course. Keep it for Sundays and special days."

"How is it that we still have that portrait of great-grandfather? How did it survive the fire at Nillacombe?"

"We have to thank Elizabeth and Henry for that. They went to Nillacombe after we came here and cleared that sitting-room of all the rubbish of the fallen ceiling. There was nothing left worth salvaging except this portrait, which was still hanging on the wall, dusty but undamaged. I remember my delight when they handed it to me. It will be yours one day, John."

"I shall value that, as I do this ring. Thank you, Mother."

Tom was standing before the fire, beneath that portrait, watching this scene with great satisfaction. His son, all of six feet tall, was a handsome lad. How could it be otherwise with such a mother. The healthy open air life he had lived was reflected in his bronzed face and muscular frame. Tom was proud of him, and of his success at the quarry, where, as Tom had hoped and expected, he had become an expert mason. It was to be hoped that one day this young man would meet a girl worthy of him, and that they would never have to experience the traumas that had befallen his parents.

It was difficult to believe that Mary Ann was now forty-six. She certainly didn't look it. True, her face was more mature now, yet her delicate skin was still so pure and soft. Her hair, perhaps a shade lighter in colour and lacking some of its former lustre, was always so attractively set. Her figure was still neat, though a little fuller. Her poise perfect, bringing to mind that statue on Down Tor's noble pedestal.

Mary Ann became conscious of his gaze. Their eyes met with some intuitive understanding. This was another milestone in their lives. How long before this son of hers would lose his heart to someone else?

"You have done far more than your fair share of work today, my love. Go and sit by the fire and tell John all about Ashburn Hall and his great-grandfather, whilst I clear these dishes and wash them up."

The spate of rumours that had been circulating in Princetown over the ensuing years, as to the fate of the prison, finally crystallised into fact. It was definitely to be reopened as a civil prison.

Work commenced immediately on the construction of new houses in the village. Tom received notice that their cottage, together with all the others in that terrace, were to be demolished, most of them now being considered unsuitable for habitation. The opportunity would be taken to widen the road and build new houses. Ironically, though Tom had been so depressed when he first saw this house, he was now reluctant to leave, he almost resented it, such a home had Mary Ann made of it.

The quarry owners had foreseen that they would have to build more houses for their workers at Foggin Tor. Accommodation was found for Tom and his family at a group of cottages alongside the track that led from the quarry to the Tavistock - Two Bridges road near Rundlestone. They bore the attractive name of Mount Pleasant. Whoever chose that name must have done so at the height of summer, for the view from them across the broad expanse of moorland down which the Pila Brook meandered, over to the hills on which King Tor was a prominent landmark, was indeed a very pleasant one, especially of an evening when the sun dipped below the horizon and the sky was blood red with the promise of another fine day on the morrow. But alas, in the winter, they were painfully exposed to the westerly gales; it was anything but pleasant then.

The house they now occupied was no larger than the cottage they had vacated. It had much the same layout. Their furniture fitted in well. Mary Ann soon had their new home looking as comfortable and welcome as the old. Much to their delight Suzannah and George were still their neighbours. But Martha and Henry, not too happy with the turn of events, or indeed with the sort of life the quarry could provide for them, had gone back to Tavistock to live.

On the far side of Suzannah were Zachariah Hicks, also a stone mason, his wife Ruth, his son Sharack, aged nineteen, and his daughters Sarah, thirteen, and Rachel, eleven.

Such was the shortage of houses that most of the tenants took in lodgers. Incredibly John Northam and his wife Elizabeth, though they were only in their early thirties, had six children, three sons and three daughters, and yet found room to take in four lodgers. That was the extreme case, but many of the houses had up to seven occupants. Suzannah and George took in two lodgers, William Gest and Edward Damerell. It was a bit confusing to have two Williams in the house. Tom and Mary Ann wondered how soon it would be before they were asked to do likewise.

It was in the autumn of the year 1850 that they moved to this overcrowded community. By midsummer of the following year they were thankful still to be on their own. It was one of those summers of long dry settled weather when the moor took on its most benign appearance and beckoned one out into its distant places. At breakfast one

Sunday John suggested that they explore the upper reaches of the Walkham River, where they had never been. He was surprised when his mother said she was not feeling too well and would rather not go today. His father elected to stay with her.

"Ask William to go with you," said Mary Ann, "but be back in time for dinner, won't you?"

But John set off on his own. There were times when he enjoyed having the moor to himself, alone in the vast open spaces. When no other voice disturbed the silence. And there *were* such days of utter silence. When there was no breath of wind; when there was not an animal in sight; when even the birds seemed afraid to disturb the peace. Yes, peace; that was what was so wonderful about it. The mind was set at rest; one's sight became more aware of the colours, the shape of the hills, the details of one's immediate surroundings. There were so many strange things to be seen, so many questions to be asked and answers to be sought at some later date.

John's first objective was to follow the peat railway-track that the Naphtha Company had constructed, at so much labour and expense, only for it to be abandoned within a year or two. He joined the track where it crossed the road just beyond the Rundlestone Inn. The valley of the Blackabrook stretched away in front of him, leading him out towards those distant hills.

He had not gone far before a branch track, at right angles to the main track, descended to the river, which it crossed on a sturdy bridge, and continued up the hill beyond to the scars of the peat ties, on the slopes of Omen Beam. He could see all that without having to follow it. To do so would have taken up too much of his time. However, a little further on, he did descend a short distance from the track to examine a group of stones. He found them to be a canopy over a well, on the capstone of which were the letters IF and the date 1568. He wondered what that signified. Who would be able to tell him about that?

Beside the track, near here, was a building, perhaps for stabling the horses, thought John. In another mile or so he came to the end of the railway, where a substantial platform had been built alongside the line, presumably where the peat was stored ready to load onto the trucks. It seemed a tragedy to John, that such a splendid undertaking had been in use for so short a time.

Beyond the platform the ground became very wet and marshy. He climbed to higher ground to avoid it and came to the Prison Leat, whose course John had often seen beside the road leading from Rundlestone to the prison. He had been told that its source was the River Walkham, some miles away. He decided to follow it. There was marsh on either side of the leat; he was glad of its dry and firm banks to walk on.

What desolate country this was just here, what an undertaking to construct a leat through such ground. He could see Great Mis Tor looming high on his left; and surely that must be the head of the Blackabrook on his right, in a featureless hollow backed by a barren hill and hazy distant tors. This was wild country, primitive, primeval, forbidding. But this was what he wanted today, to be alone with nature. There was a spice of danger and fear in it. That excited him. Now he could see the valley of the Walkham ahead, and soon the place where it made a sharp turn westward into a small gorge-like entrance to whatever lay beyond. He must walk there one day. But now he wanted to see where the leat started.

Some distance further on the leat and the river came close together, though there was still some way to go before they met. On the far side of the river he could see a stationary water-wheel amongst some mine workings. He would explore them on the way back.

He found that there were two sources for the leat, one being the entire contents of a little stream that descended a valley to the east of the Walkham. The other was a channel from the Walkham itself, at a place where the hills closed in to form only a narrow passage for the river, giving it a rather mysterious setting. What lay beyond? It cannot be far now to the source of the Walkham, thought John, but he must leave that for another day. Time was getting on.

It was easy to jump across the river here, so immature was it. Another leat, dry now, along the right bank, led him back to that water-wheel. He examined it and made a cursory survey of the other remains, enough to satisfy himself that no work was taking place here now. It seemed to have been recently abandoned. Now he hurried on his way. He was likely to be a bit late for dinner, but he knew his mother would understand.

"John is very late," said Mary Ann, "we had better get on with our dinner or it will be spoilt."

John had still not returned by the time they had finished their dinner. Nor had he two hours later, when Mary Ann said, "What is keeping him, do you suppose, Tom. I'm getting a bit worried."

"Oh, I expect he is enjoying himself so much he can't tear himself away, it is such a perfect day for walking."

But there came a time when Tom also began to feel anxious. It was most unusual for John to stay out so long.

"Which way did he say he was going?" asked Mary Ann.

"Along the peat railway track. He did mention the Walkham valley at breakfast. He may not come back the same way, of course."

"Tom, please organise a search party. He may need help somewhere; you must go before it gets dark."

"I'll go and see Zachariah. He has lived here for years. He probably knows the area better than anyone."

Zachariah suggested several directions John may have taken on his return. "Tell you what. We'll go out in pairs to look. Sharak and I will go Mister* way. You and Will go out along the peat railway. Get t'other William and Edward to go to the west of Mister and look across the Walkham valley, in case he's gone that way. But all come back before it gets dark, otherwise we'll be 'aving search parties going out for us. We can't do no gud in the dark."

Before the search parties set off, Tom asked Suzannah to keep Mary Ann company whilst they were away.

"Mary, dear, I know you must be feeling very worried. I'd feel the same, I'm sure. Let me make you a hot drink, it will help to pass the time and keep us occupied."

***Pronunciation of Mis Tor in the vernacular.**

“I used to worry about John going out on long walks when he was a boy. But he was always so sensible and took proper precautions. He always came back safely. I just can’t imagine what can have happened to him today. The weather is perfect. What sort of hidden dangers are there up that valley, would you suppose?”

“I don’t know, dear, I’m not much of a one for walking. I’ve never been up there.”

“I shudder when I think of bogs, there are plenty of those around near the heads of rivers. He didn’t say how far he was going up the Walkham, just the Walkham valley. That could mean anything.”

“Tell me something about that old gentleman in the picture up there. How come you’ve got such a fine picture? Who is he?”

Thus did Suzannah distract Mary Ann’s mind from her apprehensions. But the hours dragged. Dimsey turned to dark and they had to light the oil lamps before the first pair of searchers returned. All eventually assembled. None had seen any sign of John, or had any clues as to why he had disappeared.

“We’ll go out again at first light,” said Zachariah, “we’ll get more men and search further afield. Us’ll find ’im.”

Mary Ann stayed at home the next day, with Suzannah for company again, just in case John returned from some unexpected quarter. Never was there such a long day. There seemed no hope as party after party returned with still no news. Mary Ann began to feel ill with anxiety. Tom could find no words to comfort her, he was as worried himself. He could think of no possible explanation for the mystery.

Overshadowed by the massive bulk of Standon Hill, inconspicuous from all directions, yet with a simple charm all its own on its lowly eminence, lay a pile of rocks known as Bagga Tor, nearly four hundred feet below the summit of that great hill to the north. In between these two differing hills lay the valley of the Baggator Brook and a farm of the same name. South of the little tor another farm nestled close to the Wapsworthy Brook, an insignificant stream until it entered, with a flourish, the River Tavy below Hill Bridge.

So isolated was this little farm of Longbetor that no track capable of taking a cart led to it. Only a bridle-path from the house gave communication with the outside world. The path crossed Wapsworthy Brook at a miniature ford, and then crossed fields to Wapsworthy Farm and to the lanes from there to the nearest villages of Peter Tavy and Mary Tavy, both some three miles distant.

In this farm lived Stephen Madge, his wife Ella, and their daughter Penny. Ella's first-born, a boy, had died in childbirth. This daughter of theirs, though, had proved as capable and useful as any son could have been. She had learnt to ride their ponies at an early age, and to ride them bareback. There was no point in spending money on a saddle if it wasn't necessary. She was adept at rounding up their sheep from the moor, at the minding and milking of their few cows. She was a tall, well-built girl, with a high colour in her cheeks from constant exposure to sun and wind. Her hazel eyes sparkled in her clean-cut features. Her head was crowned with a mass of auburn hair, usually tied at the back to keep it out of the way. She wore man's garb when on her farming work, but knew how to make herself look feminine and attractive when attending church on Sundays or at social occasions at Peter Tavy.

On this particular Sunday she did not go to church, however. When she had brought in their flock the previous evening it was found that one sheep was missing. She told her father she would go out this morning and look for it. She donned her working clothes and a smock, covering her locks with a wide-brimmed hat to shade her eyes from the bright sunlight and give her better visibility.

Vaulting lightly onto her pony, she rode up through the farm enclosures, following the course of the brook towards its source, but turning off before reaching there to a gate which gave access to a stroll that separated their land from that of Baggator Farm. At the end of the stroll she guided her pony up the steepening slopes of Lynch Tor, to a cairn on the summit known as Limsboro. From there she had a clear view to the east, a vast featureless expanse of emptiness, where, in the distance, the Walkham had its source and across which it flowed between hidden banks. Yet it was an area of considerable activity during weekdays, when the peat was cut for the mines at Mary Tavy; Wheal Friendship and Wheal Betsy. The peat was stooked to dry on the higher ground to the south of Limsboro, giving to that area the name Stooky Moor.

Penny looked long and hard from this vantage point, but could see no sign of her lost animal. Away to the south lay Cocks Hill. In that direction she now set her pony at an easy trot, keeping a sharp lookout all the while.

No better success rewarded her in this area. What could have happened to the poor beast? She would go no further than Shallow Ford, to which she now descended. She let the pony drink at the ford, then followed the river upstream towards Sandy Ford.

About half way between these two points she was horrified to see a man lying face down on a scattering of stones, which she knew was the debris of an adit which had been excavated here not long ago by the miners at Wheal Prosper, further up the valley. He must have heard her approach for he lifted his head slightly and almost inaudibly called for help. She dismounted and knelt beside him. "What's happened to 'e. Be you 'urt?" Then she noticed that his right hand was twisted at an impossible angle from his wrist, that his clothes were torn and filthy. When she turned him onto his back he groaned with pain; she saw that his shirt front was covered in blood. He had a wound and a great bruise on his forehead, blood had streamed down his face. His forearms were lacerated. "Oh God, man, you are 'urt. Can you tell me what 'as 'appened?"

"I fell down a mine shaft . . . trying to rescue a sheep . . . it was on its back, in a hollow . . . the ground gave way . . . I landed on top of the sheep. It's dead . . . I would be but for her . . ."

"And you managed to crawl out through this adit?"

"Yes."

"That blood on your shirt, be that yours or the sheep's?"

"The sheep's, I suppose."

"Thank God for that. Look, I got to lift you onto my pony. It's goin' to 'urt you, but 'tis got to be done."

She went for her pony and led him as near as possible to the man. With repeated cries of "gidde down now, gidde down," she persuaded the animal to lower himself on his knees.

Then she realised that she had to do something about that broken wrist. She pulled off her smock and folded it diagonally to form a sort of sling. Then she placed it across his chest, very gently lifted his forearm, holding his hand to support it from the broken wrist, and laid it in the fold of the sling. She could see him clench his teeth with the pain it caused him.

"That 'urt, didun it. 'Twill feel better now," as she tied the ends around his neck.

"Are your legs all right?"

"The left one is, I think. My right ankle hurts."

"Now, I'm goin' to help you get up, and you got to lean on me and limp across to the horse, and get yourself astride it. Can you do that?"

"I'll try."

Standing behind him, she put her arms beneath his armpits and heaved him upright. He let out an involuntary yell of pain.

"What 'urt you then?"

"My chest."

"Now put your arm around my neck and take the weight off that right leg."

They struggled precariously over the stony ground to the horse, and with less difficulty than she had supposed, got him astride it.

"Now, hold on to 'is neck as best you can whilst I get 'im to 'is feet."

"Gidde up, now, gidde up."

She held on to the man whilst the pony rose to his forelegs. "Now lean forward," as the pony struggled upright. "Now we shall be all right."

John was not at all sure that he was going to be all right. He was beginning to feel faint and was sweating profusely. The movement of the horse aggravated the pain in his chest. His head, and it seemed every bone in his body, was aching. How much damage had he suffered? His right hand, on which he depended for his work, would it ever be any use again? Who was this girl who was helping him? Where was she taking him? He looked down at her. She had only a chemise on above her trousers. Her neck and arms were bare; she did not seem at all concerned. How far had they to go like this? The jolting was agonising. How long could he stick it out?

"How far have we to go?" he managed to ask, though even that was painful.

"Not very far, you are doing fine. Here, take my hat, to keep the sun off you." Penny walked close to the man to help him if he showed any signs of falling. The pony needed no leading, he knew the way. She thought it might help if she talked to him.

"What's your name?"

"John."

"Mine is Penny. I've been out all mornin' lookin' for that sheep what saved your life. No wonder I couldn't find 'er. Poor thing must 'ave been on 'er back all night. Where you come from, then?"

She got no answer to that question. Must be 'urting 'im to speak, p'raps.

"I live at Longbetor, small farm near Bagga Tor, if you know where that is."

She kept up her chatter, describing the scenery they were passing and anything else that came to mind. But she was getting no response from him at all. He is not looking too good, she thought, as she saw his head lolling forward onto his chest, his eyes closed, his mouth clenched tight, beads of perspiration appearing on his upper lip and chin, the only parts of his face that were not streaked with blood. His good hand was clutching the pony's mane, to help him keep his balance. That was a sign that he was still conscious.

"We'm nearly there now, I can see the farm. Pretty little stream comes down this valley. Wapsworthy Brook 'tis called, though some people says Yoledon Brook. I like Wapsworthy meself. Wapsworthy is a farm near us, much bigger than ours . . . Mother and Father will be surprised to see what I'm bringing home to them, instead of that sheep. But they'll look after you, you'll be all right in Mother's hands."

Mother and Father were indeed surprised and alarmed when they saw this apparition on Penny's horse, with bloodied face beneath her hat, one arm in a sling, and drooping forward in utter weariness. And a half-dressed daughter holding on to him.

"Whatever's 'appened, Penny, who you got 'ere?"

"The man's fallen down a mine shaft, Mother, 'es badly 'urt. Father, hold on to 'is shoulders, I'll take 'is legs. Be careful, every movement is hurting 'im."

They carried him inside to their sparsely furnished parlour and laid him on the floor.

"Get my mattress from my bed, Father, we can't get him upstairs. Then either you or I will have to ride to Mary Tavy to get a doctor."

With John more comfortably settled on a mattress and his head on a pillow, her father said he would go for the doctor, Penny would be able to look after this man better than he could.

John was only hazily aware of what was happening to him. He had periods of losing consciousness. The agony of being moved brought him to life again. Then at last the relief of being able to lie still on something soft. He was aware of his face being bathed with warm water, the wound on his forehead being tenderly cleaned. He half opened his eyes to see these two women ministering to him. The sling was removed, and then his shirt. They must be cutting the shirt off him, so careful were they not to move him more than was necessary. His arm with the broken wrist was laid gently by his side; he could not help wincing as they did so. Then they washed the blood from his chest and stomach; dried him, and covered him with a blanket. He relapsed into unconsciousness again.

He was falling, falling, falling in horrible blackness: that awful jolt as his body hit the ground; that terrible pain as his wrist broke; he cried out with the pain.

"All right, all right, young man, it will soon be over."

He opened his eyes to see a man at his side. It must be the doctor, he was setting his wrist in a splint. Then, as if in a dream, he heard him saying, "He has at least two broken ribs. I do not know what other internal injuries he has suffered, only time will tell. His ankle is badly sprained, not broken. You have done well to clean that wound on his forehead, and the abrasions on his arms. They will heal all right. Do not move him more than is absolutely necessary. I will give him something to induce sleep. When he wakes feed him only on liquids, warm milk and beef-tea. He's a healthy man, he should pull through all right. I will come again in the morning."

At last the family could attend to their own needs and have a very belated dinner. Penny related the events of the morning. Her father remarked what a good job the doctor had done, setting that wrist. "He gets plenty of practice at that sort of thing at Mary Tavy Mines, I don't doubt." Her mother was concerned about the young man's parents.

"They'm goin' to be very worrit when 'e don't come 'ome," she said, "did you ask 'im where 'e lives to, Penny?"

"Yes, but 'e didn't answer. I'm not sure whether 'e 'eard me or not. I only know he's called John."

"Where are you goin' to sleep tonight, now 'e's got your mattress?"

"I'll sleep down 'ere, in case 'e needs any help. I'll be all right in the rocking chair."

"You'm a good girl. You did well to bring 'im home like that. Nobody could 'ave done better. Poor man, what a dreadful thing to 'appen to 'im. Such a fine lookin' young man, too."

Penny changed her clothes into blouse and skirt. Thus she remained throughout the night, keeping a candle burning in case of need. He moaned and groaned occasionally. Sometimes she knelt beside him to see if he needed help, but he did not wake. But once he flung his good arm about in such distress that she held his hand to soothe him. He hung on to it with an iron grip as if trying to save himself. She wiped the sweat from his face and spoke quietly to reassure him that he was safe. It was some time before she could release her hand from his and be sure that the nightmare was over. She had difficulty in getting any sleep herself.

But when her parents came down early next morning, they were both sleeping quietly. So lightly in Penny's case that she was soon alert when she heard movements in the room.

"What sort of a night has 'e 'ad?"

"Very restless, with bad dreams."

When John woke he looked round the room with a puzzled expression. "Where am I?" he asked.

"Don't you remember coming 'ere on my pony yesterday?"

"Oh, that awful ride, yes."

"And that accident you had?"

"Did that really happen?" He looked at his wrist in its splint. "It did, didn't it. It was horrible."

"You are safe now. You'll soon be better. Where do you live, John?"

Again there was no immediate answer to that question. Then he said, "In a valley, somewhere, but the house was burnt down."

When later, the doctor was informed of this conversation, he confirmed that the patient was suffering from concussion. Not surprising really, considering that blow to the head. He re-examined the wound. "That will heal better without a bandage as long as you can keep it clean. You must stay on your back, young man, and lie as still as possible to allow your ribs to mend. You'll have to be very patient."

As he left he told Mrs Madge, "He will have to stay like that for at least three weeks. I would not advise him being moved, however much he may desire to go to his home, when he remembers where that is. It is going to be difficult for you, I hope you can manage."

"Oh, yes, us'll manage somehow. Us'll look after 'im."

Penny spent another night in that rocking chair. But it was a more restful one for both of them. There were no more nightmares. The kind attention John had received throughout the day had calmed him. This girl Penny; she had a particularly soothing influence on him.

When he awoke in the morning, soon after the room was lit by the increasing daylight, he looked across the room to this girl, and for the first time realised what discomfort she was enduring for his sake. His mind was clearing now; he was able to study her with more interest than had been possible hitherto. Her body was covered by a blanket, but he could admire that mass of auburn hair that hid most of her face, except her closed eyes. Those hazel eyes that had expressed such sympathy and kindness. That was what he remembered about her face. He wanted to speak to her but it would be unkind to wake her. Was it some thought transference or had he made some noise that caused her to open her eyes? When she saw him looking at her, she threw off her blanket and came to him.

"Do you want anything, John?"

"I remember now where I live, Penny, can you get word to my parents? They must be worrying about me."

"Yes, of course. Where do you live?"

"At Foggin Tor."

"Where is that?"

"Do you know Rundlestone?"

"Yes."

"There is a track that goes from near there to some quarries."

"Oh, I know the quarries, but I didn't know the name. I didn't know there were houses there."

"A little way along that track there is a group of houses on the right. Ask anybody there where Mr and Mrs Tremain live, they are my father and mother."

"I'll go directly after breakfast. Oh, I'm so glad you have remembered at last. You'm lookin' better too."

At about the same time a very weary-eyed Mary Ann was preparing breakfast for her dejected-looking husband.

"Where are you going to look today, Tom?"

"It is no good going up the Walkham valley again, we have searched that thoroughly. Zachariah suggests Omen Beam and the Beardown Tors area. We won't have the same number of searchers today, so many men cannot be spared from the quarry. I have very little faith we shall find him there, but I must keep trying."

Only Zachariah, the two Williams and Edward set out with Tom on this forlorn search. Tom was looking exhausted before he started, with lack of sleep and worry.

Suzannah had never seen Mary look like this before, hollow-eyed, pale of face, a wisp of her untidy hair drooping over the frown on her forehead. Her movements sluggish, her thoughts far away. What could she say to her now? There seemed to be no words of hope left.

"Mary, will you teach me how to knit?"

"I thought you could knit."

"Yes, but only simple knitting. Show me how to do the more complicated stitches."

So, whilst Suzannah practised her stitches, Mary Ann resumed some sewing. in that way they passed the time. Conversation was minimal.

They looked up at each other in surprise at the sound of horse's hooves outside.

Mary Ann, a ray of hope rising in her breast, went to the door to find a girl with two ponies there.

"Be you Mrs Tremain?"

"Yes."

"I have news of your son, can I come in?"

"Oh, thank God, thank God. Where is he? What has happened to him? Is he all right?"

She took the girl by the hand and led her indoors. "Sit down, my dear."

"He has been badly injured, but nothing that will not mend. He is with me mother and father at our farm, Mary Tavy way. We'm looking after 'im, but he must not be moved yet."

"What happened? What are his injuries?"

"He fell down a mine shaft." A cry of horror from Mary Ann as she put her hand to her mouth. "He managed to crawl out of an adit, that's where I found him. He's broke his wrist, and has some ribs broke too. That's why he musn't be moved."

"Oh, poor boy. But thank God you found him. How did you get him to your house?"

"John says you are an expert horsewoman. I've brought a spare pony with me. Will you come back with me now? It will do him good to see you, and to be able to tell you all about it himself."

"Yes, I will. But could you not have come to tell us this yesterday?"

"No, he got concussion, 'e couldn't remember where 'e

lived until this morning."

"Suzannah, can you find someone to run to Tom to tell him this?"

"Yes, I will. Where shall I say you are going?"

"Ours is a small farm between Wapsworthy and Bagga Tor. It's called Longbetor."

"My dear girl, I'm so grateful to you," said Mary Ann. "What's your name?"

"Penny."

"Wait a minute, dear, whilst I change into something more suitable for riding."

Whilst Penny was waiting she looked around the room. Her eyes rested on that portrait on the wall, as everyone's eyes always did, so unexpected was it in such surroundings. Who was that fine old gentleman?

She was bold enough to ask Mrs Tremain when she returned.

"That is my grandfather. John is named after him. Come, let us be going."

Mary Ann noticed that only one of the ponies was saddled, and that with a very ancient looking contraption.

"That is for you," directed Penny.

"Do you always ride bareback?"

"Yes, I never need a saddle. Pony and I knows each other well enough."

How well Mary Ann understood that. Both riders noted with approval how easily each other mounted their steeds.

Whilst they rode, slowly to begin with, Penny related in more detail her finding of John, of the sheep that had saved his life, of the difficult ride to her home. Of what other injuries John had, and what the doctor had said. Mary Ann admired this girl's resourcefulness in making an improvised sling out of her smock.

When there was little more to be said, they urged their ponies into a trot, climbing the slopes of Little Mis Tor, then to the east of Great Mis Tor and down to the Prison Leat, which they followed to where a path led them to Shallow Ford. Penny seemed adept at finding firm ground between the marshes. Mary Ann was shown the adit where John had been found. From now on she could sense the agony that John must have suffered for the rest of their journey.

They dismounted at the farmhouse porch. Penny led Mary Ann into their parlour, and to John, who was looking up expectantly from his mattress on the floor, a blanket over him except for his bare chest.

"Oh, my dear boy, it is such a relief to see you, we couldn't imagine what had happened to you," as she knelt down beside him; "your forehead, John, what a dreadful bruise and gash. How are you feeling now?"

"All the better for seeing you, Mother. But I am really feeling better, thanks to Penny here, who has been very kind to me, and, of course, her parents. Here is her mother to meet you."

Mary Ann rose to her feet and held out her hand to this rosy-cheeked, kindly-faced woman who came smilingly to greet her.

"How can I thank you for what you are doing for my son?"

"You would do the same, me dear, that I'm sure. Us'll look after 'im, don't 'e fret. Doctor thinks he'll pull through well. You'll take a cup o' tea, won't you, Mrs Tremain?"

"Thank you, I would love one. But please call me Mary, we don't have to be formal."

"Then I'm Ella to you. Me 'usband's called Stephen, he's out in the fields at present. Penny, come and 'elp me, leave John and his mother together for a bit."

"John, I have brought you some underwear and night-wear. You look as though you need some. Have you got anything on under that blanket?"

"Yes, but they had to cut my shirt off me. Thank you for thinking of that, I'm certainly going to need them, it looks as though I am going to be here for some time. You must have been very worried when I didn't come home."

"I have been feeling ill with worry, and so has your father, who has been out every day with search parties looking for you. It was a complete mystery when you couldn't be found. What an awful experience for you, it is a miracle you survived it."

John was about to tell of the nightmares he had had, when the tea arrived.

It is wonderful what a cup of tea can do to create friendship. By the time that gathering over the cups was over, they all felt they had known each other for quite a while. Any initial tension had soon been dispelled by John spilling his tea on his chest when he raised his cup to his lips with an unaccustomed left hand, and Penny came quickly to mop it up. A little touch of happy familiarity that warmed Mary Ann's heart.

"John, can you tell me what happened to you on that walk; how did you come to fall down that mine shaft?"

"I had been returning over Cock's Hill when I heard a sheep bleating. I found it at the bottom of a pit, on its back."

Penny interrupted to explain that sometimes a sheep is unable to recover itself from this position.

"I went into the pit to help it, but the ground gave way under us. I was clutching the sheep by its wool and just held on to it, we fell together until we hit the bottom of the shaft. All I can remember about that is a great blow to my forehead. I must have lost consciousness then."

"Oh, John, how awful. I suppose the sheep cushioned your fall, or surely you would have been killed. Go on, dear."

"When I came round I found I was able to move my head and was aware of a pinpoint of light. I remembered what Father had told me about adits. I knew I had to crawl towards that light, but as soon as I moved I was aware of the pain in my wrist and chest, and then in my ankle. All the pains were on my right side. I found that if I lay on my left side I could shuffle myself along with my left arm and left leg. It was terribly slow progress, I had to stop every now and again to rest. A cool draught of air seemed to revive me and I struggled on again."

"Is that how your left arm has got so lacerated?"

"I suppose so. I had so many other pains I don't think I was aware of that. I kept looking towards that bit of light, gradually getting larger, and eventually I was able to see the shape of the adit mouth. I knew I could make it then. When I got out into the open I could only lie still and hope that someone would eventually find me. I was quite prepared for a long wait. I was astonished that so soon I heard someone approaching. I tried to call out, but that hurt too."

"Penny has told me all about finding you and your ride home on her pony. I can see all this talking is tiring you, but I am so glad you have been able to tell me. It has been such a mystery that no one could find you. Ella, I'm so grateful to you; are you sure you will be able to manage having John here, with all your other work?"

"Oh, us'll manage. And I 'ope you will come often to see John."

"I have given no thought as to how I'm going to get home."

"The same way as we came," said Penny. "I'll come with you."

She went to fetch the ponies, leaving the two mothers to have a last word together.

As they rode through the fields Mary Ann said, "Your mother has just been telling me that you have spent the last two nights in a rocking chair, to help John if necessary. I do thank you for that. But am I right in thinking it is your mattress that you have sacrificed for John?"

"Well, yes. We hadn't any other. But father is borrowing one from Wapsworthy Farm, I shall be all right now. And if you be worryin' about John being on the floor, doctor said it is probably best for 'im, so he keeps his back straight and lets the ribs 'eal properly."

"That makes sense. It is a great comfort to me to know he is being so well cared for. You are a kind family, I could not wish for him to be in better hands."

Tom was at the door waiting for them when they arrived. Penny was intrigued to see these two middle-aged people throw themselves into each other's arms and hug each other for joy. Mary Ann then introduced Penny to her husband. "We have a lot to thank her for, and her parents. They are taking great care of John. Penny, dear, I have no dinner prepared to offer you, but you are welcome . . . "

"Yes, you have," interrupted Suzannah, "I have made something for you."

"There you are, then, come in and join us. I was going to offer you bread and cheese. This is Suzannah, our neighbour and great friend."

Tom now had the opportunity of assessing the worth and warmth of this girl who had done so much for his son.

When she had gone, Mary Ann related all she had learnt about John's horrendous experience.

"It is a miracle he wasn't killed," said Tom, "had he been, we would never have known what had happened to him."

"Tom, I don't understand how the ground could have given way under them; I don't suppose John would know either, it must have been so sudden."

"Very often a small mine shaft is capped by a large flat stone. I can only assume that the combined weight of John and the sheep must have tilted that stone onto its edge. Thank God it didn't fall with them. I don't suppose John realised there was a capstone there, it was probably covered with earth. He probably didn't know that the pit was the head of a shaft. No, he couldn't have known that. These pits look so innocent, and of course there are many that are not mine shafts. How badly has he been hurt, do you think?"

"I doubt if we shall know until he is able to move about again, that will be some weeks yet. His most serious injury apparent now is his broken wrist. Will he ever be able to use that hand again?"

"You will want to see him often, won't you? I wonder if I can persuade Mr Uren to let you use one of the horses from the stables? He has been very sympathetic and helpful when he heard of John's disappearance. He has allowed me this time off to look for him."

"Oh, I do hope you can. I was wondering how I was going to visit him."

"I'll go and see him now."

"Tom."

"Yes, dear."

"What is your impression of that girl, Penny?"

"I was struck by her naturalness. She wasn't at all shy with us, she just made herself at home with a country girl's ease. I liked her for that. She's the picture of health, a great help to her parents I should think."

"She and John are going to be thrown together a lot in the next few weeks."

"Now, what are you thinking?"

"That they are very suited to each other. Wouldn't it be natural for John to fall in love with someone who is so attentive to him, doing so much for him. You must admit she has good looks, too. We do not know the full extent of John's injuries. Who knows, he may need someone like her in the future."

Chapter Fifteen

When next the doctor visited John, only Mrs Madge was there to receive him. She left the parlour whilst he made his examination.

He noted with approval how clean and well-cared for his patient looked. After his medical tests and questions about what physical movements hurt him, and whether his bodily functions were normal, he said, "I don't think you have suffered any internal injuries, other than your ribs. You are a lucky man. How do you manage to shave and keep so clean?"

"These kind people do nearly everything for me. Mr Madge shaves me; Penny and her mother wash me where I can't manage myself. I am getting used to doing everything with my left hand, though it is a bit frustrating at times. Do you think I'll ever be able to use my right hand?"

"I have to be frank with you, I just don't know. You will have to find out for yourself, eventually, what movements you can do, and exercise it as much as possible. The swelling in your ankle is going down, but you have damaged the ligaments; they often take a long time to heal. Otherwise you are doing fine."

On his departure he said to Mrs Madge, "I congratulate you on the way you are looking after that young man. I don't think it will be necessary for me to come again until it is time to remove the splint. You are doing all the right things for him."

Not only was it frustrating for John to have to do everything with one hand; the inactivity of having to lie still and alone for much of the day was also very trying for him, the hours dragged badly. He was delighted therefore when his mother arrived one day with two books for him, *Oliver Twist* and *David Copperfield*, by that popular author Charles Dickens.

"How have you managed to come on your own, Mother?"

"I have been able to borrow one of the quarry horses, but can only do so on a Sunday, when they are not required for work there. Your father went to Classywell and retrieved Nelson's saddle from Elizabeth; she had salvaged it and always felt I would need it one day. There's kindness for you!"

"So you will be able to come every Sunday. How I shall look forward to that. The time will go quicker now that I have these books to read. It must be Sunday today, then. I lose count. I have been here a week."

"Has the doctor been to see you again?"

"Yes, he says I have no internal injuries, and apart from my wrist I should be all right. But what am I going to do, Mother, if I can't use my right hand?"

His mother was spared the answer to that question as Penny appeared with a tea tray. This was the first time that Mary Ann had seen her dressed in feminine garb. She wore a simple muslin dress in buttercup yellow, the full skirt not quite reaching to the ground; the bodice, topped with a broad white collar and drawn in at the waist, had short puff sleeves. Her hair, usually tied behind her head with any old piece of ribbon to keep it out of the way, was now allowed to hang freely about her face, thick and lustrous, shoulder length and with a natural uplift of curl at the ends. It framed a countenance that was now enhanced by a smile and a slight blush as she became aware of John's and his mother's eyes upon her.

"Did you make your dress, Penny?"

"No, Mother did, I never seem to 'ave time for sewin'."

This was a new experience for John, too. He couldn't stop looking at her. She seemed to move with so much more grace now.

Ella came in with a cake.

"Did I 'ear you say y'ould be able to come every Sunday, Mary?"

"Yes, if I may, Ella."

"You'll be very welcome. 'Tain't often us gets visitors, us'll look forward to it. 'Tis good for John, too."

Penny brought John his tea, kneeling beside him and propping up his pillows for him.

Each Sunday Mary Ann noticed this increasing devotion on Penny's part, and approved. There was little doubt that John appreciated it.

On the third Sunday John was sitting up for his tea.

On the fourth, he was on his feet and limped to greet his mother.

"Oh, this is good to see, John. When did you get up?"

"Two days ago. My legs were very wobbly at first, but they are getting stronger."

"And you have had the splint removed."

"Yes, I can move my fingers a little, but can't hold anything yet."

"You will be able to come home now, we'll have to get a trap or something to fetch you."

Did she notice disappointment in John's face? There was no doubt about the pleading look in Penny's eyes.

"Us be quite 'appy to keep 'im 'ere for a while yet," said Ella, "though I'm sure you must want to 'ave 'im with you again. Penny is 'elping 'im to walk, she'd dearly love to see 'im proper restored to health again."

Mary Ann looked at Penny.

"Please," was the only word she uttered.

How could such an appeal be refused?

Ella said to her husband that night, "I'm not sure whether we're going to lose a daughter or gain a son. Would you be able to manage the farm without 'er."

" 'Twould be 'ard. She'd be sorely missed."

"How is he goin' to earn a livin' to keep 'er? I can't see that right 'and of his being any use."

" 'Twould be nice to 'ave 'em both here; I'm willing. Won't be much good if they starts 'aving kids, though. Us 'aven't got the room."

"That's looking a bit far ahead, ain't it? They'm well suited though."

Every evening, when work was done, Penny would massage

John's ankle and encourage him to practise holding things with his right hand, and to flex his wrist. They went for short walks together, John's arm round Penny's shoulder for support. Each time the walks would be a little longer. The ankle gradually strengthened and became less painful, until he was able to walk without her support. His arm was then transferred from her shoulder to her waist, and hers went round his. The walks became a pleasure instead of an exercise. But no progress was made with that wrist. His hand was useless.

One Sunday morning they took the well-worn path through the enclosures to the gate that led on to the stroll, the path that John had ridden in such agony all those weeks ago.

"Do you remember my talking to you then?" asked Penny.

"I can't remember now what you were saying, but just the sound of your voice was helpful. It was something pleasant to balance the awful pain."

"After you told me your name, you never spoke again. I wondered if you had fainted."

"No, I knew you were talking. All my concentration was on fighting the pain, which was lessened a bit when I leant forward. But my teeth were clenched so hard I couldn't speak."

"It must have been awful for you."

"Penny, let's go to the top of that little tor. What's it called?"

"Bagga Tor. Does your ankle feel up to it?"

"It'll have to be. I want to feel I have achieved something."

It was quite a gentle climb, though the ground was rough. They found a rock on which to sit, just below the summit and looking down into the valley of the Baggator Brook. There was a little bit of shade here from the heat of the August sun.

"I have always loved tors, Penny. I get such a sense of peace, looking down from their heights. Look at that valley. What could be more peaceful than that? You can see the whole course of the stream coming down the side of that great hill. Doesn't it make you want to walk up there to its source?"

"I have done so. A boggy place it is, too. But a lovely walk 'til you get there. We'll do it one day."

It was a sign of their growing comradeship that they were content just to sit and enjoy that scenery in silence. There was no need to talk. Just to be together was sufficient. That is until the dull ache in John's wrist brought him back to reality.

"What am I going to do with myself, Penny? Even if I get some use in this hand, I'll never be able to carry out my work as a mason. It needs too much delicate control of the tools of the trade."

"Clerical work?"

"Stuck in an office? No thank you. I want to be out in the open air."

"Farmin' then. You could learn to ride a horse. Round up the sheep. You could milk a cow with one 'and. You'll learn to do all sorts of things with one 'and."

"But always dependent on help with other things. Look how much you help me. I appreciate that, in fact I love it. But I also want my independence."

Penny was silent.

"You're stuck for an answer to that, aren't you? There is no answer to it. I suppose I'll get used to it."

Penny had got an answer to it. She wanted to be his right hand. But it would not be seemly to suggest it. It was not the right moment to do so anyway. He had to make some effort to work out his own destiny.

"Come, let's go home to dinner. You 'ave your mother's visit this afternoon to look forward to."

August gave way to September. The days shortened and the weather became more unsettled, restricting these walks. But as so often happens in the autumn, when leaves carpet the ground with the warmth of their golds and browns, when the sun is lower in the sky and casts longer shadows; when the thinning foliage of the trees reveal the fantastic shapes of their branches, there are magical days of soft light and gentle airs that must not be spent indoors.

Such a day was it when Penny and John knew that within a few more hours they would have to part company. There was now no reason why John should stay any longer at

Longbetor. Apart from his wrist he was fully restored to health. His mother wanted him home again. She would be coming by horse and trap, as far as Wapsworthy, to fetch him this Sunday afternoon.

"Penny, let's have a last walk together this morning. Look, the sun is shining. It promises to be a fine day."

"Where would you like to go?"

"To Bagga Tor again."

Once more they trod that path that by now was so familiar to them. They walked hand in hand, but had little to say. Both felt emotional. They would be able to see each other again, of course, but this special relationship between them was about to end.

It did not seem nearly so far to Bagga Tor as it had on that previous occasion. Neither had the place quite the same charm for them. The sun was not so warm; the breeze, what there was of it, was cool. There was no incentive to sit and admire the view. It was too early to go home yet.

"Let's go to Cataloo Steps," said Penny.

"Where's that?"

"A path used to go past here in the old days, when people of the moor carried their dead to Lydford Church for burial. Father says it is called the Lich Way. It crosses the River Tavy at some stepping-stones where the Baggator Brook enters that river. It's a pretty place. There is a wood nearby still called Coffin Wood. Perhaps they rested the coffin there before deciding how to carry it across the river."

"Is it far?"

"Not too far. We can be back in time for dinner."

To the west of the slopes of Bagga Tor a stony lane led down to where another lane crossed the Baggator Brook on its way to Standon Farm.

"Be careful of your ankle, John, on these stones."

Beyond the lane their path became a muddy one between the boundary wall of Browsentor Farm on one side and the Baggator Brook on the other. Trees lined the brook and mostly hid it from view, but its song was ever present as it splashed and swirled its way along its rocky bed.

The scene opened out where the brook turned sharply to run for some distance parallel with the broad waters of the Tavy, forming a long narrow strip of land between them. Here were the stepping-stones, one group across the Baggator Brook, another more impressive group across the Tavy, connected by a path of river pebbles over the strip of land.

Most of the stepping-stones were awash as a result of some heavy rain. The sun reflected from the breaking waters creating sparkling diamonds amidst the blues and browns of the calmer depths. Wet stones at the water's edge glistened in all shades of browns and greys from near black to near white. Trees still in leaf dotted the strip of land and the banks of the two rivers, casting dark green shadows over the otherwise bright green sunlit grass.

Arms around each other's waists, John and Penny gazed enraptured at this scene, so magical in its isolation, so fraught with the ghosts of the past; it was not too difficult to imagine the coffin being carried laboriously and precariously across those stepping-stones.

Slowly, then, they walked beside the brook to where the two rivers met in a flurry of sun-speckled turbulence, in contrast to the silence, stillness and mysterious depths of their tree-clad banks.

"Penny, you could not have brought me to a more beautiful place for our last . . . our last . . . I can't *say* it. Penny, we *can't* leave each other. You mean too much to me."

He turned and faced her, holding her arms. He saw her lower lip quiver, a tear trickle down her cheek.

"You feel the same, don't you?"

She could only nod her head.

"Oh, Penny, my dear." They were in each other's arms, hugging each other, wet cheek against wet cheek, moist lip to moist lip. In all those months of such close association they had been so circumspect, so careful not to run the risk of spoiling such a tender relationship. Now, their unspoken love for each other knew no fetters. It was long before they could bear to release each other, there could never be another moment like this, so precious, so unexpected; it had to be savoured to the full.

"Penny, I did not know you loved me like this."

"I did not think you would ever want a country girl like

me."

"You have done so much for me, dear, I have so much to thank you for. How could I help loving you?"

"You have done something for me, too, John."

"I have? What?"

"I have listened to you speaking, and have tried to speak like you do. I don't feel I am just a farm-hand now. At first I was sorry for you, and all your injuries. Then I found I loved doing things for you, it became important to me that you should get better. It is a woman's instinct, John, that I did not know I had."

"But Penny, do you really want a man with a useless hand?"

"I would not be worthy of you if my love was not stronger than that."

"You are willing to marry me?"

"Yes, John."

"How can I provide for you?"

"We can go on living as we have been. You will learn farming, and you will learn to love the work. And you won't resent my helping you as you might someone else. We'll manage."

"You dear, lovable, lovely girl. Give me another kiss. I did not realise how delicious it could be."

They were in no hurry to leave this idyll. Only the recollection that some concern might be felt by their parents if they were over-late for dinner made them realise that they must tear themselves away from this cherished place and momentous event. Not that they hurried their return, it was such a pleasure now to walk in the closest possible contact with each other, making plans for the future, laughing over recollections of the past.

They reached the farm to find that John's mother had already arrived.

"Mother, you're early!"

"No, I am not, John, it is you who are late. You have been giving me agonies of worry again for your safety. Where have you been all this time?"

"Penny, you shouldn't have taken John so far," admonished her mother, "you are too late for dinner now."

"We did not know it was so late, Mother." Penny looked half smilingly at John, as much as to say, "You tell them."

"We have some news for you both. You will forgive us I hope when you hear it. I have asked Penny to marry me. We couldn't bear the thought of parting. We have both realised how much we love each other."

Mary Ann went to Penny and held both her hands.

"Your mother and I have already suspected that this was the cause of your lateness. We have been teasing you both. I am delighted to hear we were right. I have admired you so much for your devotion to John. You have done so much to restore his health. I shall always be grateful to you for that. You are very dear and very special to me." She kissed her affectionately. "I am so happy for you, John. God bless you both."

Ella then came to John and held his injured hand with motherly warmth. "We 'ave loved having you 'ere, John, and pleased that us 'ave been able to help you. We welcome you as the son I never 'ad. My son died in childbirth. He would have been about your age now. Will you all sit down while I go and make some tea. I can't imagine either of you wantin' any cold dinner at this hour."

"No, we've forgotten all about it."

Alone with the happy couple Mary Ann said, "John, I know it will be a wrench for you, but you must come back with me today. Your father is so looking forward to seeing you again, he has had no chance since your accident. I, too, want to have you to myself before I lose you to Penny. I don't suppose you have formed any plans for your future yet, have you?"

"We were talking about that on the way home just now," said Penny, "John is worried about not being able to provide for me, and how he can earn a living. The only thing I can think of, if Father and Mother are agreeable, is for us to live here. I hope I can teach John to love farming, as I do. Perhaps one day we will have a farm of our own."

"Your father has always said he could never be a farmer. Do you think you could be, John?"

"As long as I'm with Penny, I'll like anything."

In came Ella with the tea just then, followed by her

husband.

"Us couldn't 'elp but yer what you been discussing," said Stephen, I 'ear you two are engaged now. My 'earty congratulations. Your mother and me 'ave no objections to your living 'ere, 'tain't the first time us 'ave talked about it. In fact I welcome it, for I'm danged if I knows what I'd do without Penny 'ere."

When the time came for their departure, Mary Ann said to Ella, "You must come to us at Foggin Tor one day, can you manage to do that?"

"Oh, yes. When I goes to market at Tavistock I borrows a gig from Wapsworthy, they'm always ready to lend it when I need it."

"Then come next Friday, to dinner. You will be able to meet Tom then."

"Welcome home, son. My, you are looking much better than I expected."

"He is looking all the better for having some happy news for you, Tom."

"You have? What's that?"

"Penny and I are engaged, Father."

"Oh, splendid, I am glad to hear that. It is not unexpected, you know, I have heard rumours! Now, I've got to shake you by the left hand, haven't I? I'm sorry to hear your wrist had not mended properly."

"That's all that's wrong with me now, but it is very frustrating. I am gradually learning to do everything with my left hand, such as writing. And I can even shave myself now; that took a bit of practice."

"I'm sure it did. Come with me tomorrow and meet your old colleagues, they are looking forward to meeting you again. You can lend a hand with the odd jobs. We'll find some work for you."

John did get a good welcome from his old mates. But he was only half-heartedly interested in the 'odd jobs'. They were boring. His mind was elsewhere. To be separated from his beloved so soon after they had declared their love for each other was hard to bear. Over and over again did those scenes and happenings at Cataloo Steps pass through his mind. When was he going to see her again? Not before next Sunday at the earliest, unless she came with her mother on Friday. That was unlikely. He rather hoped not. He wanted her to himself.

Friday came at last, and so did Ella, on her own.

"Come in, Ella my dear, let me take your coat. How lucky we are to have such a fine day for your visit, it can be pretty grim here at times, as I'm sure you well know."

"Yes, 'tis very exposed to the westerly winds and gales, ain't it? Often foggy, too. I couldn't 'ave come if it 'ad been like that. I did not know, though, that there were so many 'ouses 'ere."

"And more are to be built; it is becoming quite a village, isn't it? Tom and John will soon be here. Let me show you round our little home. It is small, but in a way that is a good thing, otherwise we would have had to take in lodgers, as most of the others have to. I just don't know how some of the families manage."

As they passed from parlour to kitchen, Ella said, "What a delicious smell."

"I've made a beef-steak pie for you, I hope you will like it."

Upstairs Ella was shown the two small bedrooms, but more particularly the lovely view from the window of the rear bedroom. "These cottages are known as Mount Pleasant, but I think they should be called West View cottages, for that is their greatest asset. But I expect you know it well enough, Ella."

"No, I doan, us doan of'en come this way. What are them tors?"

"That is King Tor on the left, and Pu Tor a little beyond it. Now look at the sun lighting up Vixen Tor, usually it is not easy to see from here, being below the horizon."

"You love the ol' Moor, doan you Mary?"

"Yes, I do. I was born and bred on the Moor; it means everything to me, in spite of the terrible things it can do to you. But come, I hear the men arriving, they don't have long for their meal, I must dish it up."

Tom and Ella were introduced. There was mutual admiration in their minds. 'What a fine looking man,' thought Ella. 'So this is the kind, homely looking woman who had been caring for John; no wonder he was content there,' thought Tom. John greeted his future mother-in-law with affection.

They sat down immediately to a rather hurried meal, but all relished and praised the pie and the tenderness of the meat. Conversation was mostly about the forthcoming wedding, where and how soon it could take place.

"It can't be soon enough for me," said John, "I am doing no good here, it irks me to see my mates doing the work I used to do. I want to try this possibility of farming."

When Tom and John prepared to return to work, Mary Ann said, "Shall we walk with them, Ella? Would you like to see something of the quarry?"

But by the time they had donned their coats the men had already gone; they could not delay.

"Never mind, we can stroll at our own pace."

Arm in arm they walked along the track towards a long, massive tip of stone waste extending westward from the quarry mouth.

"That is where they are building more houses now; and a chapel I believe. Since the prison has been reopened the barrack buildings at Princetown are no longer available for the quarry workers. It has been a great problem here, housing everybody."

They had to stand aside whilst a horse-drawn wagon passed them carrying a huge piece of worked granite. "That will be taken to Tavistock by road," said Mary Ann, "and then on the canal to Morwellham, for shipment to somewhere. Isn't it amazing how these great masses of stone are handled?"

At the quarry mouth they were not allowed beyond a certain point, it was too dangerous. But Ella was able to see the huge hole now made in the ground, and the sheer face of the quarry beyond. She was astonished at its height. They watched a great block of granite on the quarry floor about to be turned over. A cable from a crane went right to the top of the cliff, then through a pulley anchored at the top, and down again to a hook-shaped piece of metal fitted into a hole in the side of the block. "Tom tells me that that hook is called a 'dog', and the hole in the block of granite is made with a pointed hammer called a gad. You see how technical I am getting! Tom loves to explain all this to me. It is fascinating, though, isn't it, to see how these enormous weights are moved. Look, there is goes." The crane took the strain and that hook or dog pulled the massive block onto its side.

"You ladies better get movin' before you gets 'urt," said a quarryman.

Confidences were exchanged between them as they strolled back along the track; little details of their past. It all helped to confirm the growing friendship between them.

"I must be gettin' back now," said Ella, as they reached Mount Pleasant.

"Come in and have a cup of tea first, it won't take long."

They went to the kitchen together to prepare the brew, then carried it back to the parlour and sat at the table.

As Mary Ann stirred the tea she said, "Penny is a very unusual name, what made you call her that?"

"Well, my dear, I've been wonderin' if I should tell you or not. But since you ask that, it has 'elped me to make up me mind. Penny is not me real daughter. When me baby boy died I was overcome with grief. But it so 'appened that some callous person 'ad left a nearly new-born baby at the door of my brother's farm. He knew of my grief and brought the baby to me. It was such a relief to me to be able to suckle it and comfort it. Some money 'ad been left with the baby. That's why us called 'er Penny."

All the while this tale was being told, Mary Ann had been holding the teapot poised ready to pour, her body rigid with suspense.

"Where is your brother's farm?" she asked in a quavering voice.

"Cox Tor Farm, beyond . . . Oh, Lord-a-mercy, Mary, me dear, what's the matter?"

Mary Ann had dropped the teapot, both hands now covering her face. A cup was smashed, the teapot spout broken, tea flooded all over the clean white table cloth.

"Mary, are you ill? Come, me dear, sit in this more comfortable chair."

But as soon as Mary Ann rose to her feet, she collapsed

onto the floor in a faint.

Poor Ella tried to lift her, but knew it was impossible. She ran from the house to seek help next door. Suzannah came to the door.

"Come with me, quick, your neighbour's fainted."

By the time they reached Mary Ann she had recovered from her faint, but was sitting on the floor, her face still in her hands, sobbing uncontrollably.

Between them they helped her to the chair, but could get no word from her to account for this grief. There was no stopping the flood of tears.

"You stay with her," said Suzannah, "I'll fetch Tom, her husband."

That took some time, for it was more than a mile to where Tom was working.

When, breathless, Tom knelt beside her, begging her to tell him what was causing so much anguish, Mary Ann at last took her hands from her face. She was deathly pale, looking drawn and haggard, her eyes full of tears and fearfulness.

"Tell us, my love, what is it?"

In a choking voice she said, "John and Penny, they cannot marry."

Tom and Ella looked at each other in bewilderment.

"They are brother and sister."

"Brother and sister? How can that be?"

"Jethro."

"Oh, God, not that fiend again." Then the awful reality of what that one word implied.

"Hell and damnation on that man," he shouted, "Ella, can you account for this revelation?"

There was shock and astonishment in Ella's eyes, as with difficulty she repeated the story she had related to Mary, and what had followed.

"Come close to me," said Mary Ann, between sobs.

They knelt, one each side of her. She held out her hands to clasp theirs, in an effort to control herself.

"Do not judge me, Ella, until you have heard all I have to say. My secret cannot be kept any longer. You must both hear the dreadful truth. I am that callous woman who left the baby on your brother's doorstep . . . Tom has just called that Jethro a fiend . . . He was . . . A huge, lustful, beast of a man . . . He kidnapped me and raped me horribly . . . "

Tom lifted her hand to his lips in sympathy, but in his heart he was living again the rage that had consumed him and made him murder that man. It was astonishing that she had kept this secret from him all this time, there had never been an inkling of this revelation.

"That baby was his . . . I hated it . . . I could not bear the thought of rearing it, and living with it, a constant reminder of that awful night . . . I had to get rid of it . . . No one knew what I had done with it. No one but my mother and father knew that I had had that baby. They kept the secret too . . ."

Tears were streaming down her face again. She withdrew her hands and once more hid her face in them, in a paroxysm of sobs and shudders. When she was able to continue, she said, in a weak voice, "The bitter irony of it is that I now love that girl . . . I have ruined her life . . . and John's. My punishment is that I have got to live with this knowledge for the rest of my life . . . What is going to happen to the two of them?"

"Ella, do you follow all this?" said Tom, "Can you understand the terrible cause of it, how awful was Mary Ann's experience that brought her to do this thing?"

There were tears in Ella's eyes, as with emotion she said, "I am bewildered. I can 'ardly believe it. Mary, me dear, do not think I judge you. I feel for you from the bottom of me 'eart. I wish I 'ad some words of comfort for you, but I just don't know what can be said, I am all upset too. I don't know 'ow I'm goin' to tell Penny."

"There is nothing more you can do here, Ella," said Tom, "It is best that you should leave us now, you have a long journey home, it will be dark before you get there. I feel concern for you. Let me see you safely on your way. You and I have now the dreadful task of telling our children this devastating news."

"God be with you," he called, as Ella drove away.

Tom turned to see a group of quarrymen coming off duty, John amongst them. He waited for him.

Dismay filled his soul as he contemplated the task ahead. He wanted to get back to Mary Ann, to comfort her. Yet he did not want John to see her in the state she was in. Anyway, it was up to him to break this awful news to John, Mary Ann had been through too much already. He must take him somewhere where they can be undisturbed.

"Hullo, Father. Ella is very late leaving for home, isn't she?"

"John, I have some bad news for you. Let's walk down towards the Pila Brook."

"Has anything happened to Penny?" he asked, with apprehension in his voice.

"No, she is all right."

"What's the matter, Father, you are looking all upset?"

"Do you remember, John, my telling you of the awful period in my life when your mother was kidnapped?"

"Yes, but I thought you didn't want to be reminded of that."

"We have always told you that your mother escaped from that dreadful man. In a way that was correct. But it was not before she spent a terrible night with him."

Tom directed his son to a convenient rock beside the brook, where they could sit, before he resumed.

"You do understand, John, don't you, what that implies? Your mother had a baby as a result of that night. It was such a traumatic experience that she could not bear to rear that baby. She disposed of it, but no one knew how. I knew nothing about any of this until this afternoon, when Ella told us that she had adopted an abandoned baby when her own son had died in childbirth. That baby is now Penny. She is your sister, John."

"I do not understand. How does Ella know it was Mother's baby?"

"By the most extraordinary set of circumstances your mother left her baby at Cox Tor Farm, near Peter Tavy. Ella's brother runs that farm. He knew Ella had lost her son. That baby took its place, she brought it up as though it was her own daughter. It was your mother who realised that it was her baby. John, my dear boy, you have got to realise it is against the law for members of the same family to intermarry. It is terrible to have to say this, but you will have to part from Penny, she can never be yours."

John was stunned to complete silence. There was nothing to be said. Life without Penny was unbearable. Life with Penny was now impossible. What was there left in life to live for?

"Come, John, dear boy, I must get back to your mother, she is terribly upset, I don't like leaving her alone, but I had to tell you this first. You have got to be brave, and face facts. How hard it is for you I know only too well. Life can be very cruel."

They reached home to find that Mary Ann was no longer in the parlour.

"Wait here, John, I expect your mother has retired to bed, she looked really ill. It may be too much for her to see you just yet."

Mary Ann was dry-eyed now, but her face reflected the mental agony she had suffered. She looked old and worn out, pale and lifeless. Tom took her hand.

"I have just told John the awful truth."

"I was dreading having to tell him. How did he take it?"

"In stunned silence. He hasn't spoken a word since."

"We'll have to take him away from here, Tom, make a complete break. I don't know where. I can't collect my thoughts."

"Do you want to see John now?"

"I don't want him to see me like this. I shall only break down again if I have to explain anything to him. I only want you at the moment. I want your understanding and forgiveness for what I have done."

"Of course I understand. There is nothing to forgive. Only one man is responsible for the evils that have beset our lives. Everything stems from him and that dreadful night. I hope he is rotting in hell."

"Tom, please."

"Oh, I am sorry, my love; but I boil with rage whenever I think of what you had to suffer that night. I have murdered that man over and over again in my thoughts."

"Tom, I am being unkind to John, leaving him alone down there in his misery. He must need some motherly love and sympathy. Tell him to come up and see me. I'll try to keep calm."

But it was only Tom who returned to her.

"John has gone out. I can understand him wanting to walk and think things out, rather than sit and mope. He is bound to take this badly. It will be a long time before he gets over it."

"Poor boy, he was so happy with Penny. I cannot think of her as my daughter, only as the girl he has fallen in love with. What a mischievous twist of fate this is, that those two should have been thrown together like this."

"We must do something to keep our minds from dwelling on these things. Let me make you a hot drink. Would you like tea or cocoa?"

"Tea, but I think I broke the teapot. You'll find another one down there somewhere."

There was a knock on the front door whilst Tom was making the tea. She could hear voices. Apprehension filled her breast.

"Oh, God, Tom, what is it?" when she saw the look on his face.

"John. His body has been found at the foot of the quarry face. He is dead."

Chapter Sixteen

It was generally assumed that John's death was a tragic accident. That he had experienced an attack of vertigo and overbalanced. But it was difficult to account for him walking along the cliff edge so soon after coming off duty.

This was not the first death that had occurred at these dangerous works. There was a tradition amongst the quarrymen that they show their respect for the dead and sympathy for the bereaved by a ritual procession to the church.

Some hundred men assembled near Mount Pleasant Cottages, lined up in two columns. They all wore white trousers and black coats. The rear six men, three on either side, raised the coffin to their shoulders. When all was ready, a signal was given and all moved forward in unison, in a slow and stately march.

Behind the coffin came the chief mourners. Mary Ann, all in black, a black veil only partially covering her white, gaunt, shrunken face, with her arm through Tom's for support. Behind them came Penny, her head bowed, her eyes averted from that coffin, with Ella and Stephen each linking an arm in hers. Then Suzannah and George, followed by Mr Robert Uren, the Works Superintendent, and many of the families of Mount Pleasant.

At certain intervals, at another sign from the funeral director, the first six men of the column stepped aside and waited until the coffin reached them. They then took over from the previous bearers, the coffin always remaining at the rear of the column. This was repeated at regular intervals all the way to Princetown Church. A very solemn, impressive, dignified and lengthy proceeding.

At the church the procession was met by the priest and the clerks, who led it to the open grave. There, the priest waited until the column of men dispersed around the graveyard and the coffin reached and was laid beside the grave. The mourners stood around it.

Then did the priest intone:

"I am the resurrection and the life, saith the Lord: he that believeth in me, though he were dead, yet shall he live: and whosoever liveth and believeth in me shall never die. We brought nothing into this world, and it is certain we can carry nothing out. The Lord gave, and the Lord has taken away; blessed be the name of the Lord."

The priest then recited the thirty-ninth Psalm.

The coffin was then lowered into the grave; Tom sprinkled earth upon it.

"Forasmuch as it hath pleased Almighty God of his great mercy to take unto himself the soul of our dear brother here departed, we therefore commit his body to the ground; earth to earth, ashes to ashes, dust to dust; in sure and certain hope of the Resurrection to eternal life, through our Lord Jesus Christ.

"I heard a voice from heaven, saying unto me Write, from henceforth blessed are the dead which die in the Lord; even so saith the Spirit; for they rest from their labours."

After the congregation had recited the Lord's Prayer, the priest gave his blessing.

"The grace of our Lord Jesus Christ, and the love of God, and the fellowship of the Holy Ghost, be with us all evermore. Amen."

Carriages took the mourners back to Foggin Tor, where they went their several ways, the intensity of their feelings militating against any gathering together.

But Suzannah noticed with what difficulty Mary was descending from her carriage. She went to assist her. She and Tom had almost to carry her to her bedroom, where they undressed her and put her to bed.

"She is ill, Tom. That lengthy procession and standing in the cold churchyard has been too much for her."

This dear woman, who had once shown such compassion for her in her time of tribulation, now needed help. Suzannah gave it unstintingly, in spite of the demands of her own household.

Ella and Stephen had noticed with what composure Penny had borne that long march and ceremony. Only when the coffin was lowered into the grave did she have to wipe her eyes. All the way on that long drive home she had kept silent, deep in her thoughts.

She had shed many tears when that unexpected and heart-rending news had been broken to her, that she and John could not marry. The shock that her real mother was John's mother, that she had no known father, had been bewildering and disturbing, barely believable. On top of all that came the greater shock of John's death. What was there left in life worth living for now? She had even contemplated ending her own, as John had done. They would be together again, then. But that was a cowardly way out; she was not useless, as John must have thought he was. There must be some purpose in her life, could she only fathom what it was. Where did her loyalties lie now, with her foster mother and father, or with her real mother? Could she ever bear to leave these two who had reared her and loved her and taught her all she knew? What were her real mother's feelings now, having lost both her children, one abandoned, the other lost in despair? But would her real mother want to see her now, under these changed circumstances? How terribly ill she had looked today. She felt a desperate desire to go to her and comfort her.

Ella was not greatly surprised when at breakfast she heard what Penny proposed to do. All her life Penny had shown this desire to help, whether it was for sick animals or humans in distress. It had culminated in her care of John. Now it was John's mother, her own mother, whom she felt she must help.

When Penny had gone, Ella said to Stephen, "That girl's place is with her own mother. Us 'ave got to be prepared to let 'er go. 'Tis goin' to be mortal 'ard to lose 'er. Will you be able to manage the farm without her?"

"I dunno. I can't imagine this place without 'er. She'm

everything to us, bain't she? 'Ow can us let 'er go?"

"We 'ave no claim on 'er, me dear, we got to let 'er do what she wants to do, an' us mustn't influence 'er."

Stephen shrugged his shoulders, shook his head, heaved a sigh and went out to his farm.

Ella returned to her chair, rested her elbows on the table and her chin in her hands. She tried to contemplate this house without Penny. It would be like blowing out the candle at night. All light and life would go out of it. She had brought such happiness and comfort to their lives as a child, and now, as a grown woman, had proved so capable and reliable on the farm. They would have to lose her to someone eventually, of course, someone would want her for a wife. It had seemed such a wonderful solution that she and John should marry and live here, that would have been added happiness. Now, bewilderingly, that was a bubble, full of coloured lights, that had suddenly burst and left nothing.

Ella could feel the tears welling up, but she brushed them aside. It was no good giving way to despair, there was work to be done. She must put a brave face on it. She must not allow Penny to see the depth of their grief, it was going to be hard enough for her too.

When Penny arrived at the Mount Pleasant cottage, Suzannah opened the door to her.

"Could I see John's mother?"

"She is very ill, I'm not sure she should be disturbed."

"Please, just for a moment, I won't stay long."

Suzannah was still undecided. Mary had slept little during the night, but appeared to have dozed off when she had left her a moment ago.

"May I see John's father, then?"

"He is out at the moment, at the works."

The disappointment in Penny's face was irresistible.

"Come then." She felt very sorry for this girl who was so involved in the tragedy that had befallen this family.

When Penny entered the bedroom she was shocked at the change in that once so beautiful face.

Mary Ann opened her eyes at the sound of her entry,

then held out a hand when she recognised Penny.

Greatly encouraged by the gesture, Penny knelt beside her and took hold of that hand.

"I had to come to see you. I could see yesterday how much you were suffering, you looked so ill. I have been thinking of you ever since. I hoped I might be able to help you."

The only response she got was a gentle squeeze of her hand.

"You are ill, aren't you? really ill. Will you let me come and look after you? . . . Please."

A moment before, Mary Ann had felt too ill and emotional to trust herself to speak. That soothing voice had a calming effect on her. That 'please' and the pleading look in those hazel eyes were so genuine.

"Yes, Penny. Come."

"I'll go back to my mother now; well, you know what I mean, and tell her, and collect some clothes. I'll be back soon. You are going to get better." She kissed Mary Ann's hand and restored the bedclothes round her shoulders.

Tom returned as Penny was taking her departure. "Hello, Penny, I did not expect to find you here."

Penny told him of her talk with her mother, and that she would be coming back later to help, if he was agreeable.

"I would welcome your help, my dear. It is good of you."

"You are not looking too good yourself."

"That may be because I haven't had much sleep lately."

A doctor from Tavistock arrived in the afternoon. He diagnosed pneumonia and prescribed the treatment necessary. The patient would need careful nursing.

Penny returned later in the afternoon and virtually took over the running of the household. She persuaded Tom to sleep undisturbed in the room that had been John's. She remained all night, fully clothed, with her mother, dozing occasionally in a chair, but mindful of all her mother's needs. She made a point of using the word 'mother', she had got to get used to that fact, and it seemed to give comfort to Mary Ann.

The next morning Penny asked Tom to return to his normal work and routine. It would be best for him and for her. With Suzannah's help she could cope. She prepared his dinner and made broth for her mother, who had eaten little for some days.

Tom obtained a spare bed and fixed it up in Mary Ann's room for Penny. Eventually everyone had better nights and more restful days.

It was balm to Penny to be kept busy. It helped to overcome the heartache of her loss. It was a relief to Tom to see with what ease Penny made herself at home here and how smoothly she managed everything. Even greater was his relief to see the gradual improvement in Mary Ann's health.

Tom had written to Linnie to tell her of their tragic loss and of Mary Ann's illness. He had expressed the hope that she would be able to come and see her daughter, whose condition was causing some anxiety. He had not mentioned anything about Penny. That revelation was too complicated to include in a letter, it was best left until it could be told face to face.

It was a fortnight before a reply arrived, by which time Mary Ann's health had improved to the extent that she could now sit up in bed, and was able to read it. It was from her Uncle Edward.

My Dear Mary Ann,

Tom's letter to Linnie received. I am so sorry to hear of John's tragic death, and of your illness. I do hope you are feeling better, for I have some sad news for you. Your mother passed away peacefully a week ago, after a short illness. I delayed informing you earlier as I knew you would be unable to attend the funeral and I thought it might be unwise when you were so ill yourself. Also the funeral occupied much of our time and thoughts. It was conducted with great sensitivity and solemnity.

I am missing her companionship very much. I do know how grieved you will be to hear this news. My sympathy to you, and I shall hope to hear soon that you are quite recovered.

Your affectionate uncle,

Edward.

Mary Ann was saddened but not unduly shocked. Her mother's visits had ceased once they had come to Princetown to live. Though they had corresponded frequently, their entirely different life styles had caused them gradually to drift apart. Yet it was another break with the past. The last link with the Cockcrofts and those far off days of Ashburn Hall was now severed. Only old Sir John's portrait remained to remind her of those days.

By degrees Mary Ann recovered her health and strength, she was eating and sleeping normally. She no longer needed night attention. Penny and Tom exchanged rooms. The thought that she was in John's room, sleeping in John's bed, gave Penny a grain of happiness. But then came apprehension. Very soon her help would no longer be required here. Once her mother was well enough to take over the running of the house, what was to become of her? Could she ever feel the same at Longbetor now? There was going to be a great void in her life, a lack of purpose.

As they lay in bed together, getting mutual comfort from their close proximity and the returning normality of their existence, Mary Ann and Tom also discussed the future.

"I don't want to stay here, Tom. I want to make a complete break from this locality."

"There are some very successful mines near Tavistock now working. Could you contemplate living in Tavistock?"

"Oh, Tom. Don't go back to mining. I don't want to lose you too. That is no life for you now, and you know it. You are an open air man."

Then, after a long pause, whilst their thoughts were roaming but getting nowhere, Mary Ann said, "What are we going to do about Penny? I can't think of her as the baby I hated. Only as John's sweetheart, and a lovable girl who has been so good to me here. I don't want to lose her either. What are Ella and Stephen thinking? They will expect her to go back to them, I suppose."

"The solution to that lies with Penny. She must be wondering about that too. We will have to have a family conference and sort the problem out. Now, go to sleep, my love, before your returning beauty gets a setback."

"Dear Tom. You deserve a kiss for that."

Though these problems were never far from their thoughts during the ensuing days, nothing more was said until Mary Ann had at last been able to get dressed and make her faltering steps down the stairs to her parlour.

Then, when Tom had returned to work after dinner, and Penny had cleared the dishes and made everything tidy in the kitchen, she came and sat with her mother before the glowing peat fire.

"It is good to see you here, Mother, and with some colour in your cheeks now. You'll soon get the strength back in your legs, and be doing all the things you used to do."

"It's thanks to you, Penny, that I've got this far."

"You won't be needing me much longer, will you?"

Mary Ann's stomach turned over at the realisation that the time had come when the question had to be decided.

"Penny, I can't bear the thought of losing you. Your devotion to John and now to me has made you very dear to me. But you have to decide what you want to do with your life. Have you come to any solution?"

"I am torn in two, Mother. I know how much I owe to Ella and Stephen. It is so strange now, not to be calling them Mother and Father. I know they love me, I don't want to hurt them. Will you be all right if I go to see them tomorrow?"

"Does that mean that you want to come back to us?"

"If you will have me, yes."

"Permanently?"

"Yes, Mother."

By the time Tom returned from work, Mary Ann had gone back to bed, a little exhausted from her efforts. She told Tom what had transpired between Penny and her, and of Penny's decision to see Ella and Stephen on the morrow.

"Mary Ann, before Penny finally makes up her mind, I think she should know all the facts of the past. All she knows at present is that she was born to you out of wedlock by an unknown father. There are still people here who know about my murdering a man and the reason for it. If she learnt that fact from someone else and not from us, she might resent having come to the wrong decision and blame us for it. We can't allow that to happen. It is going to be difficult, but I must speak to her."

"Yes, you are right, dear. Please God she will understand."

That evening Tom waited until their light supper was over and Penny had finished all her tasks.

"Come and sit down, Penny. I have something important to tell you. You are not going to like it, but it has to be said."

Is he going to tell me that he doesn't want me here, thought Penny, with a sinking feeling in her heart.

"I understand that you are about to make up your mind whether your life now lies with us or with Ella and Stephen, and that you are going to see them tomorrow. Before you come to any decision you must know more about why your mother abandoned you as a baby. It concerns your father. This is what is going to hurt you. He was a big bully of a man. I tried to fight him to prevent him kidnapping your mother, but I had no chance against a man of his size and strength, he knocked me out. When later I discovered what he had done to your mother, I tracked him down and killed him. That is what you must know, Penny, and know it from me, not someone else. I killed your father, in a fury at what he had done to my beloved girl, your mother."

Tom paused to give Penny a chance to speak if she wanted to. But she remained silent.

"Suppose someone had kidnapped you, Penny, and you suffered some dreadful thing as a result, would you not have expected John to have avenged you?"

"Yes, I would. I understand. But I am horrified at the thought that that man could be my father."

"Penny, my dear, you must now put that thought behind you. What you have to realise is that, had your mother kept you she would always have hated you. She has told me so. Instead you have been brought up by two people who have loved and cherished you. You are a product of their love, not of your father's lust and your real mother's hate. Events have turned full circle. You are loved by both families. I will welcome you here, just as your real mother does now."

"That was a kind thing to say."

"There is one more thing that may influence you. Your

mother wants to leave this district. I don't know yet where we shall go or what we shall do, but it might take you away altogether from Ella and Stephen. That will be important to you. You have all the facts now to allow you to make your decision."

It was a Sunday when Penny rode her pony back to Longbetor. Tom and Mary Ann spent a peaceful day together, relishing the opportunity to perform little kindnesses to each other. Trying to forget for a while their sad loss; to put all problems aside and get the greatest pleasure from their love for each other. It had seemed such a long time since this had been possible. Yet they could not entirely banish from their minds the thought of what Penny's fateful decision might be.

Not until late afternoon did she return. Tom saw her coming down the track to their cottage, leading her pony, which was laden with a variety of bags and packages. She had obviously walked thus, all the way from Longbetor.

The exercise and the winter wind had given her a high colour, her hair was blown awry and encircled her face in its wisps, as smilingly she saw Tom waiting for her.

"This can only mean one thing, Penny. Welcome, my dear."

Her smile broadened and her eyes lit up as she heard those words.

"Let me help you with your baggage."

Having got everything into the house, and the pony tethered where it could graze in peace, Penny entered what was now to be her home.

Mary Ann stood facing the parlour door, waiting for her. When she saw that happy smiling face she held out her arms. Penny came to them and received a warm embrace and a motherly kiss.

"I can tell by your face what you have decided, my dear. I am so pleased."

"You are looking better, Mother, have you had a good day?"

"Yes, I have. And I do feel better. And you are looking

the picture of health, if delightfully windswept. You'll want to tidy yourself whilst Tom makes some tea. Then you can tell us all about your day."

Sitting around the fire, sipping their tea, Penny began. "I knew what I wanted to do before I had reached Longbetor. I had been trying to imagine myself living again in that room, where I would always have a mental picture of John lying on his mattress on the floor. It would be a constant heartache to me. I have never known John here, it has not been quite the same. Our mutual loss seems to have made it easier to bear. Knowing what I do now, life at Longbetor can never be the same. I would be performing my tasks because they had to be done, not because I loved doing them, as I had before."

Penny sat gazing into the fire, her thoughts distracted by these memories.

"My problem was how to break this news to Ella and Stephen. To me, as I reached the farm, they were still my mother and father, who meant so much to me. It seemed heartless to tell them that I was going to leave them. I know I had tears running down my cheeks as I started to explain, but to my surprise Ella saved me from the ordeal. They had anticipated and already made up their minds that I would want to come to you. She made it all so easy for me, yet I could see from her troubled eyes it was not being easy for her. They both assured me that they could manage the farm without me, that Stephen hoped to get a young lad from Willsworthy to help them. They would be all right. My duty, they said, was to come to you. I felt very sad at the thought of leaving them, they had been so good to me. But there has to be a purpose in my life now. I believe it lies here, with you, more than at Longbetor."

"Why do you say that, Penny?" asked Tom.

"You told me yesterday, of your intention to leave here and seek work elsewhere. When I told Ella this, she said she had heard that Essworthy Farm near Sheepstor was now without a tenant. She wondered if that would be a possibility for you."

"I've always said I could never be a farmer, Penny, I know nothing about farming."

"But I do. That is where I can help. It would be a sheep farm, you know. I have lived with sheep all my life. I believe it is something that will bring peace to you both. It will also give me the purpose in life that is important to me now."

"Tom, you once said that mining was the only thing you could do. But when that fell through you became an expert stone mason. For my sake you have promised not to go back to mining. For my sake, please try this farming. You can do it. I know where Essworthy is, you'll love it there. It is not far from Sheepstor Bridge, in the Mewy valley. Don't you remember we saw it from the top of Sheeps Tor, many years ago?"

They exchanged knowing smiles.

"Yes, and that silver river threading its way through the valley. I am tempted. At least I can go and make enquiries about it. Perhaps Penny and I could visit the farmhouse and see what sort of state it is in."

Penny felt there was nothing more to be said on that subject now. She would have to wait until they had made that visit. There was something, though, which had been puzzling her ever since she had become aware of her true identity.

"Mother, will you explain how it came about that you chose Cox Tor Farm as a place to abandon me?"

"Yes, I have been wondering about that, too," said Tom, "but don't, my dear, if you feel it is going to upset you to recollect it."

"I had to choose somewhere where I was not known, and where I could not be seen. Somewhere that was easily accessible from the moor, and isolated from other buildings. You must know, Penny, that Tom spent three years in prison for his so-called crime. I was very restless and unhappy during that time. I used to go for long rides on my horse, Nelson. I got to know great tracts of moorland that I had never seen before. What is more, Nelson got to know them too. He was the most intelligent of horses. On one of those rides I discovered Cox Tor Farm, so I knew of its isolation and ease of access, when I was turning over in my mind where to rid myself of my baby. It seemed to me to be the ideal place. You once asked me, Tom, what was the quickest way from Classywell to Foggin Tor. That is the route I took. No one would see me there at night. But at Devil's Bridge I followed a line of guide stones to Merrivale. Fortunately it was a bright moonlight night. Nelson was marvellous at finding all the good ground. I only had one hand on his reins, the other was holding on to my baby. Then we climbed up to the Staple Tors, and across to Cox Tor. I tethered Nelson at the gate to the short lane leading down to the farm. This was the dangerous part, in case their dogs barked and raised the alarm. I crept as silently as I could down that stony lane, and along the path to the front door. I laid the baby on the doorstep. She had slept all this time, I had given her a good feed before we started. Then the dogs started barking. I flew along that path and up the lane as fast as I could. I'm sure I was on Nelson and away before the occupants of the farm could have roused themselves and investigated what all the barking was for. I rather hoped they would be roused, so that they would find the baby. She was well wrapped up and warm, but I felt terribly guilty abandoning her on that cold doorstep. Nelson was as eager to get home as I was. We couldn't gallop, of course, but he trotted at a good pace and knew exactly where to go."

"And you never regretted doing that?"

"No. And I don't now. Had I not done so you would never have been to me what you are now, Penny. That is what I find so very extraordinary. That I can love you as I do. There can be no doubt about that."

"Thank you for telling me. It has tired you, though, hasn't it?"

"This is the first time that I have ever spoken of it. It has made me tense, as I was on the whole of that journey. I could not afford to be seen, and I was afraid all the time that I would be."

Penny rose, knelt before her mother and took her hands. "I hope I will be able to prove to you that your love for me is justified."

Within a month of their enquiries and examination of the

farmhouse, they had moved to Essworthy. By that time Mary Ann had quite recovered her health. Once more she made a new home. Once more Tom learnt a new skill. Penny was in her element, virtually running the farm to begin with, but watching with joy the increasing interest and enthusiasm developing in her father. For want of a better word, that is what she now called him.

A legacy from Linnie helped them to stock the farm. Mary Ann started keeping chickens again, happy to do what she knew she could do.

They had visits from Suzannah, who had bewailed their departure from Mount Pleasant, but was now so pleased to see them settling to their new life. And from Ella and Stephen, who were sincerely thanked for having suggested this farm, where everything was turning out so well. Then the joyous day when Elizabeth and Henry arrived. These were friendships that could never be forgotten, even when their visits became less frequent, and new friends were made in the immediate neighbourhood.

Time healed old wounds, old bitternesses, and mellowed old memories. It became impossible to associate Penny with those memories. She could only be associated with John. The comfort she brought them both, compensated to a very large extent for the loss of a beloved son.

EPILOGUE

In June of the year 1893, the Royal Assent was obtained for the construction of a dam to span the Burrator Gorge, and form a reservoir in the Meavy valley, thus to provide an ample source of water for the towns of Plymouth, Devonport and Stonehouse.

In due course, notice was served by the Corporation of Plymouth on the tenant of a farm in this valley, that he was required 'to quit and deliver up the tenancy and possession of the lands and hereditaments situate in the parish of Sheepstor, known as Essworthy . . . ' etc.

Seated in his comfortable parlour, on the last evening to be spent in this ancient place, the old man gazed wistfully into his peat fire, the glow from which lit up his wrinkled, weather-worn face, and that of the still comely features and silver grey hair of his wife. They sat in silence, rueing the fact that they would not be here on the morrow.

Near half a lifetime had he farmed this land, since that sad day when their son had passed away. How wise had been this dear wife of his, to persuade him to take this farm. How reluctant had he been, for he had always declared that he could never be a farmer. Well, he couldn't have been, could he, without the help and encouragement of that auburn-haired, hazel-eyed girl who had taken the place of their son, and who had shown them such love and devotion. She had taught him all he knew about farming. How happy they had all been together, until at last the time came when, in her middle age, she had succumbed to the wooing of a farmer from Wakaton, and agreed to marry him. Reluctantly they had been able to carry on without her, but they had never lost touch. How welcome was the sight of her when periodically she came to see if they needed any help.

Now all this land was destined to be lost beneath the waters of a lake. These beautiful green pastures, dotted with the white of his grazing sheep. For that is how he had seen it from the top of Sheeps Tor, on that memorable occasion when he had been wooing his own beloved girl; an occasion and an incident he was to remember and be comforted by in those dark days of despair, when his only consolation was the sight and the touch of a lock of her golden hair.

Then again, they had obtained a more comprehensive view of the scene from the summit of Down Tor. Not only of this beautiful valley, flanked by its neighbouring tors, and threaded by the meandering ribbon of the Mew, but of a wide panorama of the Dartmoor hills and vales that were to mean so much to him during the years that followed. That day had reached a peak of perfection for him, when a wind-sculptured figure stood poised like a statue on the topmost rock of that tor.

These were the memories that must now be cherished, which must always remain in their minds, to ease their heartache. He knew Mary Ann was sharing his thoughts, as their eyes met and they exchanged wan smiles.

He rose from his chair, raked the ashes from the dying fire; then took both his wife's hands in his and helped her to her feet. They embraced; he fondled her silver hair, that familiar endearment that had always meant so much to them both; then led her slowly to their bed.

When, next morning, their conveyance took them over Sheepstor Bridge, across Drake's Leat, and up the steepening hill towards Wakaton, they halted for a moment for a last lingering look at this nostalgic scene. They knew, in their hearts, that they would never cease to long for those fields, for that river, for that valley of peace. How long would it be before the rising waters of the lake would hide it all; from everyone; for ever?

GLOSSARY

Adit A horizontal tunnel into the hillside for draining a mine, sometimes used as access.

Ammil A phenomenon assumed to be peculiar to Dartmoor, the word being, in Dartmoor language, the equivalent of 'enamel', when everything inanimate is encased in ice. For a fine description of the 1947 occurrence see *Dartmoor* by L.A. Harvey and D. St. Leger Gordon, page 199.

Balance bobs Horizontal lever pivoted at its centre, one end being connected to the pump rods descending the mine shaft, the other having a weight to balance the system.

Beam A suffix indicating an area where opencast tin-working has taken place, often resulting in gerts (see below). Willabeam, Caters Beam, Gibby's Beam, etc.

Black tin After the tin ore (cassiterite) has been pounded to a fine sand, the tin content is extracted by sedimentation in buddles or other means. When the water is removed a heavy black or dark brown slime is left. This is known as black tin, which is then smelted to produce white tin, in liquid form until it cools to become solid ingots.

Buddles A pit, either circular or rectangular, to which the tin ore, after it has been pounded, is directed and allowed to settle in water, kept continuously stirred, the heavy tin content sinking to the bottom whilst the lighter material is washed away.

Cloam oven A brick lined oven built into a fireplace wall, heated by the insertion of glowing peat or other hot material, until the temperature is considered right; then the ashes are raked out and the food takes their place.

Coinage/ Coining The practice of chiselling off a corner of a tin ingot (a coign) for the purpose of assaying its purity. The ingot was then weighed and stamped with the private mark of the owner, who had then to pay duty on it. (See *Tavistock Abbey* by H.P.R. Finberg, page 174.) These tin duties were abolished by an act of Parliament on 16 August 1838. (*A History of Tin Mining and Smelting in Cornwall* by D.B. Barton, page 79.)

Core Usually an eight hour shift below ground by the miners.

Dimsey Long period of twilight.

Flat-rods Long lengths of horizontal rods joined together and suitably supported, connecting the crank of the water-wheel or other engine to the pivot of the balance-bob. The system is always under tension, being pulled in one direction by the crank and in the other by the weight of the pump-rods in the shaft. They were necessary because usually it was not possible to locate a water-wheel near to the pit-head, and also the wheel often pumped more than one shaft.

Gerts Deep opencast tin-workings. An intermediate phase of tin extraction between alluvial working of stream beds and deep underground mining, when the tin lodes were traced uphill from the river valleys. Very extensive on Dartmoor.

Growan Coarse sandy material resulting from the disintegration of granite.

Launder A wooden trough for conveying water. Aqueduct.

Leat An artificial watercourse, of which there are a very large number on Dartmoor, taken from practically every river or brook. They vary in size from the small potwater leat supplying farms, etc., to those that take the major content of a river, such as the Devonport Leat, whose sources are the West Dart, Cowsic and Blackabrook rivers, and the old mine leat taken from the River Tavy originally intended for the Wheal Friendship and Wheal Betsy mines at Mary Tavy, but now used for hydro-electric purposes.

Sheer-legs Hoisting apparatus, often consisting of three poles triangularly spaced at their base, joined at the top, from where a system of pulleys (block and tackle) would be suspended.

Shippen A cattle house or cow byre, often separate from the farm building, but in the case of the Dartmoor longhouse an integral part of the house, being separated from the living quarters by a central passage.

Stamps Heavy bulks of timber, iron shod at the base, which are raised by cams on a revolving shaft, but allowed to fall by gravity on to the tin stone, for crushing purposes.

Stoping A method of hewing away the workface in a mine to reveal the tin lodes.

Stroll A space between enclosure walls, always open on the high moor end of them, to allow ease of access for the animals to take shelter if necessary, and for driving of stock to and from the moor.

Tallet A space over the shippen, often accessible by an exterior stone staircase, for the storage of hay.

Ullestor Rock Now called Roborough Rock. According to Crossing (*Guide* page 444) it is shown on an eighteenth century map as Ullestor Rock. Its present broken-backed appearance is due to the fact that the centre portion was quarried away in 1830 for road maintenance. (*Brief History of Yelverton* by Crispin Gill, page 8.)

Wharf As applied to the stopping places on the Plymouth and Dartmoor Tramway, before the word 'station' came into use on the later railways. Since one terminus of the tramway was the seafaring port of Plymouth, it was probably natural for the word 'wharf' to be used.

Wheal Prefix to the names of many Cornish and Devon mines, which were often given female Christian names. Sometimes spelt Huel in Cornwall.

Whim A vertically pivoted winding drum having radial arms attached to it and thus rotated by horses. Used for drawing ore from the mine shaft in kibbles or iron buckets.